Steel Victory

J.L. Gribble

D⬤G STAR
BOOKS

Published by Dog Star Books
Bowie, MD

First Edition

Cover Image: Bradley Sharp
Book Design: Jennifer Barnes

Printed in the United States of America

ISBN: 978-1-935738-73-2
Library of Congress Control Number: 2015943000

www.DogStarBooks.org

ACKNOWLEDGMENTS

Books should never be written in a vacuum. I could not have accomplished this without the support of many.

To my incredible writing community: Jennifer Brooks, Christe Callabro, Ron Edison, Judi Fleming, Vanessa Giunta, Kathleen Kollman, Chun Lee, Rhonda Mason, Jason Jack Miller, Erica Satifka, Deanna Sjolander, Shara White, K. Ceres Wright, Stephanie Wytovich, and everyone else from the Seton Hill University Writing Popular Fiction program (past, present, and future). Thank you for your support.

To everyone who read all or bits of this novel in its many incarnations: Sabrina Benulis, Matt Betts, Faryn Black, Greg Fisher, Glenn Garrabrant, Tristan Horrom, Adrienne Kapp, Michael Mehalek, Heidi Ruby Miller, Maryn Rosenberg, and Chris Stout. Thank you for pushing me to be a better writer.

To Jennifer Barnes and John Edward Lawson. Thank you for believing in Limani.

And to Jeffrey Coleman, Timons Esaias, Diane Turnshek, and Stacie Yuhasz. Thank you for being my mentors in literature, writing, and life.

Victory tapped the fingers of her right hand against her thigh in a steady rhythm as she watched a lone moth circle the overhead light. Each beat counted the movement of a blade as she dueled an imaginary opponent in her mind's eye. Lunge, slash, parry—launch into a forward roll, hamstring her partner—reset, en guarde. Next to her, her daywalker Mikelos made another notation in pencil on the blank sheet music spread across his lap. To him, the beat of fingers against denim in the tempo he'd set for her represented the music of a full orchestra, a hundred instruments in his head as he worked on his latest symphony.

A dock worker in a battered coverall entered the customs house's scant waiting area, heading toward Victory and Mikelos. She paused her tapping, and Mikelos looked up from his work.

"Ms. Connor?"

Victory suppressed a stab of irritation and jabbed a thumb toward Mikelos, who sat next to her on the stiff bench. "He's Mr. Connor. I'm just Victory." Wouldn't be the first time in her long life that she'd been called the name of her male companion, probably wouldn't be the last. Mikelos was smirking—he knew her pet peeves.

The dock worker lowered his eyes, scrunching a rag in his oil-stained dark hands. "Sorry. Master Rhaavi asked me to give you a message."

Victory smelled fear and hesitation twisting from his skin along with undertones she could not identify offhand. Forest and shadow. She forced herself to stay seated—the poor guy might bolt from the room. She checked the nametag on his uniform. "Go ahead, Taba."

Taba opened his mouth, but hesitated, almond eyes switching from Victory to Mikelos and back again.

"Don't worry. I promise she won't eat you," Mikelos said. His hazel eyes danced with amusement. The overhead fluorescent light tinged them a green that matched the faded streaks in his spiky brown hair. His compact form lounged on the bench, but his musician's hands twisted a loose thread at the hem of his shirt.

Victory smiled, careful not to flash fang and traumatize the young man any further. "Ignore him, please."

Steeling himself, Taba took a deep breath and said, "The, ah, river transport isn't stopping."

Visions of the two-hundred-foot-long riverboat careening into the small dock to crush the Limani customs house—and them in it—with cargo containers tumbled through her mind. Mikelos rose to his feet and shoved the roll of sheet music in a pocket of his cargo pants just when Victory realized Taba's true meaning. The riverboat intended to pass them by. "Where's Rhaavi?" Mikelos said.

Victory also stood, but Taba seemed past his fear now that he knew their reaction would not be taken out on him.

"His office. Want me to take you there?"

"Please," Victory said, as she and Mikelos followed Taba down a hallway. "You know whether he got that old radio fixed?"

"Part came down from the Brits last week, and I supervised the elf who installed it. I think that's how he got word. I wish real radio was still around." Taba hesitated.

The glass door to the back offices reflected in the fluorescent light. It picked up Mikelos and Taba's own reflections, but only Victory could see herself standing between them. "So do I. I miss cell phones even more." Victory stalked between the men, pushing her way into the back. Taba would have seen just what he saw with his own eyes. A woman of average height, with blue eyes and deep auburn hair pulled into a long braid. Paler than most, maybe, but that didn't make a distinguishing characteristic on its own.

Taba regained his equilibrium and led them through an open office area brimming with file cabinets but lacking any occupants. Taba's coworkers waited for the riverboat outside in the warm night, leaving the room with an eerie abandoned air. Light and the low fuzz of static emanated from one of the smaller offices in back.

After the Last War, traditional wireless communication became impossible because of the radiation still in the atmosphere. The elves had found a way around it, but protected the necessary enchantments. Victory suspected they wanted to keep the pesky warmongering humans from getting out of hand again. That wasn't a crazy conspiracy theory when one of the eldest elves in the city of Limani had confided that to her himself.

"Master Rhaavi?" Victory tapped the doorframe with her knuckles before stepping into the cluttered office. "Everything okay?"

The customs master sat hunched over a small table covered in old electronics. Without looking up, he raised one hand to silence them. He twisted a knob on the enchanted radio and picked up a microphone. "Limani Docks calling Roman One Three Nine. Come in, One Three Nine."

Victory sensed Mikelos hold his breath next to her. She would have done the same had she needed the oxygen.

The radio spurted more static, and after a few seconds Rhaavi set down the microphone. He wheeled his chair away from the table and back toward his desk. "That's all I've heard for the past ten minutes." He rubbed his bald head, shiny with sweat, and took a sip from the mug on his desk. "Guess you two should have a seat."

"What's going on?" Victory moved the stack of folders on one chair to the floor before sitting. "Taba said the boat wasn't stopping. How far away is it?"

"I got the first call, oh, maybe twenty minutes ago?" Rhaavi shuffled through the forms on his desk. He found the appropriate paper in a pile on his computer keyboard and handed it to Victory. "Captain of One Three Nine said he was receiving conflicting orders and that he might be late. Then he radioed in again a few minutes later, saying something about his new orders to skip Limani and continue upriver to his stop in Calverton."

Rhaavi's scrawling handwriting revealed nothing more than his report, so Victory set the paper back on the untidy desk. That made no sense. Why head straight to the British colonies north of them? Limani was a good customer, and the riverboat must have deliveries to make. At least it still had to sail past the city to continue up the Tranosari Bay toward Calverton. "We can't let that happen."

"Yeah, and what do you propose to do about it?" Rhaavi leaned back over to the radio and twisted a knob again, but it just emitted more static. "All we've got here are fishing boats. By the time we call in people to captain the yachts, the riverboat will be too far away."

Victory stood. "So we take a fishing boat. Keys?" She held out her hand, palm open.

"And I might need to raid whatever sort of armory you have out here," Mikelos said. "Victory, your sword still in the car?"

"It is."

Rhaavi still didn't move, sitting back in his chair and looking up at them in perplexity. "You two are nuts. Yeah, some deliveries might be missed, but that's the shipper's problem. People here'll complain and it'll get made up. Some British stockholder must've thrown his weight around."

"That boat is going to Calverton," Victory said, emphasizing the destination. "My sire is on that boat as a registered passenger. If it docks in the British colonies, he will be sought and killed." This time, she did bare fangs and repress a growl.

Realization dawned in Rhaavi's eyes. "That ridiculous new ban up north. I'm sorry, I didn't know he was on the boat."

"It's okay." Victory backed away. "But now we need your help. Keys to a boat, and if you have a spare firearm for Mikelos to use, that might be handy."

The customs master darted around his office, opening a safe in the corner and retrieving a revolver and a box of bullets. "This is all the weaponry I've got here, but you're welcome to it. The keys to the boats are hanging on the wall in the main office. Taba!"

The dockhand poked his head back in the office from where he'd been lurking outside. "Sir?"

"Get the *Good Choices* gassed up and ready to go." Rhaavi passed the gun and ammunition over to Mikelos. "This pistol has been in my family three generations. I want this back, you hear?"

Mikelos tucked the box under his arm while he inspected the revolver. "My word," Mikelos said, popping a moon clip into the cylinder.

"Are you sure you don't want to call anyone for backup?" Rhaavi said. "You're in the Mercenary Guild, right?"

"There's no time. We can't afford to miss the boat and let it go up the Tranosari. I'll grab my sword," Victory said. "Meet you by the boat, Mik." He passed the roll of sheet music to her before following Raavi.

She jogged out of the customs house and across the small parking lot toward her electric town-car. So much for a simple evening, reuniting with her sire Asaron after his latest mercenary contract in the Roman holdings to the south. Perhaps catching up on news and gossip over dinner in town. She opened the passenger door to dig around in the glove compartment after dropping the sheet music on the seat. Good, she had left her stiletto there after loaning it to her daughter Toria last week. She buckled its sheath around her left forearm, then flexed and rotated the arm to settle it.

Victory had given up her own mercenary life decades ago, retiring to the independent city of Limani after the Last War. Following the upheaval of the city's political system almost eighty years ago, her quiet life vanished when she received a permanent seat on the ruling council representing the city's vampires. However, those vampires consisted of her and Asaron, and she had lost when they drew straws. These days, she used her sword to stay in shape and train new Mercenary Guildmembers, not for defense.

She unlocked the trunk to withdraw her beloved hand-and-a-half bastard sword, sheathed in a battered leather scabbard. She would wield it with pride to protect that vampire who'd saved her life for the first time eight hundred years ago.

Before he shoved the *Good Choices* away from the dock, Taba looked caught behind words he couldn't express. Victory scooted to the other side of the prow. "What's wrong?"

"You, ah, want me to come? I might be able to help."

His scent of fear returned, crisp and dark, overlaying the fishy aroma from the nearby boats. "No, kid, we'll be okay," Victory said. She gave him a closer study. He had broader shoulders than the more common varieties of werepanther usually did. "You're a, what?"

"Leopard, ma'am," he said. "Sinai Clan."

That explained both his dark skin and shoulders, and he hadn't even reached his full bulk yet. "You're also young, Taba," she said. "Strong as I'm sure you are, no. Don't worry, we've done this before. But thanks. And call me Victory."

"You're welcome, Victory," Taba said. "I'll be here when you get back."

At that, he pushed the small fishing boat away from the dock. Mikelos started the engine, and with a low rumble, they headed out over the river.

"We may have done this before, but that was a long time ago." Mikelos' low voice carried just over the engine and wind. "We should have brought the leopard."

"And get him killed?" Victory scanned the dark water for the slow-moving barge's lights. "The Sinai Clan is dying out over here, and no one knows how they're faring in Old Europa. Genevieve would have my head if anything happened to that kid." The head of the werepanthers in Limani was protective of her clan. The wolves might have the reputation for being a close-knit pack, but the cats had their own protective instincts.

"True, very true," Mikelos said. "See anything?"

Brilliant summer stars and a waxing moon bathed the world in pale silver, reflected back again by the undulating surface of the river. A faint golden glow caught her eye in the distance downriver. "There! Cut the engine."

The low rumble faded into silence. "How're we going to reach them?"

"It's hugging this shore," Victory said. "We can drift to them. We're shielded by the front of the barge itself."

Using an oar to steer, they kept themselves head-on to the barge until it came within reach short minutes later. The growl of the engines camouflaged any splashes they made.

Victory uncoiled a line of rope and lassoed one of the barge's cleats. Limani had been the scheduled first stop, and the transport rode low in the water, laden to the maximum limit with dozens of massive shipping crates. After pulling the smaller boat toward the barge, she secured them together so the sides wouldn't scrape and betray their presence.

"I'm going up." She double-checked her weapons and reached for the barge's hull. "You coming, or do you want to stay here and guard our retreat?"

"No close-range weapons." Mikelos left the stern to give her a boost up. "One shot, and the whole crew will be on us. I'll stay here and be ready to drive the getaway car. Give a shout if you need me."

"You'll hear more than shouting if I need you." Victory hauled herself over the edge and onto the barge's deck. It was a good thing she hadn't dressed up to welcome her sire home—grime from the side of the hull now streaked the front of her jeans, and she had a feeling it was only going to get worse.

With one last wave to Mikelos, Victory darted between the large shipping containers stacked in the front of the barge. She made her way toward the rear of the vessel, where the working and living quarters for the crew should be.

The real question concerned Asaron's location. They were nearing Limani, but had not yet passed it. He might not even know his travel arrangements had changed. If all else failed, she could sit tight in hiding and wait for the mayhem to start when her sire figured out his new destination. Even before the British colonies had begun their crusade against vampires, echoing their European homeland's long-held discrimination policies, Asaron refused to travel there. Something about a girl.

But she had no guarantee Asaron was still loose on the riverboat. The captain might have ordered him restrained at once upon learning his new orders in order to prevent said mayhem. Either way, Victory needed to find him now.

Could it be possible to take over the boat and force it to dock at Limani? Rhaavi didn't seem too concerned, and she wondered how often he let deliveries slide. She paused, placing a hand against the side of a container that was damp with evening dew. The customs master was right—this was a commercial shipment, and she didn't want to open that can of worms considering her political position in the city. But if Asaron landed in Calverton, he would have mere hours.

She kept to the shadows when she neared the rear of the barge. If only mythology and legend were reality, and she actually had some form of psychic connection with her sire. Instead, hearing heartbeats warned her of anyone approaching, her one main advantage.

Speaking of which—the dull roar of blood echoing through a heart's chambers alerted her before she heard the gentle rhythm of the crewmember's footsteps. She kept between two containers in the last row, sinking to her heels. Her right hand found its way to the hilt of her sword.

A shaggy-faced man in no apparent uniform wandered through the space between the cabin bulkhead and cargo. Making a split-second decision when he passed by, Victory lunged from the shadows and grabbed the back of his coat, then hauled him between the containers.

She pushed him up against the sturdy metal, bracing her forearm across his throat. "Don't scream. Don't make any noise." She dug her arm into his neck, not enough to cut off air or circulation, but enough to show she meant business.

He didn't even try to open his mouth, and his eyes shone with fear. The man nodded his head a little.

"Good," Victory said. "I have no intention of hurting you if you tell me what I need to know. I'm not a pirate, and I only desire one thing on this boat, something that does not belong to the Empire. Understand?"

"Yes'm." Just a whisper, but the reek of too many days on the boat with not enough toothpaste washed over her. "You're here for the vampire, then?"

"Smart man." Victory released him a tad, but stayed tense, ready to restrain him if needed. "You know what will happen if this boat continues to Calverton with him on it?"

"He'll die," he said. "Cap'n knows this, but made us lock him up anyway. Said we couldn't afford trouble. But Asaron don't deserve that. He's been a good passenger, playing cards with the crew and the like."

"Well, I'm here to relieve your captain of his problem," Victory said, "and I don't want to give you any trouble either. So you can either take me to him, or tell me where he is."

"I'll tell you, and then you better do something with me," he said. "So I can tell Cap I resisted."

"Fair enough," Victory said. He asked for it. It was obvious Asaron had made quite the impression, which surprised her not in the slightest.

The man gestured toward the back of the boat, from the direction he'd come. "Follow the side all the way to the back, then take the first door you come to. Asaron's locked in the second cabin." He paused, looking apologetic. "I don't have a key, and I don't know who's keeping it."

"Thank you very much, but that won't be an issue." Victory released the man, taking a step back. "Asaron and I are in your debt." He looked up, meeting her eyes for the single second she needed. "Sleep."

The crewman dropped like a stone when he was hit by the mental push behind her command, and Victory grabbed him before he could thud to the deck. She lowered him into a comfortable sitting position, arranging his arms and legs enough akimbo to appear like he'd put up a fight before losing. Lying in the shadows, he wouldn't be seen with a casual glance between the containers. She knelt next to him, recovering a bit of strength. Age brought added gifts to vampires, and she had discovered this one over the past few years. Asaron had urged her to improve it, saying practice would make it easier, but she was uncomfortable messing with people's brains.

She peered outside the cargo area once again. With no one in sight, she crept out of hiding and headed to her left. The crewman had given perfect directions, leading her through a deserted section of the riverboat crew quarters. The outside door proved unlocked, so Victory knelt low before pulling it open. She peeked around the corner, but the passageway stood empty. Without unloading to do in Limani, the other crewmembers would be enjoying a quiet night before getting to Calverton around dawn.

Hugging the wall, Victory darted to the second door. She pressed her ear against it. Movement inside, footsteps pacing, no heartbeat. Asaron. She tried the knob, but the man had been right. Locked, and she without any tools to fix that. That was the problem with spur-of-the-moment adventures—no time to pack the essentials.

She rapped out a staccato beat on the door with her knuckles. The movement inside halted. She knocked a second time, repeating the code.

Relief washed over her when she heard the answering pattern. She backed away from the door, ready to kick it in. Drastic, but she didn't see many other options unless she wanted to hunt down the captain for the keys. Mikelos would have to be ready to go when they came tearing back.

A door farther up the hall opened.

"Hands on your head. Now! Back away from the door!"

Victory raised her hands to either side of her head. She pivoted on her heels to confront the new arrival.

The crossbow aimed at her chest gave her a start. The crew had done their homework about fighting vampires and this man had come prepared. Shot with any accuracy, the crossbow's wooden bolts were as hazardous to vampires as to anyone else. He kept a handgun holstered at his waist, but it must contain normal bullets rather than silver if he preferred the more unwieldy weapon.

The man dressed better than his more helpful crewmember, and when he shifted the crossbow to get a comfortable aim, Victory caught the glint of gold at his collar. She had the honor of meeting the captain, then.

He eyed Victory with a mixture of hatred and revulsion, a look she hadn't felt in her own civilized city for years.

She heard a muffled shout from back on deck. They must have found her unconscious friend. Victory wasted no time when the captain's fierce attention broke, diving for his legs. They crashed into the hallway wall.

He cried out in pain when they landed in a heap. The crossbow clattered to the floor. He made a quick grab for the holstered gun, but Victory was the quicker draw, snapping the stiletto into her hand and pressing it to his throat. He met her eyes and flinched away, looking to the side. But he dropped the drawn pistol.

With slow movements, Victory untangled herself from the man's legs and crouched over him. Eyes not leaving his, she groped for the discarded gun at his side. Once she had a firm grip, she replaced the knife at his throat with the pistol. With a twist of her wrist, she resheathed the stiletto.

Rising to her feet, aim never wavering, she favored her prisoner with a glare honed by centuries of proving herself against larger mercenaries. "I want the keys to this cabin."

The captain conceded defeat, lying on the floor as he did. Careful not to make sudden movements, he reached a hand into his breast pocket and withdrew a single key.

"Place it on the floor and push it over to me."

He followed instructions, and Victory knelt to scoop up the key, never taking her eyes or gun off the captain. Taking a step back and reaching behind her, she slid the key into the doorknob.

With a small *snick* she felt more than heard, the door swung inward. "Asaron?"

A deep voice answered. "Right here, girl."

She almost sagged with relief. "Grab your things, we're out."

"Way ahead of you." A hand gripped her shoulder, and her sire darted past her into the passageway and to one of the other closed cabin doors. She focused on the captain at her feet but caught a glimpse of Asaron's long red hair before he disappeared again.

More shouts from outside. They'd found Mikelos. "Asaron, we have to go!" Time to rescue the rescuer. She tilted her head toward Asaron's former prison. "Into the cabin with you," she told the captain at her feet.

He scooted across the floor on his rear into the small cabin. She gestured with the gun. He scooted back another few feet. She stepped forward to pull the door closed and lock it once again. That should help keep the barge off their tail for a short time once they made their escape.

Asaron emerged back into the hallway. He wore his familiar long leather duster over jeans and plain black shirt with his ever-present rucksack slung over one shoulder. Two sword belts looped over his other arm. Victory recognized the distinctive iron hilt of Asaron's Schiavona, but not the other wrapped in fabric. "Bit overkill, don't you think?" She led him back outside onto the deck. Asaron remained silent.

The rear of the boat was deserted, the deck railing and river spread out before them. She tossed the key into the water and listened for more shouts. "See anything?" Having Asaron at her side made her that much more confident. She had absolute faith that Mikelos could hold his own no matter what came up, but Asaron's military experience dwarfed even her own.

"Nope," Asaron said. "Got a boat?"

"How else do you think we got here? Mikelos is driving."

"Could have been magic if you had the kids. Let's get out of here," Asaron said. "If you hadn't noticed, they're not too vampire-friendly."

Victory led him back around the side of the boat. All the noise came from where she'd left Mikelos. They ducked between cargo containers, dashing through the maze toward the opposite end of the boat.

"Move, and we'll cut your line. Where's your friend?"

When she heard the voice ahead of her, she halted Asaron with an arm across his chest. She crouched and poked her head around one of the containers, not wanting to attract attention quite yet. Three men stood at the deck railing with their backs to her. She couldn't tell whether they were armed.

Then she heard Mikelos. "I don't know what you're talking about." She recognized that tone of voice. Her daughter used it on her all the time when she tried to act the innocent. Now she knew where Toria got it from.

Mikelos continued, "Your captain made the arrangements for me to ferry a friend out here for him since you weren't stopping in Limani." Oh, she knew where he was going with this. She would smack him later, after she thanked him for stalling so well. "Guess he didn't want to share."

Her cue. Straightening, Victory strolled out from between two of the metal containers wearing her best innocent look. "What seems to be the problem here, gentlemen?" She flashed them a charming smile and sauntered toward the railing.

The center sailor sneered at her, revealing few teeth. "Who're you?"

"Just a visitor. You can check with your captain. He should still be in his bunk." Ignoring the men, she looked over the edge of the deck down to Mikelos. "Ready to go?"

Mikelos gave a curt nod before pulling loose the rope knot tied to their little boat.

When Victory swung one leg over the railing, the man of poor dental hygiene grabbed Victory's arm. "Not so fast, girl."

She smiled again at the man holding her arm, this time flashing a bit of fang. He yelped and jumped back. "I'm quite fast, thank you," she said before dropping down to the boat, landing with a small rock of the vessel. "Take that as you will, but my husband might be a bit insulted!"

Asaron appeared next to the men at the railing above her. He tossed his rucksack and both swords down to her, then pitched himself over the edge of the boat to dive headfirst into the water.

"See ya," Victory said up to the gaping sailors. She shoved the boat from the side of the barge when Mikelos revved the engine.

One of the sailors above her drew a pistol from his belt and took aim. "Get down!" Victory dropped to the deck, and a bullet whizzed past her head.

More bullets hit the water around them. Good thing Asaron didn't need to come up for air.

The small fishing boat drew away at top speed, such as it was. There were a few more shouts from the crew, but they weren't being paid to keep vampires prisoner. Victory was not inclined to complain when the shots ceased. Water lapped at her fingers, and she raised her head.

"This isn't good," Mikelos said.

The boat listed to the side when Asaron hauled himself on board. "Hey, Mik," Asaron said. "Thanks for the rescue."

"You might have been better off in the water," Mikelos said, still staring at the bottom of the boat.

Victory followed the line of his stare. A bullet had cracked the hull, allowing water to flow in.

The fishing boat limped to the nearest shore thanks to frantic bailing and a lot of luck.

Asaron might be safe, but they weren't out of the water yet. It had been a long day already if Victory was making puns that terrible, even in the safety of her own head. When the hull scraped sand, Mikelos cut the engine and Asaron jumped out. Water soaked them all from the knees down at this point, so Victory sacrificed her boots to help her sire. Between the two of them, they dragged the boat onto shore.

Asaron collapsed back onto the sand, and Victory avoided the temptation to join him. "How are we doing on gas?" she said.

Mikelos was examining the bottom of the boat as water drained out. "Not the problem. We might have enough to get back home at this point, but the boat itself isn't going to make the trip. It's not a leak. Looks like the bullet found a weak spot and now we've got a long crack."

"Where are we?" Asaron propped himself up on his elbows. "And I don't suppose either of you knows what time it is? I lost track, being locked up the past two days."

Studying the lay of the stars, Victory said, "Not long till sunrise. As for where we are, I'm with you."

"Daywalker?" Asaron gave Mikelos an expectant look.

Mikelos shrugged. "We passed Limani while you two were playing around on the boat. I lost track once the sailors found me." He turned in a slow circle. "Nothing looks familiar. I'd say we're no less than five miles from home, but that's too far to walk in the time we've got left."

The small sandy shore led to dense trees in the full leaves of summer, but held no landmarks Victory recognized. Mikelos was right—they had no way to ensure they would make it back to Limani before the sun. She eyed the boat sitting lopsided on the beach. "We're making camp here, then."

"Camp?" Asaron rose, and it was her turn to be on the receiving end of expectant looks.

"You, Asaron, and what shelter?" Mikelos said.

Victory pulled off her wet boots and socks and padded across the sand in her bare feet. Placing a hand on the side of the boat, she said, "This."

"And how to do you propose to manage that, daughter?"

Now he was just teasing. This was not the worst situation the two of them had been caught in with the rising sun. "Toria told me about the time your truck broke down last summer," Victory said. "Stranding you guys in the middle of the Wasteland. The farmhouse."

Now that had been luck. Victory had traveled her share of the edge of the Wasteland, the flat desolate plain that stretched from west of Limani across the bulk of the continent and permanent reminder of the Last War between the British and the Qin. Now the land was home to dust and scrub and lingering radiation, unable to support more than limited life. The burnt-out husk of an ancient farmhouse had saved Asaron's life. Now this boat provided the same gift.

Asaron favored her with a proud smile. "Good thinking."

Putting their strength to use, they dragged the boat toward the trees while Mikelos scouted out two full-sized tree trunks close enough together. It took all three of them to flip the boat and brace it against the trees.

While Asaron tied the arms of his coat around the boat's cleats to create a curtain, he said, "I'm still amazed we came across that house when we did. Talk about a godsend."

Victory stuffed brush around the cracks between the boat and the forest floor. Any extra cover would be useful, and it was a good thing the branches above them were dense. "I still can't believe anyone used to live out there for you to find a house in the first place."

"There used to be a lot more subsistence farmers in that area. Toria's birth family was one of many."

Victory swallowed back a snort. "Family. Right." She hated to think what Toria's life might have been like before she and Mikelos adopted her.

"Just because the elves said her father would become an abuser doesn't mean it was set in stone," Asaron said.

Victory shoved in a final handful of leaves. "Good luck you found her when you did." Bandits had burned the farm and killed the parents, leaving the months-old baby to the elements. Not in any position to raise her himself, Asaron had brought the child to his progeny and her daywalker. Years later, they learned the elves had marked Toria for eventual "rescue" from her birth parents. Pure coincidence led

Asaron to the site first. More memories of her last trip to the Wasteland swam to the surface of her mind. Dirt and rocks, strange animals, a desolation where nothing proper could grow or live. "Thinking of Toria growing up out there is terrifying."

Mikelos wrapped his arms around Victory, drawing her head to his shoulder. She hugged him back, giving him a quick peck on the cheek.

Asaron finished tying up a sheet of canvas he'd found stowed beneath one of the seats. Between it and the coat, they would be protected from direct sun. He stepped away from the boat, surveying their handiwork. "I suppose it will have to do," he said.

Sire and progeny were both seasoned campaigners and had often traveled with humans or others immune to the sun's rays. Both of them had been in worse spots, with much less time to cobble together a shelter. This ranked right up with a luxury hotel. "Guess there's not much else we can do," she said.

Asaron looked over the river to the east. The stars had faded as the sky transitioned from black toward midnight blue. Dawn approached. "Guess not." She heard a hitch in his voice.

Liar. Asaron never could hide anything from her. "Hey," Victory said. She disentangled herself from Mikelos' arms and approached her sire, placing a hand on his shoulder. "What's wrong?" Centuries ago, a client had nicknamed them Sun and Moon. Considering his fiery red hair in comparison with her darker locks, and the way he towered a foot over her, she had not been inclined to disagree.

Asaron captured her hand and gripped it tight, tracing her fingers with his thumb. "I was locked in that cabin after we left port in New Carthage."

"That's what, a three-day ride?" Mikelos said.

"Closer to four, with all the stops." Asaron gazed over Victory's head. She glanced over her shoulder and realized he was giving her daywalker a hungry stare.

Realization dawned. "Four days, with no food?"

"Three days, after they locked me up and took everything I had bottled," he said. "Bottles were gone when I grabbed my stuff after you broke me out. I'll have to get Toria to charm me more when we get home."

No wonder Mikelos looked like the evening special. But this was an old conversation. Mikelos belonged to her. Sire or not, vampires did not share daywalkers. She squeezed his hand. "Will you be okay?"

"Yes," Asaron said. "Been through worse." His eyes turned back to the imminent sunrise.

So had she, though it was never fun. But if Asaron thought he could handle it, Victory wouldn't argue. "C'mon, let's get settled."

He nodded once, dragging his eyes away from the sky and ducking under the canvas. Before she could follow, Mikelos grabbed her again. Always a tug of war in this threesome. "Yes, love?"

"I can't sleep under there with you," Mikelos said. "Not while he's like that."

"I know," she said. Not just a tug of war, but a never-ending process of soothing male egos. A hundred years later, it still wasn't any easier. Pulling Mikelos behind her, she followed Asaron under the boat and settled herself into a corner. "Okay," she said. Asaron had stolen the prime spot, lounging against one of the trees next to his belongings. She would have to be content with hunching over for this conversation. "Now for the real story. What the hell was that little escapade about?" Mikelos lay on his stomach, stretching his legs out of the covered area into the open air.

"Did I tell you how much I appreciate this, daughter?" He tried to appear innocent. It failed, since his face was only about three feet from hers.

She met his look full on, aware of how unsettling an intent look from her could be. Mikelos could meet a vampire's eyes, but Asaron didn't live with a companion who stared him down on a regular basis. No escape behind coyness this time. Not after dragging her who-knew-how-far away from the city on what was supposed to be a normal evening. "Don't even try to pull that. I want to know why I just risked our lives to save your sorry old ass. Why the sudden trip home?"

"Have some respect, girl. This sorry old ass can still whip yours. But I do appreciate the timing."

"So talk, then," Mikelos said. "Why were you in the Roman colonies to begin with? Max said the Guild contract was sealed and wouldn't give us any details. Then you disappeared last month, and we didn't hear from you until Toria told us we needed to meet you at the customs house tonight."

"I should have taken the train instead of setting foot on that boat. But as for why—" Asaron pulled the second sword out from under the pack next to him and laid it in front of Victory.

She unwrapped the cotton to reveal the hilt. "Toria's rapier! I was wondering where it went."

"She also didn't tell you that it broke." He held up a hand before she could demand explanations. "It's all better now. She asked me to get it fixed for her, and that's what I did. I'm friends with a good smith down in the Grand Strand, so I figured that was the best place to take it."

"But why wouldn't she tell me?"

"She didn't want you to be mad that she'd broken Jarimis' sword." Asaron took the blade back and rewrapped it. "I was actually about to head west to look into some deaths when I got quite the panicked message from her. Something to do with science and alloys." The elder vampire made a face.

Victory could commiserate. Like her sire, she'd never understood her daughter's fascination with the modern.

Asaron continued, "So since I wasn't the only one looking into that case, I promised Toria I'd get it fixed. Then it showed up in my hotel room in two pieces. I figured magic had to be involved somewhere at that point."

"But why would she think that I'd be angry at her?" Victory said.

"My fault," Mikelos said. "I flipped out once when she let a friend play Connor's cello. She is terrified of hurting the relics from those that we loved. And Jarimis was your progeny."

A guarded look crossed Asaron's face. "I would have been gone longer, but there's been news from the south. Bad news."

"Is there any other kind?" Victory said. "Let me guess: something about the secession of the new Emperor?"

"Politics." Mikelos snorted. "Romans are crazy. I grew up in the capital, and I still don't understand them."

"Things have changed, but not that much. Since the Emperor didn't have a son himself, the heir was chosen from his nephews," Asaron said. "And who the senators approved wouldn't have been my first choice."

Her sire paid more attention to global politics than she did these days, since he still made his living off warring factions. "Why?" Who wasn't important, Victory knew, but rather the motives behind the choice.

"Humans are beginning to forget about the war that created the Wasteland," Asaron said. "The Romans weren't involved, and the Senate in Roma wasn't directly affected by the results. The imperialist faction won."

"So?" Mikelos said. "That's always been the case on the continent. The colonies have spread as much as they can. The southern Wasteland is even more uninhabitable than ours."

Asaron shook his head. "There's still north."

Victory froze. "But north is Limani."

"And that is where the Roman Army is currently marching."

Sun broke over the horizon. This was not the sort of news Victory needed when she wasn't safe at home. Asaron would have to meet with the city council to share this information, and they'd need to start coordinating with Max Asher, head of the local branch of the Mercenary Guild. Mikelos squeezed her hand, and Victory realized she'd frozen in thought.

"Is the army going to get here today?" Mikelos said. Asaron shook his head. "Then both of you sleep, and we'll raise the alarm tonight."

Mikelos might be Victory's best friend and lover, but daytime guardian was the daywalker's original job description. She handed him her sword and he ducked out of the shelter to settle against another nearby tree.

She curled up next to Asaron, entwining her fingers with his. Asaron completed her family, and with them, Limani could stand up to anything.

Toria closed her eyes in brief dismay when thunder rolled through the apartment. That wasn't supposed to happen. When the glassware in her impromptu laboratory stopped rattling on its shelves, she peered at the beaker and dagger in her hands. The silver solution coating the bottom and sides of the beaker had transformed into a black chalky substance. The blade didn't look much better. Useless, now. She plunked both items back on the counter and pulled off her lab glasses.

"What the hell?"

At her partner's query, the containment spell collapsed around her in sparkles of violet light. When the last vestiges faded, Toria waved her glasses at the doorway. "Hey."

Kane stepped into her lab—also known as the corner kitchen of their apartment—with an over-exaggerated hesitant expression. "Am I in danger of being blown up?"

"Not today," Toria said. She eyed the charred mark on the countertop. Yet another sample had proven a failure. She exchanged her glasses for the beaker and crossed to the other counter, making sure not to scuff the chalk lines on the tile floor with her feet.

Kane stayed well away from her work area, choosing a stool from the sitting area of their open-concept apartment. "What happened to 'I will not set things on fire without my partner present'?"

Toria washed and rinsed the beaker, then brought a damp sponge back to the other counter to dab at the black soot mark. "You had plans. With a boy. So this is me entertaining myself while you're out on hot dates." Some hard scrubbing removed most of the mark.

"You could have gone with Mikelos and Victory last night and stayed back at the house. Mikelos would have cooked for you this morning," Kane said.

"But then the whole sword thing would have come up," Toria said. "It's embarrassing." Not only had she broken her sword and had to ask her grandfather to get it repaired, but the sword had been an antique that used to belong to one of Victory's progeny. She wasn't looking forward to her mother finding out. "So. Your date. Any good?"

"He was okay," Kane said, running a hand through his close-cropped black hair. "Really, really old-country British, so he freaked out when he figured out I was Victory's foster son. In the middle of brunch. Also embarrassing."

"Sorry, hon," Toria said. She was, honest. Her partner was tall, dark, and drop-dead gorgeous. And still got more dates than she did, even considering his more limited dating pool. In a perfect world, she and Kane would have lived happily ever after together, but their relationship had been closer to that of siblings from day one. But no time to dwell, she had work to do. "The day is still young. Want to help?"

Kane left his safe spot to come closer to her workspace, dragging the stool behind him. She knew he wouldn't be able to resist her latest chemistry project, even if he was often limited to note-taker and general observer. Still more interesting than hoity-toity British boys. "What are you up to now?" He eyed her neat row of vials containing different variations on the silver goop she'd just discarded.

"Well, I figured out why my sword broke," Toria said. "Simple, in the end, and I should have realized it a long time ago." Any middle-school kid with a chemistry set knew the answer to that one. Or hobbyist jeweler. Or self-taught metallurgist. All of which she was, to one degree or another. "Why is silver mixed with copper in most jewelry?"

"Umm . . ."

He did this, acted the dunce to make her feel better. She loved him for it. "It's mixed with copper to make the piece stronger. Silver on its own is too soft a metal to retain its shape against hard wear and tear," she said, rearranging the vials on the counter again. She pulled her glasses back on, and gestured for Kane to grab his own pair hanging on the wall. "So what did I do that was so inordinately stupid?"

"I was never clear on what you did in the first place." After donning eye protection, he picked up one of the vials and watched the silver solution slide around inside. "Just that you converted part of the metal in your sword to silver."

Toria plucked the vial out of his hand and returned it to its original place. "Yeah, when we were young idiots, and I thought I knew what I was doing. Before I knew as much about chemistry and metallurgy as I do now. I analyzed one of the shards, and frankly, I'm surprised it lasted as long as it did."

"How so?"

She pointed to a spot on the floor, and Kane moved his stool and then parked himself as instructed. "Because I had the damn proportions completely wrong." She clenched her fist at her side. It would be a long time before she stopped berating herself for this. "I thought I could willy-nilly mess with the steel and that my magic would retain the strength of the blade. I was so stupid."

"No, you weren't," Kane said. "Just young. You said it yourself, you didn't know as much as you do now. And I assume now you're trying to fix the problem?"

"Yeah." She unstopped the vial at the end of the row to pour the silver solution into the clean beaker. "Grandpa took the hilt when he left. He said he'd take it to a smith he trusts and get a new blade forged for me."

"Then Asaron'll bring it back good as new. And we'll redo the spell we did in high school, but you'll get the proportions right this time, and it'll be your old sword again. No problem."

She could feel another tension headache coming on, despite her partner's soothing presence. Toria scuffed both hands through her short hair. "You're right. I should have gone with them to pick him up. What if the boat was late, and they got stranded during the day?"

"Then it's a good thing Mikelos is perfectly okay in the sun," Kane said. "It'll be okay, love."

She swirled the silver in the beaker. Damn his logic. "Yeah, I guess."

"They'll bring him home. And your sword. Now show me what we're going to do to make it even better than it was."

After being wrapped up in each other's souls for ten years, he knew how to manipulate her. Not that it was difficult to make her talk about her true passion: mixing the two volatile sciences of chemistry and magic. "Well," she held up the new beaker, "this is a formula I'm still attempting to perfect." She gestured to the remaining vials. "Those are the latest variations I mixed up this morning."

"Do I want to know what's in them?"

Toria had banned him from helping her play with chemicals due to his incurable inability to measure with any precision. He was a terrible cook, too. "The new idea is that instead of weakening the steel of a blade by converting a percentage of it to silver, I should coat the blade with a microscopic layer of silver instead. Bond it to the steel so well it can't even be scraped away."

"So what are we doing here, exactly?" Kane said.

Toria picked up another small blade from the counter—a broken throwing knife, this time. "I've been trying to figure out the best way to bond the silver alloy to the steel of a blade."

"Magic?"

"Of course." Toria held the beaker out to Kane. "And I've gotten used to working with the extra magical properties the silver gives me. It takes too much concentration to pour the alloy on the blade and get it to cover evenly at the same time. So you pour, and I'll spread."

Uncertainty clouded his face. "If you think so."

Her fascination with mixing chemistry and magic always left him a bit puzzled, similar to the way his own passion for literature made no sense to her. "You'll be fine, hon," she said. "Help me set up the containment spell, and then pour when I tell you to."

He grasped the beaker between thumb and forefinger and looked unsure how tight to hold the glass. She gave him an encouraging smile, and he relaxed. He would trust her. He always would.

What she and Kane formed was unique in Limani—a warrior-mage pair. Before Kane, Toria was just a regular mage. A bit precocious for her age, but nothing special. Before Toria, Kane had zero magical ability, despite both of his parents being mages. But when they first grasped hands at age twelve, their energies meshed with such completeness that the jolt of power even activated Kane's latent magical ability. Together, their power was so stable that they had control over their abilities that most mages took decades to achieve. Some bonded mages took advantage of that control to expand the reaches of their power, becoming legends in magical circles. Toria and Kane, on the other hand, had decided on the more traditional road of warrior-mages after bonding, focusing their extra time on martial arts, swordplay, and tactics and apprenticing themselves to Limani's Mercenary Guild.

With Kane helping her, she could place the load of the containment spell on him and concentrate on spreading the alloy. She shouldn't have juggled both magical processes at the same time. Her lapse of mental control over the containment circle had resulted in the earlier thunder as her power echoed through her affinity element of storm. She didn't have enough concentration for the circle while doing two other things requiring such physical dexterity.

They locked gazes. Toria nudged the mental switch in her head that allowed the world around her to flare into real color. Every time she used her magesight to illuminate the world, she wondered how mundane humans could stand such bland surroundings. But now her silver vials glowed, and the beaker Kane held gained more depth of light and shadow than seemed possible. The knife in her open palms shimmered with electricity, the result of a charm she placed on all of their weapons to protect them from rust.

Kane overshadowed every other magical object in the room. His fluid emerald aura enveloped him, shimmering over his deep brown skin and representing the powers of earth he aligned with. While both of them were mages, and all mages could affect the magical power inherent in the world to an extent, Kane's true talents lay in growth and healing.

She tuned out her own familiar aura by habit but knew Kane saw her body encased in a delicate crystalline structure glinting deep violet, deceptive in its strength. The power of her own element of storm reacted with the leftover electrical charge in the room, and she smiled when the hair on their arms stood on end. Her alignment with storm allowed her to manipulate the power that flowed through all people and objects, from the electrical power of a storm or a wall outlet to the bioelectricity in all living beings.

Other mages aligned with air, water, and fire, rounding out the so-called circle of planetary life. Warrior-mages could come in any combination of the five elements, but Toria and Kane counted themselves lucky that storm and earth worked so complementarily with each other.

Toria's personal shields fractured, then spread out to form the framework of a globe around them, using the chalk circle on the floor as a guide. Kane's fluid aura expanded to flow in and around the prismatic shapes of her shield.

A small sigh escaped her lips, and Toria recognized the matching look of contentment on Kane's face. She felt Kane pour more of his energies into the shield and took the weight of powering her half of it. She remained connected to the energy, but now it was Kane's responsibility to maintain the containment spell. When they shared magic, they were as close as two hemispheres of a brain, working in harmony to accomplish one goal.

She paused for Kane to regain his own internal equilibrium. He opened his eyes and held up the beaker. "Ready?"

Toria grasped the knife's hilt, holding the blade horizontal. Kane tipped the beaker, and her thick silver formula oozed toward the edge of the glass.

Her entire being centered upon the point where liquid would meet metal. Toria felt her perception shift in a way she had not expected. Her vision tunneled, and the blade of the dagger magnified hundreds of times in her sight, more precise than a microscope. But it had depth, not the flat look of a sample smashed between two glass slides. The blade wavered in her hands, making the world appear as though it shook in a violent earthquake. A wave of dizziness passed over her.

Everything stilled when the silver liquid touched the blade. Then a brilliant flash of pure white light left Toria blinking away shadowy negative images. Uncontrolled power surged through her. She heard the familiar sharp crack of thunder, and the world went black.

Kane shouted her name in the distance. She no longer sat on her stool, but instead found herself sprawled on the tile floor. Her left shoulder ached where she'd landed on it. Heat warmed the skin on her cheeks and forehead in marked contrast to the cool floor.

"Toria!"

Kane's hands wrapped around her upper arms and tugged. The strange warmth got hotter, and an odd smell met her nose. Had she mixed some compounds wrong?

Her eyes shot open when all of the pieces fell together. Kane stood above her, shouting her name and attempting to haul her across the floor. She pushed herself up, banging the top of her head into Kane's chin. They both yelped in pain.

Broken glass surrounded her, and the alloy oozed across the floor. Blue flames leapt from the silver liquid, gushing a thick white smoke toward the ceiling. The knife lay discarded nearby, the blade charred and black.

"What the hell happened?"

"You tell me!" A note of panic marked Kane's voice. A screeching noise drowned out the rest of his words when the smoke detector kicked in.

Toria pushed herself off the floor, ignoring the complaints from her aching body and the ringing in her ears. She must have cracked her head on the floor when she fell, too. She staggered across the kitchen to grab the fire extinguisher off the wall. This was not her first incident. Kane took cover on the other side of the kitchen island when Toria pulled the pin on the extinguisher and sprayed the unnatural blue flames with thick white foam. She had done this too many times.

The fire went out fast, and Toria thanked her luck that she'd once again not burned down the small apartment building. They surveyed the mess.

"You have a habit of doing that," Kane said, pitching his voice over the smoke detector, but calmer in the absence of fire.

She didn't have the energy to shout back. The metal extinguisher clanged on the counter where she set it down. She rubbed her sore shoulder and hoped the noxious metallic taste in the air faded soon.

They stared at the mess of evaporating foam and scorched metal staining the tile floor. With a last disgruntled beep, the smoke detector stopped screaming. "Well, then," Kane said. "We should probably work on this before the stains set in the tile."

"What do you mean, 'we'?" Toria said. "I'm pretty sure this is my project and my mess. And definitely my fault."

"Nah." Kane pushed up his shirtsleeves. "Once again, we forgot our power doesn't just double when we work together."

"Yeah. It quadruples," Toria said. She opened a tall cupboard in the corner of the kitchen, revealing their stock of cleaning supplies. "I was so determined to get results. Are you sure it isn't you who should be the scientist?"

"Thank gods I'm not." He caught the roll of paper towels Toria tossed to him. "Let's pop open all the windows after we're done here and head out for the afternoon while the air clears."

The cleanup went quick, a matter of mopping up foam and soot. Toria shoved the charred knife into a drawer that collected random scraps of metal. "Want to help me again tomorrow? Or do you have another date with what's-his-name?"

"I doubt there will be more dates with Duncan," Kane said. "Oh. There was something else that happened this morning. We were, ah, asked to leave the first restaurant we went to."

Toria paused in her scrubbing to quirk an eyebrow at him. "Dress code?" That didn't seem likely, when she took in Kane's black slacks and green collared shirt.

"Nope," Kane said. "A sign that basically said 'no nonhumans.' And since there was a bright flash of blue light when I walked in, I guess mages qualify. Which is ironic, since they were using magic as a detector."

Toria stared at him. "That's the most ridiculous thing I've ever heard. Where was this?"

"Café Lizzette, off Main Street. We ended up at that Castillian place a few blocks down."

"Isn't Café Lizzette owned by Emily Fabbri?" Toria remembered the campaign posters all over downtown—Fabbri had been elected as a human representative to the city council in the last election cycle. Interesting.

"I think so. We got out of there pretty quick," Kane said. "But I'm curious to see which mage set that charm. Up for an adventure today?"

"Definitely," Toria said. "There aren't that many mages in Limani, and I want to know who's selling out."

"Me, too," Kane said. "Between the vampire bans up north and the werecreature segregation in the Roman Colonies down south, we can't afford that bullshit in Limani."

Bullshit indeed. Toria resumed her work on the scorch marks. This was her home, and she adored Limani's independent spirit. She and Kane might just be college students, but there were few mages in Limani, and they were the only warrior-mage pair. That gave them some pull, and she was going to pull threads and see what unraveled.

What else was she going to do on summer break beside set fires in her kitchen?

In simple black script, the sign in front of Café Lizzette read: *Humans welcome. Patronage discouraged from all others.*

Toria read the sign a second time, waiting for the meaning to sink in. "But that's . . . that's outrageous! Isn't that illegal?" She turned to Kane. "Please tell me it's illegal."

He leaned against a lamppost and shook his head. "I did some research while you were showering. It's not. The city council was created with the idea that this sort of prejudice wouldn't exist, so there aren't any laws to actually combat that. Awful logic."

Toria was about two seconds away from marching into the café. "I don't understand. The last census showed that barely a fifth of the population was a mage, werecreature, or elven. It's not like we're overrunning the place."

"To some people, even one is enough."

"So Emily Fabbri owns this place? One of the new councilmembers?"

"Yep," Kane said. "That's why I'm worried."

"Mama wasn't happy with the election results." They stared at the restaurant. Toria's skin crawled at the notion of this sort of prejudice, especially since the city had almost descended into civil war less than five years ago when the werepanthers sued for fair representation on the council. She knew she'd grown up in the rather rose-tinted world of Limani, but this bordered on ridiculous. Scratch that. Insanity.

Worry for her mother also itched in the back of her skull. No one had answered at the house when she'd called, which meant they hadn't made it home last night. She kept telling herself that the boat had been late and the three had been stranded at the docks. It wasn't like Mikelos not to call them, though.

"That's it," Toria said. "This is so not cool." She strode forward, reaching the door of the restaurant before Kane could react. A last look over her shoulder before entering revealed that Kane still leaned against the lamppost. Fair enough. He could come to the rescue if this ended in tears.

The bell above the door rang when she entered, and as Kane had reported, a shimmer of blue light washed over her. She reached out with her own magic to search for a taste of the caster. But a waitress pounced on her right away, breaking her concentration.

"Hi, I'm Paige, and I'll be your server today. How many in your party?" She grabbed a handful of menus from a small rack before Toria could answer.

"Um, just me, thanks. Is Ms. Fabbri available?" Toria attempted to match the girl's vapid smile and disarming look, wishing for Kane's better acting skills. She noted the eclectic artwork on the walls. "I'm a local artist and wanted to talk to her about displaying some of my work."

"That's so neat! She's in her office," Paige said, replacing the menus. "I'm sure she would love to talk with you! Wait a sec." The waitress swept back through the restaurant, weaving between tables.

Toria peered out the front window. Kane now lounged on a bench in front of the music shop Mikelos frequented. He slouched, but she knew her partner in and out. One eye was on the restaurant and he was ready to move at the first sign of danger.

"Can I help you?" The frosty voice prompted Toria to turn back to the dining room. A blonde in her mid-thirties glared at her.

"Ms. Fabbri?" Toria held out her hand. "My name is—"

"I know what your name is." She ignored Toria's attempt at politeness. "And I know who your mother is. I trust you noticed the sign on your way in?"

Straight evidence of this woman's bigotry shook her. She meant every bit of her discrimination. Well, Toria could match that chilliness. "Your sign is what I'd like to speak with you about today, ma'am." Her parents raised a polite girl, even if this woman didn't deserve it.

"Good. Then you'll realize that not only do I have nothing to talk to you about," Ms. Fabbri said, "but that you're also not welcome here, *mage*." The title sounded nasty spilling from her lips.

Any thoughts of civility fled Toria's mind. "What the hell is your problem, lady?" Her voice rose, and nearby diners were staring.

"People like you." Fabbri's eyes shone with fury. "Freaks who have too much power for their own good, and who lord it over normal humans!"

Now that was too much. "Lord over what?" Toria said. "When has a nonhuman ever affected your life in any drastic way?"

"I joined the council so that I could prevent them from abusing their power. But instead I found it was already too late." Her neglect to answer the question did not escape Toria's notice.

"Too late for what?" The woman made less and less sense. "How did you even get elected to the council when you obviously have no idea how it's run?"

"I know exactly how it's run—by representatives of a minority of the population who hold a majority of the power."

The bell above the door jangled when a new patron entered the restaurant, but Toria paid the new arrival no heed. She didn't have the patience to remind Fabbri that those minority representatives cast votes worth half those of the human district representatives. Every high school civics student knew that. "If you're this nuts, the council's going to kick you out 'cause of your own stupidity." She started when a heavy hand landed on her right shoulder. She twisted her head, startled to see one of Limani's finest frowning down at her.

"What seems to be the problem here?" For once, the phrase didn't seem quite so cliché. The police officer looked stern.

Fabbri beamed at him. "Thank goodness you arrived in time, officer," she said. "As you heard, this young woman entered my establishment to threaten me."

Toria's temper itched to spill out, but she bit her tongue. She'd been set up. The charm had alerted Fabbri, who must have called the cops before she even left her office.

His hand felt heavier on her shoulder, fingers digging into her skin. "I did indeed hear that. Perhaps the young lady and I need to have a talk about respect. And your name is?"

"She's Toria Connor." Fabbri answered before Toria could even open her mouth. "She's the daughter of the Master of the City."

Frown deepening even more, the officer said, "I see. The daughter of such an upstanding member of the city should understand that she needs to set a good example for her peers."

"Then I will leave her in your capable hands, sir." Now Fabbri was just simpering. "I need to attend to my customers."

Toria was disgusted. Her hands clenched into fists, and she fought back every instinct to throw up a shield and repel the policeman.

"Of course, ma'am." His grip tightened another fraction on Toria's shoulder. "Allow me to escort her out."

The grip released, and he nudged her forward. Toria held her head high as she preceded the cop toward the exit. Paige the waitress stood in her spot next to the menus, jaw hanging open. Toria ignored her.

First she almost blew up her apartment. And now she might get arrested. At least Kane was outside, not in here with her stupidity.

Mama is going to kill me.

Kane had come to Toria's rescue, as usual, and scrounged up both the best and worst possible adult to get her out of this mess. Dr. Lena Joensen, dean of Jarimis University, where Toria and Kane had both just finished their sophomore years. She was the second dean of Limani's local university, personally picked to succeed the founder, Victory's progeny Jarimis. And since Jarimis University included students from both the British and Roman colonies, the dean maintained one of the unelected city council seats along with Victory. She'd also taken a personal interest in the education of the young pair. When Kane had showed up at the small police station with Dean Joensen in tow, the police released Toria into her care after a lecture on "appropriate public behavior" and "representing her mother in public."

Now Toria and Kane leaned against each other on a bench outside the station while the dean finished filling out paperwork inside. It didn't matter that she hadn't been arrested, the damage was done. The few cops and visitors in the station now knew the Master of the City's daughter had been there. Rumors would spread.

"Thanks, hon," Toria said after soaking in her partner's calming presence.

He tilted his head and kissed her temple. "Still couldn't reach Victory or Mikelos at the house."

At last, Dean Joensen exited the station and sank onto the bench on Toria's other side. Toria forced herself to look at the dean. But the older woman stared across the parking lot, her expression unreadable, as she brushed an errant silver lock behind her ear.

"Um . . . I'm sorry?" Toria knew it wasn't enough. Another potential rumor: Dean Joensen bailed out a simple university student because she was the daughter of the Master of the City. Talk about favoritism. "I didn't mean to lose my temper. But she set me up."

"No harm done, Toria. You're not in any permanent trouble."

"People will talk."

"So let them talk. We can hope the smart ones will wonder what happened and see the sign on the restaurant." Dean Joensen patted Toria's knee. "And that those same smart ones will start to rethink who they have elected to Limani's ruling council."

Now she began to get it. "You don't like her either, do you? That's why you came when Kane called."

"I was given a seat on the city council after I became dean of Jarimis University," Dean Joensen said. "Because so many of the students are citizens of the Roman and British Empires. I'm their voice while they live in our city, another check on Limani's neutral position between the two colonies. Jarimis never sat on the council because Victory already had a seat, and many people couldn't distinguish Jarimis the dean from Jarimis the vampire. I've always followed your mother's example of quiet neutrality. But I wasn't about to ignore Kane's call for help. I suppose I've finally backed myself into a corner."

"Because your spot on the council is permanent." Toria compared her recent experience with scattered memories. "Mama has complained about that same thing. It looks like you guys have a lot of power because you weren't elected, but at the same time, you can't make too many waves because otherwise you'll be accused of abusing your power. That's what Ms. Fabbri was harping about."

"Exactly."

"You would have come for any student who called," Kane said.

"But not two students such as yourselves. Not Limani's warrior-mage pair, who happen to both be children of current and former councilmembers," Dean Joensen said. "Did you know that Victory and I have only seen each other once outside of the council chamber since Jarimis died? For your parents' funeral, Kane."

"Have things gotten so bad that two councilmembers can't even socialize without suspicion?" Kane said. "Mom and Victory used to see each other all the time, even before Toria and I bonded."

"The problems picked up when your parents passed away. You both have taken Legacy of the Modern World, yes?"

Toria and Kane heaved identical sighs. "Yeah," Toria said, "we got it out of the way our first semester."

Dean Joensen laughed. She knew full well that Toria preferred her science courses and that Kane would live in the literature department if he could. "Not your favorite class, was it?"

"Give me a scientific equation any day," Toria said. "Don't ask me why some jerk two hundred years ago did what he did."

"I'll try not to," Dean Joensen said. "But you know why the existence of Limani is so important."

The small city-state of Limani on the New Continent had been founded as a Greek colony, modeled after the multiple Greek city-states that funded the expedition. Less than ten years later, the last major Roman expansion had swallowed all vestiges of the independent Greek cities. Now either empire to the north or south could use their colonial forces to take over the city by moving in a few battalions of soldiers and announcing they were now in control. Limani's regular military defense consisted of the handful of civic police officers, the small branch of the local Mercenary's Guild dedicated to Limani independence, and one former mercenary playing politics as the Master of the City.

But the tiny city-state acted as a neutral zone between the two territories. The city was situated where the safe zone outside the Wasteland bottle-necked at the coast between the north and south, barely fifty miles away. Any hostile act by either side could once again result in all-out destruction, with Limani at ground zero.

Toria could have recited all of that by rote, but instead compressed the speech into "Limani acts as the barrier between the two colonies. What does that have to do with you and Mama not spending time together? Didn't the council even play poker games a long time ago?"

"Once upon a time. Your mother took money from the other members on a regular basis," Dean Joensen said. "Her constant winnings were the reason they eventually stopped. Jarimis warned me when I first took my seat on the council, but I still found out the hard way." She rose to her feet and faced Toria and Kane. "You will tell Victory what happened today?"

"Oh, she'll know," Kane said.

"Anything in particular you want me to pass along?" Toria asked.

"Tell her what happened to you today. Tell her what type of person Limani has elected to rule it, and that we need to do something about it."

Now Toria wished she had paid more attention to Victory whenever her mother spoke of the council. Fabbri had been elected with two other new councilmembers. Were either of them also spreading this hate through the city? They still needed to find the mage who had charmed Café Lizzette. "We're with you," Toria said.

Victory wasn't sure what woke her first—the last of the sun's rays setting over the forest or Mikelos' shout from outside their makeshift shelter. She scrambled to her feet after Asaron and ducked out from the tarp behind him in the dimming evening light.

Asaron drew his basket-hilted sword, the Schiavona he had wielded for hundreds of years, and took up position next to Mikelos. Her daywalker already braced himself with the pistol readied, though pointed at the ground. Victory heard another crash through the nearby underbrush. Mikelos glanced back at her and twitched his head toward where her sword leaned against a tree. She snagged it and drew the blade in time to hear a familiar shout.

"It's just us!" her daughter called out. "Don't shoot!"

Victory and Asaron lowered their swords and Mikelos barked out a laugh. "Stealthy you are not, daughter!"

The tall form of her foster son, Kane Nalamas, ducked under a low branch and emerged into view, followed by her adopted daughter. "That was kind of the point," Kane said. "Didn't feel like getting skewered today."

He staggered when Asaron clapped him on the shoulder. "Good call, boy," Asaron said. "A good skewering is never fun."

Victory lowered her sword and embraced Toria. "How did you even find us?"

"Tracking spell in the hilt of my sword," Toria said, pointing at their small shelter. "I can find that thing down to a three-square-foot radius."

"It's true," Kane said. "We've played scavenger hunt with it a few times, and even mage shields can't hide it from her. As for how we knew you were out here, we went by the house looking for you and found a rather frantic message on your answering machine from the customs master."

"So we headed to Merc HQ and grabbed long-distance wheels, enabled the tracking spell, and headed out for the rescue," Toria said. "The SUV is back on the road, less than a mile away from here."

"That's my girl," Victory said, squeezing Toria's shoulders again. "I wasn't looking forward to the walk."

Asaron ducked back into their shelter and returned with Toria's sword. "I believe this is yours, Granddaughter."

Toria made grabby hands at the weapon and all but hugged it when Asaron relinquished it to her. "Thanks again, Grandpa. I owe you one. Speaking of." Toria reached into her backpack and pulled out two canteens that she handed to Asaron and Victory. Asaron popped the cap of the charmed bottled and chugged down the preserved blood. Once drained, Victory handed over her own bottle and he repeated the process. She could wait. Her sire had had a rough few days.

"Let's head home," Mikelos said, accepting a bottle of water from Kane's pack. "Have to call Rhaavi and tell him we owe someone a boat."

"Indeed," Victory said. "Did we miss anything today?" Toria did not hide a dramatic flinch.

"Well," Kane said. "You could say that."

"You did *what*?"

Her mother's demand echoed off the tile floor of the large kitchen. Next to Toria, Mikelos rubbed his ear. All five of the family gathered around the table while Toria, Kane, and Mikelos ate a late pasta dinner and Victory and Asaron nursed mugs of blood.

"Um, can I ask which one you're most mad at before I start defending myself?" Toria refused to be too put out. If Victory had really been angry, she would have stormed off to cool down on her own. Instead, her mother seemed more in shock than anything else. Understandable.

Victory shook her head in slow disbelief. "Burning down your apartment, I can understand. You've done worse."

"Almost burning down the apartment." Even while admitting to the havoc she wreaked, it still wasn't fair to say Toria had done any real damage.

"Okay, almost burning down the apartment," Victory said. "No, what concerns me more is that little stunt at the restaurant."

"It was a bit of a drastic measure, Toria," Mikelos said.

Toria jumped to her own defense. "It's not my fault the lady was a jerk to me. And I had no idea she would call the cops the second I walked into the place."

"Ooh, scary mage alert!" Kane's quip caused a ripple of laughter, breaking the tension around the table.

Her mother matched her smile. "You're right, love. The police involvement was not necessarily your fault. But it might have been something you'd suspect."

"But nothing bad happened," Toria said. "I wasn't arrested. Nothing went on any sort of record. And by her actions, Emily Fabbri proved in front of everyone in her restaurant that she is prejudiced to the point of extremism."

"And the question we must now ask is exactly how far she will take that prejudice," Victory said.

"When's your next council meeting?" Asaron said.

"Two nights from now." Victory tilted her chair back. "Half an hour after sunset. Which means I believe I will be calling on Dean Joensen tomorrow evening." She stole a sip of Mikelos' beer. "And afterward, perhaps some coffee at Café Lizzette might be nice."

It was going to be a fun evening.

Soon after sunset the next evening, Victory drove out to Jarimis University. She still had some time before the dean was expecting her, so after parking near the administration building, she took a few minutes to wander over to the Garden of Remembrance that overlooked the river. Various friends over the years had described the gorgeous sunsets over the Agios River. Mikelos even taped one onto a vid-disk for her a few years ago, but her family informed her that it could only truly be experienced in person. The river was just as beautiful by starlight, however.

Even she donned tank tops in summer weather this warm, and a light breeze brushed over Victory's bare shoulders as she wound her way through the garden. Water splashed in a small fountain, the stone spout in the shape of Toria's rapier. She knelt at the edge of the basin and ran one hand over the bronze plaque— Victory's personal contribution to the garden established by the college.

IN HONOR AND LOVING MEMORY OF JARIMIS
BELOVED PROGENY AND FRIEND

A sudden flash of memory. *Jarimis standing before her, arms wide to encompass the river and surrounding land. His tousled black hair made even wilder by the wind blowing off the water. "Like my new project?" he said. "It's time I stopped trying to be a mercenary like you."*

Laughter interrupted her reverie, and she raised her head in time to see a trio of students attending summer classes wander into the garden from the direction of the history and social sciences building. A blanket hung over the young man's shoulder and the girls clutched paper bags that clinked to her vampiric hearing. They must be cutting down to the shore for the traditional student pastime.

The three froze when they saw her. Victory rose to her feet and smiled at them, careful not to show fang. But they returned hesitant looks. Then, the young man said, "You're Victory, aren't you?"

"So somebody did actually attend my orientation lecture," Victory said, hoping the teasing note in her voice would relax them. Every fall, Victory gave the same short talk Jarimis used to make about the importance of education in this post-Wasteland era, also including a brief speech on the university founder's life.

Their nervousness at stumbling upon Limani's Master of the City seemed to fade. The young man even gifted her with a tentative smile. "I'm a History major, so I thought your talk was really interesting. I've been to some of your other lectures, too. You're a good storyteller."

Unexpected, but welcome, praise for her skill as a guest lecturer in the History department. "Thanks." Then she made an offer that surprised even her. "If you ever want to get together and talk about anything specific, just ask my daughter or Dean Joensen. They'll get you in touch with me."

He flushed. "That would be awesome. Um, it was nice to meet you." His two companions fidgeted beside him, not as comfortable conversing with Victory.

"Have a good evening!" she called after them. Speaking of the dean—Victory dug her old pocket watch out of her jeans and saw it was about time for her meeting. After one last sweeping look over the now-deserted garden, she cut through the bushes in the direction of Lena's office.

"Victory!"

Dean Joenson waved Victory over. As she approached, the dean grasped the railing and rose from her seat on the main steps of the building.

"You're looking well, Lena." After accepting a hug, Victory studied the woman with a critical eye. "Arthritis acting up again?"

"As always," Lena said. "Though it's not as bad as it could be. I'm not looking forward to the humidity later in the summer. And you're lucky I was going to sleep in before the council meeting tomorrow night anyway. Else you'd never had gotten me out so late."

"I've said time and again that I don't mind if the meetings are during the day," Victory said. She took Lena's arm, and the two women headed toward the parking lot.

"Yes, but then you'd be stuck in the council building during daylight hours." Lena paused as Victory unlocked the town-car and held open the passenger door. "After the werepanther attack a few years ago, you annoyed the clerks endlessly until you could safely leave. I don't think they'd stand to have you around on a regular basis."

"It's true," Victory said. She pushed the ignition button, and the electric engine hummed to life. She pulled out of the parking spot, remembering to turn on the headlights when she caught up to another town-car in front of her. While she could see with almost perfect clarity at night, the rest of the city, with the exception of perhaps the eldest werecreatures, could not.

Deciding the true purpose of their meeting could wait a bit longer, Victory asked after Lena's son in Calverton. The women made small talk about their families during the trip into downtown Limani, enjoying the chance to catch up. Victory realized that aside from hurried greetings before and after the biweekly council meetings, they had not had the chance to truly talk for over two years.

Not bothering to hide down the street, Victory pulled into a parking spot in front of Café Lizzette. Emily Fabbri might have gotten away with throwing a young warrior-mage out of her restaurant, regardless of the mage in question's parentage, but she could not risk pulling the same trick with fellow councilmembers. This late in the evening, many of the diners were university students. They knew their dean, and Victory was almost as recognizable.

"That's interesting." Lena pointed toward the music shop. Propped in the window was a handwritten sign: *No Nonhumans Please.*

Victory cut the town-car's engine and sat forward, comparing the two signs. "That's not interesting. That's a really bad sign." Her voice contained a hint of snarl at the end, despite her inadvertent pun. "This crazy idea of Fabbri's is spreading. Also, Mikelos is going to be really pissed off. That's where he buys all his sheet music."

Lena laid a hand on Victory's arm. "I know you probably want to go marching in there like your daughter did. But please remember that we must be the stronger side in this situation."

Her grip tightened on the steering wheel. "I know how to be good."

"Yes, but please do." Lena patted her shoulder. "Ready to go in?"

"Not much point in putting it off, is there?" She helped Lena out of the town-car, handing the keys over to the other woman with a wink. "Just in case."

They entered the restaurant accompanied by a blue flash of light. Victory hadn't heard such ominous bells since walking into a bar populated by vampire-phobic werewolves a few decades ago in Fort Caroline, the capital of the southern Roman Colonies.

This time, hostility filled just a few of the stares. Her own hackles were up, and she wished for the days when the wild world remained a good enough excuse to wear her sword everywhere. With the possible exception of the two werepanthers in a booth toward the back—she thought she recognized them from the incident a few years ago—she was many times stronger and decades more experienced than anyone in the room. Having a solid blade in her hand would have reassured her. But in this situation, carrying a weapon would get her barred from the restaurant sooner than her blood.

While Victory surveyed the room, Lena handled the pleasantries. The first obstacle, getting into the restaurant at all, was crossed when the dean greeted the young waiter by name and asked how his finals had gone. Confronted with such familiar authority, he'd had no choice but to lead the two women toward a booth in the back. It did not escape Victory's notice that he placed them right next to the werepanthers, and that all of the surrounding booths and tables sat empty. The rest of the diners were seated in the front of the restaurant. They both acknowledged the fact in silence. Victory was irked. Lena seemed more thoughtful.

The waiter took their coffee orders—cream and sugar for Lena, black for Victory—and handed them menus. Instead of heading into the kitchen, however, he disappeared into a side office after promising to come back for their orders.

"Off to warn Fabbri already," Victory said. "And I was actually hoping to enjoy dessert before things went to hell." Just because her body couldn't gain any nutrients from regular food didn't mean she didn't enjoy the sweet stuff on occasion.

Lena stared past Victory, her lips pursed. "Don't be too offended, but I don't think he recognized you. It was probably the blue light when you walked in." She closed her eyes. "And speak of the devil. Looks like we don't even get our coffee tonight."

Victory twisted in her seat in time to see Emily Fabbri marching across the floor between empty tables. Their fellow councilwoman stopped at their booth, her eyes shooting daggers. "Can I *help* you, ladies?" she spat.

No, not daggers. Long spears. With vicious barbed ends, and possibly poison. Victory made a show of surveying her menu. After shutting it, she smiled back up at Fabbri, intentionally showing fang. The human woman hid a flinch, but Victory didn't miss the slight tension of her body. "Yes, thank you. I'll have a slice of your carrot cake. Cream cheese icing, I hope?"

Fabbri placed both hands flat on the table and drew forward, invading Victory's personal space in an attempt to recover ground. Victory's estimate of the human lowered another few notches. She never saw signs of intelligence in antagonizing a vampire. Fabbri's attempt at intimidation fell flat as her gaze slid across Victory's left cheek, unable or unwilling to meet her eyes.

"Otherwise, I'll take one of your apple turnovers," Victory said, ignoring Fabbri's hostility.

"Look, you beast," Fabbri said. At that derogatory comment, the werepanthers at the next booth both turned to look. "It's obvious where your 'daughter' gets her stupidity from since apparently neither of you could read the sign on the door."

It took just a gentle push with one fingertip against Fabbri's shoulder to move her out of Victory's personal space. "I'm going to ignore that insult to my daughter and ask you to never get that close to me again. Your breath leaves much to be desired to those with heightened senses of smell." Lena kicked her foot under the table, warning her to play nice. "By the way," Victory said. "You are aware the two young ladies in the booth next to ours are panthers? Having trouble reading your own sign?" Her last sentence dripped with more sarcasm than she had intended, but the woman was too easy to goad. Lena could berate her for it later, but right now she would have her fun.

A slight flush reddened Fabbri's cheeks. "They were let in while I was running an errand outside of the restaurant. That waitress has already been let go."

Lena had observed the heated exchange without comment, but this forced her to put in her two cents. "You fired her?"

"Of course I did." Fabbri sniffed her disdain. "The girl could obviously not be trusted to keep the unsavory elements of Limani out of my restaurant. I run a respectable establishment."

Relaxing against the padded booth, Victory caught the restaurant owner's eyes with her own. This time Fabbri did flinch away. "And you were able to tell that the two ladies behind me were werepanthers, how exactly? I know I have these silly fangs to give me away, but it's not like werecreatures have tails while in their human form."

In a stiff voice, Fabbri said, "One of my assistant managers recognized them from a dance class. Since they were already halfway through their meal, I allowed them to stay."

"Only so you could collect their bill at the end of their dinner." Lena's tone dared Fabbri to argue.

"At least be consistent in your prejudiced policies, Fabbri," Victory said. "Otherwise no one will respect you."

"That's it." Fabbri stepped back from the table and pointed at the door. Her raised voice attracted the attention of most of the diners in the restaurant. "Get the hell off my property. Or I'll call the police."

"I'm insulted!" Victory's sarcasm was on full force, maturity be damned. "You'd preemptively call the police on my daughter, a partially trained warrior-mage, but not on me, the vampire Master of the City. Lena, shouldn't I be insulted?"

"You should definitely be insulted," Lena said. "I don't believe Ms. Fabbri has the proper respect for your strength."

"Is that supposed to be a threat?" Fabbri said. "Because I will call the authorities and have both of you arrested."

Victory slid out of the booth. "Don't bother. We'd be long gone before they got here anyway." She held a hand out to Lena, who levered herself to her feet. Pitching her voice so it carried to the rest of the diners with attentions riveted on the unfolding scene, Victory said, "Have a good evening, Ms. Fabbri. Next time, we'll be sure to come back when you do have fresh carrot cake. I was so looking forward to it."

She walked past the tables and toward the entrance. Victory was sure the poison-barbed long spears had now turned wooden and fought each other for a place through her heart. She imagined Fabbri smashing a chair and attacking her with one of the table legs, but then dismissed the image as too direct for the human's subtle hatred. Evidenced by her call to the police when confronted with an angry Toria, she was much happier allowing others to do her dirty work.

Soon they were ensconced back in the town-car. Victory was deep in thought, frustrated by the woman she was forced to work with.

"It wasn't that bad," Lena said. "You didn't even lose your temper."

"Oh, it was tempting." Straightening in her seat, Victory scrubbed her face a few times. "I am not looking forward to facing her tomorrow night."

"Neither am I. Shall we make some calls in the morning?"

"If you take Daliana and Lorus, I'll get in touch with Max, Tristan, and Genevieve," Victory said.

Lena could handle the representatives of Limani's elves and other werecreatures. Victory would deal with the head of Limani's Mercenary Guild and the much higher-strung wolf and panther representatives. The panthers were still touchy regarding politics, terrified of losing their hard-won council position.

"Not a problem."

"I want to call Tristan before it gets too late," Victory said, turning the key in the ignition, "and I'll see whether I can get Toria or Kane to call Max for me. Ugh, it's going to be an early day tomorrow."

She caught Lena's small smile, then pulled back into the street. At this point, she just wanted to go home and gather her family for a much-needed conference. Now that she had firsthand evidence of Fabbri's behavior, she wanted to compare notes with Toria and get Mikelos and Asaron's thoughts on the situation.

Perhaps it had been a blessing in disguise when the werepanthers had rallied years ago. No time to think then, just to act. She and Asaron had grabbed their swords and headed for the trees to stop the major wave of fighters. Mikelos, Toria, and Kane had held the house and defeated the ringleader who hunted for Victory's blood. Then, the enemy had been clear. Now, things were much more muddled.

41

The buildings of downtown Limani faded into dark trees, the gradual change from city limits to surrounding countryside marked by a lone sign indicating JARIMIS UNIVERSITY—3 MILES. Every time she and Mikelos considered downsizing to a smaller house within the city, this drive reminded her of why she could never leave the manor. Her traditional title might have been the Master of the City of Vampires, but it was all of Limani that was hers.

"Come on, kid." Fosca circled Toria's prone body. "What have they been teaching you in that fancy school of yours?" The middle-aged woman was a traveling mercenary based out of Limani. She had accepted Max's request to work with Toria with uncontained glee.

Being called "kid" stung. Toria began to regret her rash quip concerning their respective ages at their first bows. The bruises now decorating Toria's body from the flat of Fosca's practice blade drove home her mistake. If Maximillian Asher had been surprised at the unexpected appearance of two of his more errant Guildmembers when they'd asked to borrow wheels from the Mercenary Guildhall's garage, he hadn't shown it. Instead, he had extracted a promise from them to return as soon as possible for training. When they had arrived as promised, he'd set them to spar with a few older members hanging out at the Hall on this lazy summer afternoon. Max never let her spar with Kane, claiming they got enough practice together and that he didn't want them to get too complacent.

"I'm majoring in Chemistry." She wished herself safe in a lab right now. Pain shot through each limb, and she staggered back to her feet once again. It was true—she was more out of practice than she liked to admit.

"And you think you're gonna be a warrior?" Fosca snorted and launched back into the attack.

"I. Already. Am." Toria retorted with each parry, defending herself. But two blows later, Fosca knocked Toria's feet out from under her once again. "Ouch." That had wrenched her ankle something fierce.

"Sure you are." Fosca knelt next to her. "When I was your age, I was earning a living with my sword. Not playing grown-up." She gripped Toria's wrist and helped haul her to her feet once again. Then, without bothering with a formal end to the bout, Fosca turned on a dime and sauntered across the training floor toward the locker room.

Okay, so she was out of shape. She'd spent the last semester juggling four classes and an independent study. Some things slipped to the wayside, such as her daily practice spars with Kane, who had also been dealing with his own overloaded schedule. When they had sparred, it had been at the college's athletic center. Neither had been to the Hall in almost two months.

Toria started her cool-down stretches, replaying the disastrous sparring match in her mind. She and Kane had work to do. If trouble was coming for Limani, they needed to be ready.

Though Victory had been teaching Toria the art of the blade since she could barely walk, and had been their primary weapons teacher after Toria and Kane bonded, she had allowed Max to lure the coveted pair into a Mercenary Guild apprenticeship while they were in high school. The beginnings of their journeyman phase had been completed the summer after high school graduation when they accompanied Asaron through the edges of the British Colonies and into the Wasteland. Now their official Guild training was on hold while they attended Jarimis University, but Toria knew after those four years, they'd be sent out on their own. Kane kept pushing for going south to the Roman Colonies, but Toria had her mind set on Old Europa and visiting Victory's stomping grounds. The debate still continued.

Toria turned half an ear to the spontaneous hand-to-hand combat lesson Max was giving Kane on the other half of the training room floor. If Toria was out of shape, Kane was even more so. He would always be able to run rings around her with his formal magic skills, but she had years more combat training.

If Fosca could knock her around that much, then Kane was sure to need some serious work. They would have to buckle down this summer.

Toria heard the mini-lesson end while she attempted to plan a summer training routine Kane wouldn't hate. She included a little magic-focused time to appease him, though the real reason was so she could continue work on her new sword. He could help recast all the offensive and defensive spells that had decorated the old one.

"Having fun?"

She opened her eyes to find the partner in question standing over her, a wide grin on his upside-down face. "Always."

"I wish I was as bendy as you are. How do you even do that?"

"Very, very carefully." With measured precision, she raised her legs from where her feet touched the mat above her head until they pointed straight at the ceiling. Rolling back on her shoulders, she used her momentum to push off the ground and land on her feet. "I think I'm part cat."

"That would explain your love of naps, but not your fear of mice," Kane said. They set off across the mats, giving a wide berth to two men sparring with long staffs.

Toria stepped on her left foot with care and rubbed at the bruise forming on her right shoulder. "Damn, she really got through my guard a few times."

"What the hell happened?"

"I think Fosca was spoiling for a fight," Toria said. "Either that, or Max wanted to teach me the evils of falling out of shape." That still didn't justify Fosca accusing her of being a spoiled child.

Kane wrapped an arm around her shoulders, letting go when she winced. "Poor girl. By the way, Max wants to see us."

"He beat us to the punch," Toria said. "I was all set to march to his office after we got cleaned up."

"I think we still have time to shower." Kane wrinkled his nose at their sweaty clothing. "And I'm sure hot water would do you good."

"Yeah, wouldn't do to meet the head of the Guild looking like this." She traded a mournful look with Kane outside the women's locker room before heading inside.

Toria beat Kane to the lounge by scant seconds. She still made a show of relaxing on one of the deep couches, reveling in her uncommon punctuality. She received a gentle bat on the back of her head for her efforts.

"C'mon, Max is probably waiting," Kane said.

Toria followed him out of the front lounge of the Hall and up a secluded flight of stairs to the administrative section of the building. They emerged in a hallway right next to Max's office, startling the retired merc who acted as his aide-de-camp by their sudden appearance.

Shaking her head at them, the aide waved them toward the door. "He's there, go ahead and knock."

"Thanks, Liliah." Toria rapped her knuckles against the wood, Kane lurking behind her.

After a muffled welcome, the pair pushed the door open to be confronted by a large empty desk in the center of the room.

"Over here." Max had also showered and changed back into street clothes; his damp silver hair still clung to his scalp, revealing the small pointed ear tips that reminded Toria of his own mixed heritage. He stood off to the side of the room at the large picture window overlooking the training room floor, studying a pair of men sparring with wooden practice knives.

"You wanted to see us?" Toria said.

"I believe it was the two of you who first wanted to see me." Max turned away from the window and gestured to two couches on the other side of the room, ignoring the chairs in front of his desk. "Have a seat. Would either of you like a drink?"

Max plucked a bottle of water from a small refrigerator hidden in a sideboard. Kane accepted it with thanks and settled next to Toria. Max took a seat on the couch across from them.

After stealing a sip of Kane's water, Toria said, "You're right. Mama asked us to speak with you about some problems that might come up tonight at the council meeting."

"I figured you two didn't just show up out of the blue today to get some random practice in," Max said, "but you did need it. And you got into a fight with Fosca, why?"

"She started it!" Toria backed down from Max's smirk. "I don't know what happened, sir. She accused me of being a spoiled brat and not being a real fighter."

"You're not a real fighter," Max said. "You're barely a journeyman. You'd do best to remember that."

"Yes, sir," Toria said. "We'll be back more this summer to train." Kane nodded agreement.

"Good. Then I presume the real reason you're here is to speak with me about that little incident at Emily Fabbri's restaurant the other night?" Now an amused glint appeared in Max's eyes.

Toria groaned. "So the stories have started spreading already?"

"Not stories, necessarily. Let's just say that had you gotten into any physical trouble with either Fabbri or the police, you had some friends in that restaurant with you," Max said. "A few of the Guild were there eating a late lunch. They came straight to me afterward, to warn me both of that detestable sign out front and about your confrontation."

"That's good to know," Toria said. "I'm kinda glad it didn't turn into a fight. I was way too tempted to smack Fabbri. She's lucky she called the cops on me."

"But have you heard about what Victory and Dean Joensen did last night?" Kane said.

When Max shook his head, Kane outlined Victory's experience with Emily Fabbri the night before. "So now everyone's pissed off, and council tonight should be lots of fun."

"To be a fly on the wall," Toria said.

"And to think that last month I was bored and wishing for a distraction. Like when the werepanthers attacked the building." Max tilted a knowing eyebrow at the warrior-mage pair. "Wasn't that the last time you two tried to come to a council meeting?"

"Hey, our luck isn't quite that bad," Toria said. "But since the dean dragged me into this, I'm curious to find out what happens."

"I still have the mini-recorder I borrowed from Jordon for the interviews I had to do last month for my English class," Kane said. "We could give it to Victory and have her sneak it in for us."

"I'm not hearing this," Max said. "Council sessions are closed."

"And when have you known us to do anything wrong?" Toria said.

"More times than I care to count, yet you two always seem to wiggle out of the consequences," Max said. "I wish I had half your luck."

"Unfortunately, I think it comes with her," Kane said. "None of it's managed to rub off on me."

"But at least she's entertaining. Another question: do either of you know when Asaron will be back in town?"

"He's here now, actually." Toria's turn to play storyteller. She recounted how her parents rescued her grandfather.

"Good. A few journeymen finished their rotation in the Roman Colonies and brought back word of recent military activity." Max placed his empty water bottle on the floor beside his seat. "It could just have to do with one of the nasties that keep coming out of the southern Wasteland, but I wanted to speak with Asaron about it. See whether he'd been in the area recently and get his opinion."

"What's going on?" Kane said.

"I don't really know," Max said. "Apparently I need to include more training in group tactics. The kids could only report a few groups of soldiers heading north. They didn't actually see the groups, so I don't even have numbers to work with. I was hoping Asaron might have heard something."

"I don't know when Grandpa was down there last, but it never hurts to ask," Toria said. "Come over for dinner tonight and ask him. That way you can talk with Mama before the council meeting, too. You could show up together. That would really get Fabbri pissed."

"Devious child." Max shook his head. "You take after your mother. Remind me never to cross you. I'm sure you'll get worse with age. But I will accept the dinner invitation. We have work to do."

Dull. Dull, dull, dull.

Victory had expected this meeting to begin with a bang, but instead everyone tiptoed around the issue at hand. With fifteen councilmembers, the tiptoeing resembled a herd of elephants in a crystal shop. Two of the elected human members hadn't even known about the current situation. Genevieve and Tristan, pack leaders of the leopards and wolves, respectively, hadn't before she called them. Lena took control when the head of council requested a rational explanation of recent events, and Victory was content to sit back and try to ignore the broken spring in the seat of her chair.

She zoned out, rather than jumping in and giving her own two cents—or three, or four, she had plenty—and risking the impression of being too close to the subject at hand. Instead, she set her eyes on Lena and let them glaze over, to drift to the end of the council hall where the seal of the city of Limani was painted in luscious colors on the far wall.

Two boats brought the first colonists to settle Limani over five hundred years ago. Now the golden *Toxo* and *Peristeri* rested on a background of blue seas and silver sky. They brought freedom and civilization to the shores of New Europa when the settlers established a city-state in the style of their Grecian counterparts. For the most part, the spirit of independence and community ran strong in Limani.

But as Victory knew from over a century of living there, it wasn't always the case. Once Lena finished, the opening riposte was presented.

"This behavior is unacceptable." The barest hint of a low hiss, evidence of his reptilian other self, underlay Lorus' pronouncement. The council's representative of werecreatures other than wolves and panthers curled his hands into fists on the table.

Emily Fabbri sat opposite him, staring back in matching fury. "I have received multiple complaints from my constituents, and every single one of them demands something be done about your blatant offenses against Limani's community."

From her seat farther toward the head of the table, Victory could see Lorus' elongated pupils. Soon he would be flashing fangs even longer than hers. It looked as though she would lose the bet with Max made over dinner. She had expected

Tristan to lose his temper first. Limani's most powerful male werewolf did not get his position in pack hierarchy by taking things lying down. Of course, Max had bet Victory would be the first to lash out, so perhaps now she could keep her twenty bucks.

Victory realized she had missed Fabbri's retort when Tristan's deep voice resonated off the council room's walls. "You are a lying bitch!"

She prepared to jump into the fray when Tristan's apparent insult roused the meeker human councilmembers to attention. Lucia Stein, the eldest member of the council, leaned to whisper in Fabbri's ear. Victory's vampiric hearing picked up her reminder that to Tristan, "bitch" was just another term for a lower-ranking female. Still an insult, but not as great as it could have been.

Instead, Victory shifted to her right. "What did I miss?"

Out of the corner of her mouth, Lena said, "Emily is blaming her sign on fights breaking out in her restaurant. Pay attention, girl."

Only she and Asaron could get away with calling Victory that. Outliving every other citizen of Limani with the exception of the more reclusive elves had a few privileges. And with privilege came responsibility. Fabbri mouthing off again directed her attention back to the present.

"My restaurant is private property! I have the right to deny service to anyone I choose."

"What, like 'No shirt, no shoes, no service'?" From where he lounged at the opposite end of Victory's side of the table, Max radiated a veneer of unconcern. "But now it's 'No humanity, no pure blood, no service'?"

Fabbri looked down her nose at him. "Humanity has nothing to do with it. And I don't see what your concern is. My policy doesn't affect you."

"Please." Max smirked at her. "Do your research. I don't just age well, I'm one-fourth elven, darling." He toasted her with his glass of water.

She blanched, and faced the head of the table. "Don't we have better things to discuss tonight, Alex?"

Alexander Sethri, human head of the Limani city council, had sat in impartial silence. He eyed Fabbri over his steepled fingers. "I think that while there is such dissent amongst our ranks, anything else we review tonight will be tainted by our strong emotions. And believe me, Emily—they are very strong." He lapsed back into quiet calm, his disapproval made known.

"What are you looking for here, Fabbri?" Time for one of her fellow human representatives to speak up. Soren Abramson looked up and down the table. "For us to back your idiotic notions simply because you're afraid of anything different?"

"I am not afraid of them."

Victory swallowed the snort that threatened to erupt. "Please. You called the police on my daughter, a half-trained warrior-mage, before confronting her yourself. The only reason you didn't do the same to me was because it's bad politics to have councilmembers fighting in public."

"I didn't call the police on you because you didn't storm in looking for a fight," Fabbri said. "You at least have a reputation for civilization. I could not be sure about your daughter." The biting emphasis on her last word showed her true opinion of their relationship.

"And what makes you so sure Torialanthas would cause trouble?" Toria's given name rolled off the lips of another heretofore-silent observer. Daliana, this decade's representative of Limani's elven population, had watched the debate with the same aloofness she possessed during more routine discussions about traffic laws and residential codes.

"You mean beside her history of violence? The girl was a killer before she even graduated from high school!" Fabbri lit with success, the pleasure at being able to pull this trump card evident in her voice.

"You go too far, Fabbri." With surprising defensiveness, Tristan beat Victory to the punch.

But if ever there was a time to speak in her daughter's defense without seeming too biased, this was it. "The death that resulted at Toria's hands was that of a criminal." Victory kept her voice even, but her short nails dug into her thighs under the table. "Toria acted in order to protect her family." She smiled at Fabbri, allowing a hint of fang to show. "But you wouldn't get that, would you? Since you were just elected to council less than six months ago."

"Elected is the key word there," Fabbri said. "I earned my place on this council. What have you done besides live for a long time?"

"You mean beside doing her job keeping Limani safe from vampires who see humans as snack food free for the taking?" Lorus said. "What, exactly, have you done for this city, Fabbri?"

"My position on the council is not under debate here," Victory said. "Your decision to discriminate against other citizens of Limani is."

"Emily, your actions do contradict the oath you swore when you joined the council to uphold the values that make Limani a peaceful community," Soren said. "And that's grounds to impeach you."

"You wouldn't dare," Fabbri said.

"I would." Max raised a hand. "I would impeach you. Then kick you out of the city on top of it. While I don't think the others would agree to exile you, I think I might have a little bit of backup for the impeachment."

"Seconded," chorused Victory and Tristan.

Max held out his hands in a "what can you do?" shrug. "And there we go. The proposal is on the table."

"No one has been impeached by the council for over fifty years," Lena said. "Victory, do you remember the proper procedures?"

Since she was the sole member of the current council to be present at that last event, it was a logical question. Victory shook her head. "That was a long time ago, and it was because Quinn murdered someone. Another councilmember. It wasn't a hard decision to make, so I don't remember the details. Alexander, you must have reviewed those council procedures more recently than any of us."

"I don't know the exact procedures offhand," Sethri said. "I do know that an impeachment cannot occur during the same meeting as the proposal in order to prevent us from being ruled by our emotions instead of common sense."

"So we break to review the policy," Soren said. "I'd say this calls for an emergency session for tomorrow night."

"As do I," Lena said. "Despite how in favor I am of this impeachment, I'd still rather it be done correctly."

"That is one representative from both the elected and appointed sides of the council," Sethri said. "Seems fair enough to me. Anyone else have any complaints?" Fabbri raised her hand. "Beside you, Emily." She put her hand back down with a fierce glare toward the head of the table. "It's settled then. I hereby call an official council session tomorrow night led by Lena in order to follow proper impeachment procedure." He made a note in the book in front of him without waiting for any argument.

Victory made her own mental note to thank Max the next time she caught him alone. She had resolved to bring up the issue of impeachment had no one else gone that far. However, if the idea had not been seconded, her place on the council could have become tenuous indeed. No other vampires lived in Limani to replace either her title of Master of the City or accompanying seat on the council. Max had a strong hold on his leadership of the local Mercenary Guild, but she knew he would have no regrets if forced to pack up and move on. He would probably follow through with his threats to finally retire to live out the rest of his life with the elves.

No drastic steps were needed. Instead, she noted her strongest backers. Now the problem would be to make the impeachment stick. Fabbri's humanist superiority would be more difficult to argue than Quinn's murder.

The elitist tone in Fabbri's voice dragged her attention back to the present. "Now that this nasty business has been decided," she said, "what are we going to do about the Roman army marching toward Limani?"

Asaron rapped on the doorframe to the den soon after Victory and Max left for the council meeting. "Travel gear. We've got work to do."

Roused from the book on tactics she'd snagged from Max's office, Toria blinked up at Asaron. "What?"

"Max gave me a mission," Asaron said.

She stood, placing a slip of paper in the book to mark her place. "Does this have to do with the Roman troop movements he mentioned to us?"

Asaron escorted her through the kitchen and to the bottom of the stairs, explaining, "I hope it's just simple training maneuvers. But I'm not inclined to take anything from them for granted now."

Toria paused. "Kane coming with us?"

"You do come as a matched set. I'll grab him from the library. You've got ten minutes."

"One problem. The only gear I have here at the house is from two years ago. The new set from my latest growth spurt is back at the apartment."

"You're a smart girl. You'll figure something out."

A few steps up, Toria halted and looked back at Asaron again. "Does Mama know we're going?" Mikelos had ensconced himself in his studio most of the day, but had headed into town after Victory left with Max, muttering about a replacement C string. Toria knew from long experience that once he and the proprietor of the local music supply store started talking, her father might be gone for hours. If Mikelos was even let in the shop. Victory had warned him about the sign in the window over dinner, but Mikelos was determined that friendship would win out.

Chagrin crossed Asaron's face. "You actually think your mother would let me take you anywhere near an army? Why do you think we're leaving while she's at council?"

"Good point. We'll leave a note." She bounded up the stairs when Asaron headed back down the hallway in search of her partner. Starting an expedition by night was never her first choice, but she'd grown used to it during her previous journeyman stint with her grandfather.

Once in her old bedroom, Toria ransacked her closet for something suitable since her leather armor was stored in the supply trunk at her apartment. She and Kane hadn't lived in this house since starting college. Jeans replaced her cutoffs, and a black long-sleeved shirt went over her skimpy tank top. But her old duster was here, and after buckling on her belt with its various supply hooks and pouches, she snagged it from behind her bedroom door.

Toria met Kane in the hall coming out of his old bedroom. He was attired in a similar fashion, though he'd scrounged up a set of his old leather pants. He trailed after her back downstairs, where Toria pushed open a set of grand double doors off the main foyer. Since the beginning of Victory's occupancy, the wooden floor of the old manor house's formal ballroom had supported more martial forms of footwork. After joining with Kane and becoming a warrior-mage, she spent even more time in this room than in the magical workroom in the attic.

Kane pulled their swords—her returned rapier and his own elegant, curved shamshir—from the bags they'd left in the corner while Toria rummaged in a chest on the other side of the room for sword harnesses. Next came the knives, which they strapped to belt, ankle, and wrists. Toria had just turned to eye the locked cabinet in the far corner of the room when Asaron poked his head in.

"Ready to go?" he asked

"Once you tell us where we're going," Kane said, sheathing the shamshir across his back.

"And," Toria said, "are we going to need guns?"

That stopped Asaron short, and Toria remembered that to the ancient vampire, firearms were still a modern novelty. Victory told her once that she'd had to more or less pry his crossbow out of his fingers to get him to pick up a musket for a try.

Then again, Asaron probably also viewed them as a passing fad. Part of the massive spell the elves cast over the world after the Last War prevented the creation of new firearms. Bullets were easy enough to manufacture—lead, steel, silver, whatever form needed for whatever creature needed fighting. But these days, guns were disappearing from normal wear and tear.

Her mother wasn't a huge fan of guns either, but she kept a small stock in the locked cabinet in the most discreet corner of the training room. There were a few small pistols she and Kane trained on, along with a rifle and antique shotgun. Even a peculiar submachine gun picked up by Asaron in his travels and "forgotten" at the manor.

"I think we'll be okay. Just a scouting run. The Roman army shouldn't be that tough."

Kane swallowed back a snort of surprise. "The Roman army? We're not chasing that lead. Are we?"

On occasion, Mikelos imagined that music flowed through his blood and soul the way his daughter manipulated magic. But in his case, music was not what he had been born to. Instead, it had rescued him from a short life before he burned out into obscurity.

After being expelled from the Roman orphanage upon reaching his majority, Mikelos earned a scant living singing on street corners. One night, a young man swept out of the darkness to give him so much more. The vampire Connor welcomed him into the world of music and darkness, teaching him the art of the violin and transforming his entire world. Vampire and daywalker had formed a string duo that dazzled the elite of Old Europa's society for almost two centuries. Mikelos transformed from homeless orphan to pampered musician. He had a family, even if it was a bit unconventional. He was happy.

Then Connor disappeared. Mikelos was left adrift once again, mortal, in a world changing faster than he could keep up. So he crossed the sea and settled in Limani, hoping to live out the rest of his days in anonymity, no longer connected to the famous concert pair long vanished across the ocean in a different world.

But Mikelos never lost his music. Taking Connor's name for his own, he returned to his roots, playing street corners for spare change to supplement his day job. A few years passed, and then another vampire blew into his life. Once again, Mikelos found himself a daywalker, a human for whom time stood still. But now he was a true partner, and Victory cherished him for bringing intimacy to her cold life just as he treasured her for bringing meaning back to his.

Violin case thumping against his thigh, Mikelos pulled the strap of his messenger bag higher onto his shoulder to balance the weight of the two bags. Hans had finally kicked him out of his music shop a few minutes before, citing that some people did sleep during the night. He'd also promised to pull the offensive sign from the window, which Mikelos considered a win. Mikelos left the High Note with one C string and several books of new music from the British colonies. The night had been a success.

He wandered toward the center of Limani. Though the night was warm, it was still late. He encountered a few pedestrians, people on their way home from evening jobs of their own. He passed the City Hall, noting by the lights shining from the upper windows that council must still be in full swing. Mikelos was anxious to know the results of the meeting, but he would have to wait until Victory finished inside. He couldn't help but hope Victory and Max put that awful woman through the ringer.

He had walked the few miles from the manor to Jarimis University, catching up on some exercise, and then taken the last evening shuttle into town. He planned to wait until council was over and ride home with Victory. He ripped a page out of his music notebook and left her a note under the windshield, letting his partner know not to leave without him. She would check his usual haunts.

Message left, he headed for the first—the nightclub Twilight Mists, one of the few havens for the younger adults of Limani. Walking toward the club, he imagined he had gone back a century in time, and that he was heading home from work to join a friend's band before returning to his empty apartment. Victory opened the Twilight Mists decades ago, trying her hand at a civilized business after the constant stress of the mercenary calling. She first found him in the club, and both of their lives had been forever changed.

The front door opened and a group spilled out, laughing and shouting into the night. Loud music washed across the street.

"Mikelos!" The doorman greeted him by name and clasped his hand.

Mikelos hiked up his bags once again. "Hey, Radek. Busy night?"

"Not too bad," Radek said. "School is done for the summer, so every night will be busy and not just the weekends. Might be too crowded for you." Another group of customers walked up behind Mikelos, diverting Radek's attention.

Mikelos headed inside the club, pretending not to hear Radek calling his name. He didn't feel much like chatting tonight. Dancing would keep his mind off of the council session, and the random visions he kept having of Victory lunging across the table and throttling Emily Fabbri. Entertaining though it was, he didn't think that particular scenario would end well.

"Are we sure this is a good idea?" Toria said. "I mean, we could run right into scouts. We are not exactly stealthy like this."

Under the dim light of the half-moon, Toria could not see Asaron's smile, but she heard his low laugh.

"The river crossing is a few more miles away." Kane pulled his horse abreast of hers. "What's wrong?"

Toria steered her own mount around a stone in the road, taking advantage of the time to compose her thoughts. "Well, after we cross the Agios River, I know of a place to the south where we can camp during the day. And we will reach it before dawn. But any farther south is out of our usual range. What are we going to do during the day?"

They'd borrowed horses from the stables kept by Limani's Mercenary Guild for just such missions. None of the small electric town-cars that the majority of Limani's citizens owned had the range for excursions too far out of the city's limits, but they traded distance for speed.

"What do you think I did before trucks were invented, child?" Not quite under his breath, Asaron said, "Modern times have corrupted the youth. It's a shame."

"I have no problems being corrupted," Kane said.

"I'm sure you'll muddle through. You're—" Asaron broke off, reining his horse to a halt.

Toria and Kane followed suit, trusting he would not stop for less than a good reason. She resisted the urge to ask what was wrong. Instead of trying to peer into the surrounding darkness and figure it out for herself, Toria cast out with her own special senses.

Keeping her permanent physical shields intact, she lowered the mental blocks that prevented her from being overwhelmed by the magic she could see flowing through the world. She tuned out the brilliant emerald shields surrounding Kane, and ignored the uncomfortable black hole where Asaron should have been.

"See anything?" Kane had gone the same route, and stared at the trees lining either side of the road. "And by the way, you're going weak in the rear."

"Thanks." Toria caught the loop of power her partner threw and reinforced the shielding behind her back. She sometimes forgot about what she couldn't see. Kane had a similar problem with the area below his knees.

"Hush." Asaron's tone was more absent-minded than irritated. They stilled at the command. Then, the elder vampire relaxed his alert stance. "That was odd."

"What's going on?" With the apparent danger past, Toria banished her magesight. She had nothing.

"Anything out of the ordinary?" Asaron gave the partners an expectant look.

"You mean with magesight?" Toria shook her head. "Just Kane's shields, his sword, and your necklace you still won't tell us anything about."

"Not important right now, Toria," Kane said.

Unrepentant, Toria ignored him. They were still on home ground, and if Asaron already saw bad signs, it didn't bode well for the mission at all.

"I must be getting old. Let's get out of here," Asaron said. "The night's not getting any younger, and we've still got a river to cross."

They once again pointed their horses down the road. The darkness made Toria sleepy, and her mind drifted toward the past. They had headed north with Asaron the summer after they graduated high school on their first journeyman tour. The first bout of trouble they ran into was a late-night summer storm. Asaron lost track of time, and the clouds blew away to present a sun already beginning to rise. The scramble to set up camp and get the vampire under cover had not been pleasant.

"Penny for your thoughts?"

Kane startled her out of her reverie. "Just remembering the Calverton trip and trying not to fall asleep."

"That was wild, wasn't it?" Kane said.

"Victory and I have had our share of close calls," Asaron said. "But that was one for the books. I wish these things wouldn't happen so often."

"Often for us or often for you?" Toria said. "Your definition of time can get a bit warped, Grandpa. Like Mama's. You talk about things that happened three centuries ago like they happened last week."

"Time is strange for those who live for centuries," Asaron said. "Vampires are forced to realize that events they are part of today can have reverberations decades in the future while also living in the here and now."

Kane took a swig of water from his canteen and tossed it to Toria. "Must be even stranger for Mikelos, then."

"Indeed," Asaron said. "My daughter's daywalker does not live in a life ruled by the change of the light."

"But he does live by his connection to Mama," Toria said. "He told me once that the three years he wasn't bonded to a vampire were the hardest of his life. He said that sometimes he worries about me growing up. I think he's afraid of change."

"And he wouldn't be the first daywalker to have that particular phobia," Asaron said.

Toria took point when the conversation turned more philosophical. The more intangible aspects of life were Kane's specialty. The chemist in Toria lived in the physical. She nudged her chestnut mare forward, and the sounds of the others' low voices retreated behind her.

Soon she could scent water in the air. They'd headed south to where the Agios River could be forded on horseback. Max had requested that Asaron not use the ferry closer to Limani—he didn't want to alert any more people than necessary to where they were headed. The original settlers chose their building site because of the defensibility of a peninsula. But since that made leaving difficult, on occasion it had its downsides.

Next she heard flowing water, and small waves lapping the shore. Though Asaron must have heard the river long before she did, she couldn't resist calling out, "We're almost there!"

The Agios River that ran next to the university was a wide expanse of water. By that point, various other water sources had merged with it. Now, however, it was more of a wide creek masquerading as a river, with water shallow enough to ford on horseback with just the risk of damp boots.

The rushing torrent of springtime had slowed, and the current was firm and steady. "Let's go," Asaron said. Taking the front of their trio, he urged his mount to step forward into the water.

Kane's followed suit without a problem, but Toria's mare seemed to have an inherent dislike of the water. Once she reached the point where the water met the narrow band of sand and mud alongside it, the mare planted her feet and snorted in derision. "Oh, come on, girl." Toria nudged the horse's flanks with her heels. "I'm not going to get off and push you."

But any effort to press the horse forward resulted in her skittering to either side, rather than any farther forward. Laughter reached her ears, from across the river where her companions waited for her. "Enjoying this, are you?"

"Of course!" Asaron called back. "But we don't have all night, Toria!"

Rather than waste time with a response to her companions, Toria said to the horse, "I promise I'll feed you an apple when we get across." Another loud exhalation of air met her bribe. "Carrots?"

"Toria!"

"I'm working on it!" It wasn't her fault her horse was hydrophobic.

Nothing else to be done about it. She swung out of the saddle and stepped back to glare at the horse as a rush of displaced air over her head stirred her hair. A crossbow bolt thudded into the tree trunk next to her, straight through where Toria's mounted torso should have been. She yelped and lunged forward, grabbing the mare's reins to haul her back into the woods. The horse jerked and gave a grunt, letting Toria know she was most annoyed. But the mare wasn't panicking. A second bolt followed the first, sailing farther into the woods before snapping against a tree.

Trees. Trees meant cover. Toria's brain dredged up everything it had ever learned about combat and she scrambled toward cover. The horse followed without protest. Probably since she now headed in the opposite direction of the water. Pulling the mare farther into the trees, Toria threw the reins over a low branch.

Now the shouting registered. The bolts had come from the opposite side of the river—her family had to be in more trouble than she. She wanted to dive into the river herself and help them out, but Asaron would be appalled by her lack of common sense. So she forced herself to pause and draw power straight from the air to strengthen the shields surrounding her. Then she crouched low and snuck back toward the edge of the forest.

Across the river, Asaron slashed out with his sword, keeping three attackers at bay. Her grandpa could take care of himself, so her eyes sought her partner.

"Bastards! Get off! Ow!"

Kane wasn't faring as well as Asaron. The writhing figure on the ground under two others in dark clothing must be him. A last stranger held the reins of both horses, a crossbow slung across his back.

Toria crouched and placed her left hand on the ground. She pushed a small tendril of power out through her palm and into the earth, threading beneath the water. Nature provided the current, and the water surged through her magical net.

She had never tried this particular tactic before, so she wasn't prepared for the spontaneous rush of energy that backwashed along her line of power. She shunted the overload back into the earth, a quick and dirty way to discharge power.

Kane's steady stream of insults cut off when he howled in pain. That overrode Toria's instincts and instead of the earth, she shoved the power through the constant link binding her with Kane.

Her physics didn't fail her. The sudden influx of electrical power caused a negative reaction with Kane's shields and shocked his attackers off him with a few hundred volts of electrical power. Her professors would be proud.

The real-world result was messier. The last of the power overloaded Kane's shields and rebounded to Toria, and the world went black.

Mikelos paused inside the Twilight Mists to let the bass of the music reverberate through his body. Ten o'clock was still early by youth and nocturnal standards, so the club was filling up. He inhaled in appreciation, capturing the scent of an old building that had seen sweat and smoke and music for over a hundred years. The new owners of the club had updated the décor, but the place still held many fond memories.

He first trained in classical music three hundred years ago, but time had broadened his tastes. His younger Roman street-rat self would sing anything for a penny or bread crust. His famous self once refused to play accompaniment for an operatic soprano who might be more popular than he. Now he appreciated the modern beats and synthetic sounds not possible from a classical orchestra. In his old age, he had relaxed and learned how to have fun. After he left his violin case and messenger bag with the disinterested coat check girl, Mikelos headed straight for the dance floor.

Many of the patrons were students from the high school and university enjoying the start of summer break. Toria would have known more of the people in the club, but he did receive waves from the group of young werewolves in human form lounging on couches in a corner and recognized a lone elf already spinning across the dance floor in the center of the club. What was her name? Lyri? Syri?

He reached the elven girl during a song change. She paused at his approach, though her hips still swayed in time to the subtle beat.

Mikelos put on his best court manners and gave her a sweeping bow. "May I join you, milady?"

She looked him over. She appeared to be about Toria's age, not much older than twenty. In reality, she must be closer to Mikelos' three centuries. "It would be my pleasure, daywalker."

With a cascade of harsh drumbeats, the music launched into a faster rhythm. Mikelos caught the girl's hand and spun her around to the whistles of the wolves. Other dancers began to leave the floor, leaving them plenty of room. Mikelos thought nothing of it, instead taking advantage of the space to spin his partner around.

He'd started relaxing into the rhythm when the speakers cut out, leaving a ringing silence after the loud music. Mikelos and the girl froze. Two men approached them, Radek and the second, burlier, Twilight Mists bouncer.

"We need to ask you and your friend to leave," the unfamiliar one said. Standing behind the bouncer, Radek shot Mikelos a helpless look.

"I'm sorry, were we dancing inappropriately?" He directed his question to Radek. Not much was too inappropriate at this club, and that was part of the appeal.

The other bouncer answered in Radek's place. "New company policy."

Next to Mikelos, the girl heaved an aggravated sigh. "You have got to be kidding me. Here, too?"

She was right. Fabbri's prejudice was spreading. This was ridiculous. Mikelos hated to play this card, but— "You do know who I am, right?"

"You're not human, and that's all we need to know."

"I'm sorry, Mikelos, Syri," Radek said, "but there's nothing I can do. You need to leave."

"Well, shall we?" Mikelos offered his elbow to Syri.

"Wait, you're giving in?" she said, ignoring his gesture. "Can't you call Victory? I know what she'd have to say about this happening in her club."

"But it's not hers anymore, remember?" Every occupant in the club stared at the confrontation. The wolves rose to their feet in unison. This could get ugly, and he wasn't in the mood for a fight. "C'mon." When she started to protest again, Mikelos took her arm and walked toward the coat check.

When he passed them, one of the werewolves grabbed his shoulder. "We can't tolerate this."

"We can and we will, at least for tonight," Mikelos said. "You know that jerk is going to order you guys out next."

"Two guys." He bared his teeth in the bouncers' direction. "We could take them."

"I can't order you to leave with me, but I can tell you that starting a fight would be a really bad idea." Mikelos pulled out of the werewolf's grip. "Victory's in council right now, figuring out how to put an end to this. Beating the crap out of some humans tonight would only hurt what she's trying to do." He said the last bit through gritted teeth.

The wolf looked at his three friends, then at the elf. She rolled her eyes in exasperation. "Fine," he said. "We're with you, for now. Let's go."

With all in the silent club still staring at them, Mikelos led the wolves and elf to the coat check. The girl yawned while she handed over everyone's possessions before returning to her book, and they left. Both bouncers followed the small group all the way to the exit, shutting them out with a resounding *bang*.

Once they rounded the corner back toward the center of town, the elven girl stopped in her tracks. "No way," she said. "Why would they let us in just to toss us back out? I'm going back." She turned, and two of the wolves snagged her by the arms.

"No," Mikelos said, voice firm, "you're not. I was serious when I said that Victory was working on this right now."

She pulled out of the wolves' clutches. "You'd better be right, daywalker. The elves won't stand for this."

"You think the wolves will, girl?" The lone female werewolf sniffed in disdain. "Tristan in on this with Victory?"

"As far as I know, they're all working on the problem," Mikelos said. "I'm sure the results of tonight's council meeting will be spread. If the problem isn't dealt with, then we can think about taking more drastic measures."

"I should hope so." With that, the elven girl spun on her heel and stalked down the street.

"Syri got dumped right before you got to the club," the female wolf said to Mikelos. "She's having a crappy night. Otherwise she wouldn't have agreed to dance with you."

"Oh, that's nice to know." The evening was getting stranger by the minute. "I guess I'll go camp out by the council building and wait for Victory. Take care, all."

The lead wolf clasped hands with Mikelos, and they said their goodbyes before heading away. Mikelos watched them fade into the darkness before making his own way through the deserted Limani night.

Since they met after normal business hours and the rest of the building had cleared out, the council locked the front door. Mikelos didn't mind waiting outside in the pleasant night. He settled onto the wide stone steps leading up to the Grecian building and started his new book, but the silence grated on him. A little music wouldn't hurt anyone in the quiet business district. He flipped the latches on his violin case and drew the instrument out with reverence.

He got bored with fingering drills after a few minutes and switched into a reel. But a reel could not be played sitting down, and soon Mikelos stood at the top of the steps. After the reel, he slowed it down and launched into a more classical piece, one of the first he had ever played in concert. Lit by the council hall's permanent spotlights, the building behind him transformed into a full orchestra, the street became an adoring audience. In the corner of his field of vision, he could almost see the flashing bow of Connor's cello.

"Hey, freak."

His bow skittered across the strings with a harsh shriek. Mikelos lowered the violin to his side before facing his unwelcome visitor. The unfamiliar bouncer from the Twilight Mists came up the side steps, with an even more pronounced sneer.

"Can I help you?" Had the guy followed him here? Mikelos didn't want a confrontation while this tired. Not on the council steps.

The bouncer took a step forward, forcing Mikelos to back away down a step. Not his first choice of action, but the guy had horrid breath tinged with alcohol.

So, drinking on the job and leaving early. What were the new owners of the club letting their employees get away with these days?

"I don't appreciate the way you talked to me back there." The bouncer looked down his nose at Mikelos. "You need to learn some respect for your superiors."

Mikelos stifled his laugh. "Thank you for informing me, then. I'll keep that in mind." He moved toward his bags but meaty hands shoved at his chest. Mikelos pinwheeled his arms for balance and backed down another few steps.

The other man followed, staying too close for comfort.

Not good. "Now that was uncalled for, sir," Mikelos said. He couldn't fight with his violin in hand, and taking his eyes off the man to place the violin and bow down seemed a bad idea.

"'Sir' is right," the man said. "I'll teach you some manners yet."

Though tempted to comment on the man's own lack of education, Mikelos didn't go there. "Fine, lesson learned," he said instead. "Now let's both go home and say that you've made your point."

"I don't think so, you freak." He stepped forward once more, his invasion of Mikelos' personal space complete.

He couldn't even think of more than one derogatory name? This wasn't going to end well. "No, I don't—"

The bouncer reached out, and instead of grabbing Mikelos, snatched the violin away. He smashed it with full force onto the edge of the steps behind him without missing a beat. The fragile antique wood shattered on contact with the concrete.

Mikelos' heart broke. It wasn't his first instrument, but it was his oldest. Connor had given him that violin. Mikelos dropped the bow and lunged for the other man with a wordless scream.

The man met his attack with a ready fist, bashing his knuckles into Mikelos' jaw. Mikelos' forward momentum carried him into the bouncer's chest, and they both tumbled down onto the stairs.

Mikelos rolled off the man and reached his feet first, spreading his weight across two steps. He licked his lips and tasted blood. He'd done his best to avoid a physical fight with this guy, but now all bets were off. His daywalker bond with Victory meant he was stronger and faster. This man had destroyed one of the things most precious to him. He could kill the guy, if he wanted.

He wanted.

The other man also got to his feet, rubbing the back of his head where it had bounced against the edge of the stone steps. His eyes met Mikelos' eyes, and he growled.

Oh, Mikelos wanted. But it would destroy what little ground the nonhumans of Limani had against this new crusade. Mikelos would be banished for murder.

Dammit, he would have to pull his punches.

Mikelos shot out with his own fist, catching the bouncer in the solar plexus. At full strength, he would have cracked the man's sternum. Instead, the man yelped in pain and fell backward.

After landing on the stairs, the bouncer kicked out a leg, catching Mikelos' knee and pulling him off balance.

Mikelos' knee bounced off the edge of a step with a sickening crack. Now his leg wouldn't hold him when he tried to rise, and Mikelos staggered. But the last step wasn't where it should have been, and he crashed to the sidewalk.

He landed with all his weight on his arm and hip, his knee screaming in pain. Before he could compensate with the opposite leg, a shoe met his forehead, snapping his body back to the ground.

A kick connected with Mikelos' chest. This time the pop came from a rib, and the next shot landed at his stomach.

He shouldn't have pulled his first punch. He couldn't get to his feet while the blows kept coming. Mikelos covered his head with his arms and curled around his torso, pulling his legs up to his chest.

Putting what lung strength he could past a broken rib, Mikelos let out a scream. "*Victory!*"

Mikelos braced his uninjured hand on the ground, but that was a mistake. The man's boot heel smashed down again, followed by the sickening sound of bones in his fingers breaking. He had been through worse in three hundred years. This human, this single human, couldn't kill him.

He hoped.

The council chamber erupted into chaos.

Councilmembers began demanding explanations or protesting, per their nature. Gloating, Fabbri sat back in her chair. Victory ignored the exclamation Lena made to her, instead meeting eyes with Max down the length of the table.

Max shrugged. "Hey!" he said, raising his voice over the others.

Next to him, Lorus quieted, but the others paid no attention. Then, Daliana snapped her fingers once. A brilliant white light flashed in the room, startling everyone into silence. She gestured toward Max, giving him control of the room once again.

"Thank you, Dal," Max said, staring at Fabbri. "Now what the hell are you talking about, woman? My source said it was only a few troop movements."

"I do hope you were planning on sharing this with us, Max." Sethri's dry voice held a hint of rebuke.

The mercenary mimed shock. "Of course!"

Victory came to his rescue. "Max consulted with me before the meeting. We already have someone checking the situation out." Her ears picked up the strains of violin music. She relaxed knowing Mikelos was near, even if outside the building.

"Who?" Soren asked.

"My sire Asaron graciously volunteered to be Limani's eyes," Victory said.

Fabbri snorted. "Because he can be trusted."

"He is also being accompanied by the warrior-mages Toria Connor and Kane Nalamas." Max paused. "Not that you probably think that's much better. But at least you can't claim they're not full Limani citizens."

Despite her shock at Max's addendum, Victory kept her mouth shut. It seemed he and Asaron had laid plans in addition to those they'd let her in on. But now was not the time to act like a worried mother. Right now, solidarity was key. "Both Toria and Kane are journeymen of Limani's Mercenary Guild. They are obligated to return with a proper report."

This time Fabbri rolled her eyes, but even she couldn't argue. The devotion of Limani's native-born mercs to their home was legendary. It wasn't just because they were on the payroll as a reserve battalion—one of the first lessons new trainees learned was the history of the Wasteland and the importance of Limani's location between the Roman and British colonies.

Victory also trusted Asaron. He had been a mercenary or soldier for most of the two millennia of his life, and while she had kept to mercenary work for private citizens rather than armies, he had forgotten more about the military than she ever knew. Including tactics and camp life, two things that would tell him exactly what the Romans were up to, depending on how large the group was, how they were provisioned, and which direction they were headed. A few small parties meant they had set out to kill Wasteland beasties plaguing a western town. A company or two could indeed be the field maneuvers Max suspected.

A large force marching straight toward Limani could mean just one thing. Victory didn't need her own years of mercenary work to tell her it wasn't the Emperor coming for a visit.

"My mercenaries are on a covert mission to check things out," Max said. "All I know right now is that there is a force of soldiers. I don't know how many or why. That's what the mission is for. They're not planning on contacting the Romans or even letting their presence be discovered at all. They'll be back in no more than a handful of days. We can even have another emergency council session to hear their—"

The door at the end of the council chamber slammed open, and a city clerk rushed into the room. Victory's heart beat once in surprise, and her hand jerked toward the sword she did not wear at her side.

"Mr. Sethri!" The clerk who stayed late for council meetings halted when he realized he had the entire room's attention. Then he scurried to Sethri to whisper in his ear.

A scream came from outside. Her name. Victory leapt to her feet, her hands gripping the table. No time to make excuses. She dashed for the door as Sethri spoke to the rest of the room. "A man just attacked Mikelos Connor outside our doors."

Victory burst from the council building—Tristan, Max, and Lorus right behind her—to see a strange man kicking a prone figure at the bottom of the steps. She all but flew down the steps and tackled the man to the ground. The force of her blow knocked them clear into the street. The man's body went limp when the back of his head connected with the pavement.

Victory untangled herself and shot to her feet. Lorus and Tristan headed toward her, ready to restrain the attacker. Max knelt by Mikelos, and Victory dropped to cradle Mikelos' head in her lap. Her daywalker was unconscious. Blood smeared his face, his left hand was a mess, and his right leg bent at an unnatural angle.

Daliana knelt next to Victory and placed her hands on Mikelos' chest. Her gentle touch shimmered with golden light. "He's weak, but he'll live. Some broken ribs, but no serious internal injuries." She gave Victory an apologetic look. "I'm sorry, physical healing isn't my strong suit. I can feed him power, but not much more."

"Lena's calling the ambulance," Max said. He laid a hand on Victory's shoulder. "We shouldn't move him."

"I know." She bit her bottom lip, tasting blood when a fang pierced skin. Wounds were nothing new to her.

Max squeezed her shoulder. "He'll be fine."

"Yes." She smoothed Mikelos' lank hair and felt a patch sticky with blood. Of course he would be. He was her daywalker; he could survive anything. They would get him to the hospital, the doctors would do what they could, and she would get some of her own blood into him to strengthen their bond and speed his healing. Things would work out. But right now, she was numb. She stared at Daliana's hands, wishing she could will her own strength into them.

The other councilmembers gathered on the steps. Victory wanted to demand information from Fabbri, but she couldn't jump to conclusions yet. Maybe Mikelos had just been mugged. Right, that was likely.

A groan of pain caught her attention when Lorus and Tristan hauled the stranger to his feet. "Let go of me, freaks!" He struggled in their grasp. "Did I kill the bastard?"

No, not a random act of violence. Victory almost jumped at him again, but Max snatched her wrist and held her firm. His low voice spoke into her ear. "He's not worth your time or effort."

She sank back to her knees. Attacking this man would invalidate everything she said in council.

The man laughed when she backed down. "Yeah, that's right. Too afraid to take me on without your little bitch?" He tried to shake off his captors, but the werewolf and weresnake kept their hands wrapped around his upper arms.

"Shut up or I'll hit you myself." The feral growl accompanying Tristan's threat made the man's struggles cease.

Lena pushed her way through the crowd of councilmembers. "The ambulance is on its way, Victory. They'll be here soon." She spared a nasty look for Mikelos' assailant. "I gave the police a ring, too, and they should be right behind. How is he?"

"He's banged up pretty bad," Max said, "but he'll live. Daliana's doing what she can, but we'll need the hospital."

Lena's furious eyes flashed in the light from the council building. "This can't be a coincidence. Has he said anything incriminating?"

Almost on cue, the attacker started pulling against his captors' grips again. "He threatened to bite me! The freak can't do that! Help!"

Max smirked. "Oh, yeah."

"Um, Victory?"

Genevieve stood near them at the bottom of the steps. In the werepanther's hands lay splintered pieces of wood, strings curling out like cat whiskers. "I couldn't find the bow." She looked stricken.

"It's here," Sethri said from farther within the crowd. He picked up the unharmed bow from the steps and brought it to Victory. She gathered the fractured pieces under one arm and collected the bow. The weight in her arms tugged at her heart. This needless destruction would hurt Mikelos more than his own injuries.

"Ow! Stop that!" Lorus smacked his prisoner on the back of the head. "Tristan, put your claws away and stop being a jerk. Maybe he'll stand still. What should we do with him, Alex?"

Victory wondered the same thing. Under her breath, she said, "I know what my vote is." Max shot her a grin.

Sethri studied the man in silence, then said, "Fabbri!"

The crowd of human councilmembers shifted to reveal the woman in question. Fabbri remained where she was, arms crossed and hip tilted. She exuded overeager innocence. "What? You think I had something to do with this?"

Victory perked up. She heard sirens in the distance.

"Do you know this man?" Sethri's tone was level.

Impressive. Victory would not have been so polite.

"I've never seen him before in my life," Fabbri said.

"You told me not to let that freak or his daughter into the club!" the man said from the street. "I got rid of some wolves and an elf slut, too."

The glow from Daliana's hands stuttered as she let out a hiss.

"I didn't tell you to beat him bloody, you idiot." So Fabbri damned herself. Victory would have laughed had she not been so furious.

"This doesn't look good, Emily," Sethri said. Victory could tell he was beginning to lose the calm that had amazed her. "I should—"

The loud siren from the ambulance turning the corner drowned out his words. Max jumped up and waved the vehicle in. Like Lena promised, a police town-car followed close behind. The paramedics hopped out of the ambulance right after it screeched to a halt. Two women shooed Victory, Max, and Lena out of the way, but didn't interfere with Daliana's flow of healing power. Victory let go of Mikelos' hand with reluctance and stood, but continued to hover over the medics. They checked his vital signs and splinted his hand and leg, preparing to move him onto a gurney. The medics knew their job and would take care of Mikelos well. She knew Limani Central hired the best. She was the hospital's best benefactor, because they kept her in fresh bottled blood. Her reassuring thoughts rang hollow when Mikelos groaned, even in unconsciousness, at the movement of his injured leg.

The shouts of the attacker distracted her. Tristan and Lorus handed him over to the two police officers, who exchanged the werecreatures' vice grips for steel handcuffs.

"You can't let them do this, Fabbri!" His head hit the edge of the town-car roof with a muffled thump. The cops weren't being too careful with this one. Good. He shouldn't get consideration. "Those freaks deserve—!" The door slammed shut on his further complaints.

"Quite the imagination for insults, that one," Max said. "Practically a sailor. He almost made me blush."

His sarcasm did little to cheer her, but she appreciated the effort. The medics now loaded the gurney into the back of the ambulance, Daliana climbing in beside one of the medics while the second headed for the driver's door.

Victory was torn. The council was still there, and the meeting would continue, now that they knew Fabbri had more influence than just the sign on her restaurant's door. "Lena?"

She smiled at Victory. "Go. Take care of Mikelos."

"We can deal with Fabbri," Max said. "I'll let you know what happens as soon as the meeting's over."

"Thank you." These were true friends. Lena hugged her, and she clasped Max's hand. The ambulance's lights began to flash, and she dashed to the passenger side. Right now her place was with Mikelos.

A heavy object bludgeoned Toria's skull. Again. Again. And again. It didn't stop when she brought her hands over her head, and she realized the pain came from within, the fiercest headache she'd ever had. Her eyeballs were on fire, and her brain throbbed.

She risked cracking open her eyes. Darkness met them, and she fought down momentary panic. *It's nighttime, girl. Chill out.* There was dirt under her cheek, and a rock dug into her side.

Kane! She had to help Kane. Toria scrambled to her feet when memory rushed back. Her head screeched in pain at the hasty action, and she listed to one side, struggling for balance. If the Romans were still nearby, they were done for. She fell to a knee, then pushed herself up again, trying not to retch from the roiling in her stomach. She peered across the river, but couldn't see through the haze of pain. Her hand sought the rapier at her side, but met empty air.

She fell to her knees again, clutching her stomach in her arms and shutting her eyes. That was it. She made a prime target and couldn't do a thing about it.

But no attack came. Her stomach calmed, now that she wasn't thrashing about, but the headache did not ease.

"Ugh." The inside of her mouth felt like cotton, and there was grit plastered to her cheek. But she didn't feel on the verge of passing out, so she raised her head and opened her eyes again.

The river spread before her, the woods to her back. There was the road. If not for the landmarks, and the strange footprints in the mud on her side of the river, she wouldn't have been able to tell that a battle had raged here.

No Romans. No horses. Nothing.

Of course, any Romans still around would have shot her when she began flailing around like a maniac.

"Kane!" Her voice echoed across the water. "Asaron!"

A testy owl hooted from the trees behind her, and the river continued to flow. Other than that, no response.

She pushed herself to her feet and turned in a slow circle, squinting into the darkness. The moon had set, so she had been unconscious for at least a few hours. Now, faint starlight lit the night. She dug a small glass bauble from one of her belt pouches and held it in her palm.

Focusing her intentions on the bauble, she nudged it with her mind. Pain lanced between her temples. Toria doubled over, but managed to remain on her feet.

The spell infused in the glass activated. Amethyst light sputtered out, dimmed almost to nonexistence, and then steadied to its set brightness. A cool amethyst glow bathed the area around her.

Concentrating on the comforting familiar light persuaded the pain behind her eyes to fade to a manageable pulse. Now Toria took more rational stock of her situation. Her light revealed no bodies across the river—Kane and Asaron must have been taken. Reaching deep within herself, she still felt the bond in her soul connecting her to her partner. She would be able to tell if he died. The bond was faint with distance, but still had Kane's unmistakable trace. And if Kane lived, that boded well for Asaron's survival, too.

Unless her partner had done something stupid. No. She wouldn't go there.

Now for supplies. There was no sign of her horse, even after she walked the edge of the woods and whistled for a few minutes. Either the Romans had taken the mare, or she'd given up on her crazy mistress and headed home. Guess that meant a walk back to Limani.

Weapons? The horse hadn't disarmed her before wandering off, so the Romans must have searched her. Her knives were gone, along with the small amount of money tucked in one of her pouches. They hadn't made a thorough search—the rest of her money was still tucked in the hidden pocket on the inside of her duster.

That left her sword. She had ignored the absence of its comforting weight, but could pretend no longer.

"Bastards!" She scooped up a rock from the edge of the river and sent it hurtling through the air. It landed with an ineffectual splash, but still made her feel better. Asaron would never forgive her for losing the sword after everything he went through to get it fixed. Why hadn't they taken her with them? Maybe she'd managed to disable a few of them and they hadn't had room. The thought consoled her, but not by much.

Toria stared across the river, trying to ignore the tap dancers in her skull. Everything in her urged her to go south, track the damn Romans, and rescue Kane. Yes, he still lived, but for how long?

She was at the edge of the water, waves lapping at her boots, before she realized what she was doing. "No, Toria." She didn't even have a water bottle, much less weaponry. Her magic was strong, but a rescue attempt would be a lot easier with a blade in her hand.

With great reluctance, she pulled herself away from the water's edge. No, she would have to return to Limani for aid. And painkillers. At least she'd accomplished their mission. The Romans were close to the city, and she had to bring the warning.

Toria distracted herself from her head by gripping the glowing glass even tighter in her hand. The power in the bauble strained, and the light guttered like a candle, then went out. When she attempted to reactivate the spell, sharp pain lanced her between the eyes and she doubled over again.

She hoped dawn came soon. It would be a long, agonizing walk, but daylight at least meant she wouldn't trip over everything.

The second Mikelos' eyelids began to twitch, Victory shot out of her seat by the window and across the hospital room to his side.

"Victory?" His voice grated.

"Hush, love, you're safe." She squeezed his uninjured hand in reassurance and pushed the call button by the side of his hospital bed. "We're at Limani Central, you're okay now." As okay as he could be with a leg brace, a splinted hand, bandages around his ribs, and a nasty bump on the back of his head. Victory still seethed inside, but she shoved the feelings down. Right now she needed to stay calm for Mikelos, not have a temper tantrum and start throwing furniture around.

A nurse poked her head into the room. Victory gestured toward the awaking Mikelos, and the nurse disappeared again. The doctor would come soon—her continuous flow of money to the hospital played to her advantage tonight.

Mikelos' eyes centered, and she returned his smile, brushing his hair off his forehead. He managed to raise his head a few inches and look down his body. A sheet hid him from the waist down, but there was no mistaking his bandages. "My hand—?"

"Ah, awake?" The doctor handling Mikelos' case bustled into the room and nudged Victory out of the way to check on his patient. "Hello, Mr. Connor, my name is Dr. Preston. May I call you Mikelos?"

Mikelos nodded once, and squeezed his pale lips together in pain. He let his head fall back against the pillows.

Victory tensed, but the doctor had things well in hand.

"Easy, Mikelos," he said. "You've had quite a night."

She stared in fascination while he did mysterious medical things involving shining a light at Mikelos' pupils. Visions of doctors from centuries past haunted her, wielding saws to "fix" knee injuries like the one Mikelos had suffered. Mikelos would receive special treatment due to his connection with the hospital's best patron, but battlefield experiences of spilled blood and severed limbs still lived in her vivid memories. She'd confessed these to Daliana earlier when Mikelos was being patched up, but the elven woman had just patted her hand and told her that memories were potent things before heading downstairs to her office. Truer words were never spoken, especially when spoken by the hospital's chief psychiatrist.

She ran her hands through her hair, pulling it into a messy bun. Dawn was approaching, and between the council meeting and Mikelos' attack, it had been a long day.

Dr. Preston finished probing at Mikelos' side. "The good news is that your ribs are bruised, but none of them are broken. Three bones in your hand are broken, but those are splinted and will heal with time. We've also ruled out a concussion." Victory had heard his summary of her daywalker's injuries, but the doctor stepped back to include her when he spoke to Mikelos. "However, you also tore the anterior cruciate ligament in your knee, so we're going to have you pretty happy on pain medication until we can schedule surgery today. Ms., erm, Victory has assured me that you will heal faster than a normal human, but we're still going to take every precaution against further aggravation of your wounds." He picked up the chart hanging at the end of Mikelos' bed and flipped through it, making a few notations.

Mikelos reached for Victory, and she stepped closer to take his hand again. "How much blood?" He traced the small bandage decorated with blue stars on the inside of her wrist where she had made the tiny incision with a scalpel snagged from a closet. The night nurse had balked at Victory's request for the medical supplies, but calling Daliana back upstairs had bypassed the issue.

"A few teaspoons," she said, entwining her fingers in his. "You'll be on your feet in no time. We'll reevaluate in a few hours and see whether we can avoid the surgery." She kept repeating it to herself: her daywalker was strong. He was not a normal human. Mikelos would heal even faster than Toria had when she broke her leg a few years ago.

"There will be the matter of some necessary physical rehabilitation, but, um, yes." Dr. Preston's discomfort rose, as it had earlier when Daliana helped Victory cut her wrist to collect the blood. Victory pitied him, but there wasn't much choice. It wasn't like any of the doctors here knew anything beyond the basics about vampire or daywalker physiology. Since they were the only two permanent residents of the sort in Limani, it wasn't a specialization in much demand. He would do the best he could under the strange circumstances. He cleared his throat. "But until then, we will take excellent care of you." Saving him from further awkwardness, the pager at his side chirped its insistence. Dr. Preston mumbled his excuses after checking the number.

"Thank you, Doctor," Victory said, but he had already fled the room. "Poor guy. But he's a good doctor. Or so Dal assures me." She couldn't keep the suspicion from creeping into her voice.

Mikelos smiled up at her. "That's my girl." His voice slurred.

He was crashing, hard. The pain medication must be kicking in, and combined with the extra work her shared blood was doing to help heal him, it was no surprise. Healing took a lot out of anyone. Victory tried to lighten the mood. "So, you didn't put up a very good fight. When was the last time you even picked up your sword? I'll have to put you back in training with the kids when you're better."

"The guy?" Mikelos' eyes were half open, but he still managed to look questioning.

"In police custody," Victory said. "He's got his own set of bruises. I tackled him halfway across the street to get him off you. And Tristan and Lorus got to manhandle him a bit. Probably a bit more than necessary, but I wasn't about to stop them." She was nervous, so she rambled. And she was doing it in her head, too. Gods, she must be tired.

"Good. Love you." At that, Mikelos drifted off, and his grip on Victory's hand relaxed.

"I love you, too." Victory placed a gentle hand over his heart to feel the steady, reassuring beat in his chest. The door to the hospital room opened, and she raised a hand to silence the visitor. Not that Mikelos would wake for anything at this point. She pecked a kiss on Mikelos' lips before standing to greet the newcomer.

"How's he doing?" Max said, his voice low.

"About as well as can be expected." Victory gestured for the mercenary to join her on the other side of the room. She reclaimed her perch on the windowsill, and Max took a seat in the uncomfortable plastic chair she had been ignoring earlier. He was welcome to the hideous thing. "He didn't ask about his violin."

"He might not remember, and that's probably a blessing," Max said. "It'll hit him pretty hard later, but now he needs to concentrate on healing." He shifted in his seat, already uncomfortable, but he would never give in and move like she had. He was more stubborn.

"You're right." Victory rested her head against the cool glass and stared out across the empty hospital parking lot. "So what's the news?"

"This guy who attacked Mikelos, Edward MacClellan, has been charged with assault and destruction of property," Max said. "Unfortunately, no one can prove whether he intended to kill Mikelos, and MacClellan isn't talking until he gets a lawyer."

"Figures," Victory said. "And I won't be surprised if he gets one. How did the rest of the meeting go? Are Fabbri's ideas restricted to her, or has she spread this nonsense?"

"Everything I've seen in the past few days says so. She's just the most vocal. And being on the council might make her the de facto leader."

"The vibe I'm getting isn't so much that she wants more power," Victory said, "but that she wants it out of our hands." She spoke in general terms, speaking for all of the nonelected councilmembers. "She doesn't seem fond of you, either. Even though you're human. Well, mostly."

"Mostly." He traded smiles with her. "But it's not surprising," Max said. "Politically, we're on your side."

"But does she want the power to be in the hands of only those who have been elected to the council instead of appointed? Or does she want it only for humans?" Things weren't making any sense. Maybe Fabbri was plain nuts. But an argument against the woman's sanity based on whom she let in her restaurant wasn't quite good enough.

Max studied Mikelos' still form. "MacClellan implicated Fabbri in Mikelos' attack. I think it's safe to say she's pro-human, not pro-elections. And when I left the station, the police were about to call the new owner of the Twilight Mists for questioning. This might be even bigger than we think."

"It is bigger than we think," Victory said. Another soft tap came from the half-open door where Daliana had appeared. Victory waved her in, and the elven woman ghosted across the floor to join them.

Max shifted to the side of his chair, and Daliana perched on the arm. "Ain't this a regular party? What do you mean, hon?" Max asked.

Ignoring him, Daliana said, "How is he doing?"

"Okay," Victory said. "He woke up enough to talk to the doctor, but then he conked out again. I thought you were finally heading home?"

"I took a quick consult in the ER for an elven patient," she said. Her face was grave, and she hesitated before going on.

"Spit it out, girl," Max said.

"Things are getting bad. Three more people have been brought into the emergency room within the past hour. Two werewolves and an elven girl," she said. She shook her head in silent anger. "All beaten as badly as Mikelos. One of the wolves even more so, his back might be broken." Daliana pulled a flier out of her pocket and smoothed it flat. She looked it over again before holding it up for them to see. "He had this."

The crumpled paper had almost ripped in half. One corner had soaked in blood, now dried to a flaky brownish tint. A simple flier, with an advertisement for a meeting.

DATE: JUNE 27TH

TIME: 6:00 PM

PLACE: TWILIGHT MISTS

WHAT: INFORMAL TOWN HALL MEETING REGARDING THE STATE OF THE LIMANI CITY COUNCIL AND ITS MEMBERS. ALSO FEATURED WILL BE A Q&A SESSION REGARDING CURRENT PUBLIC POLICIES AND THEIR EFFECTS ON LIMANI CITIZENS.

SPONSORED BY: LIMANI HUMANISTS
REFRESHMENTS WILL BE PROVIDED!

"Okay," Victory said. "That bad vibe went from worse to horrible." The location of the meeting outraged her more than what it planned to discuss. When she'd sold the club after almost a century of ownership, she never expected it would be used like this.

"Damn." Max took the flier and studied it. "Yeah, I'll second that. This comes off as a civil gripe meeting, but if they're already attacking people, this is going to get a lot worse before it gets better. Impeaching Fabbri and getting her off the council might not fix this."

"We can't assume these Humanists are directly responsible for the attacks," Victory said. She hated to play devil's advocate. Under normal circumstances, that would be Mikelos' job, but right now he wasn't in any position to do it. "These could be more punks operating on their own."

"One can only hope," Daliana said. She rose from her seat and began pacing the room.

The elven woman was one of the calmest people Victory knew, able to handle anything with finesse. She had never seen Daliana so worked up. Again, these weren't normal circumstances. "Well, you said MacClellan was charged. Have they questioned Fabbri?"

"That's the other problem," Max said.

Daliana stopped pacing, and both women stared at the mercenary.

"She didn't," Victory said.

"She did."

"Hell," Victory said.

"Did what?" Daliana asked. "Explain. Or is this some sort of fighter code I'm not privy to?"

"She disappeared," Victory said. "When?"

"We don't know. We were busy controlling MacClellan," Max said. "He tried to kick the glass out of the back window. You two left in the ambulance. By the time both vehicles were off, half the council had wandered back inside, and I figured she'd gone with them. Lena thought she was still outside with me."

"Perfect." Victory groaned in exasperation. "Is there going to be an arrest?"

"I asked the cops to stay on the lookout since MacClellan implicated her," Max said, "but once he shut up, they decided there wasn't enough evidence. Never mind that the whole council heard what she said to him."

"So no arrest warrant?" Daliana said.

"Nope."

"But you do believe that Fabbri set up the attacks?" The elven woman's green eyes flashed in fury. Victory didn't want to know what she'd seen in the ER to rouse her this much.

"Hell, yeah," Max said. "MacClellan didn't strike me as the type to be imaginative enough to pin this on anyone else. The bastard is proud of what he did."

Victory resisted her immediate urge to go on the hunt. "So what do we do now?"

The three stared at each other. Max spoke up first. "I'd say it's time to call a meeting."

Toria learned in junior high geography class that the southern portion of Limani's territory had the sparsest population. The reality had never sunk in until this walk home, the sunlight fading around her. Her head still ached, her feet felt like they were being stabbed by hot pokers, and the last time she'd had water was from a small stream at least five miles back.

She cut through woods to get from the road to the manor. Her spirits lifted when she saw her driveway. She felt moisture on her cheeks when the house came into view, and Toria raised her hands to her face.

She laughed, realizing that she was crying in relief. Exhaustion and dehydration were a dangerous combination. Only the gods knew where Kane and Asaron were now. But her parents would be home, and they would make everything better. A childish sentiment, but one Toria clung to while she entered the security code to open the back door. The Romans had even taken her keys.

"Mama!" Toria clutched the doorframe when air conditioned coolness washed over her. Dirt and grime coated her. She needed to dredge up the energy to shower before she could collapse.

No answer. "Dad!" She shut the door behind her, but still no one came running. Maybe they were out? The plan was for Max to tell Mama of their mission at the council meeting last night. They had no reason to expect them back this soon. But what kept Mama out late enough that she had to stay elsewhere for the day?

The kitchen wavered in front of her. With no way to contact her parents, there was no point in going back out and randomly searching. Driving in this condition would be suicide, so she dismissed that idea right off.

Max! Toria used the counter to pull herself over to the kitchen phone. She dialed his direct number at the Hall from memory. She didn't care whether he'd be angry that she bypassed his aide.

The line rang for a bit. Then, "Hello, you've reached the office of Maximilian Asher. I'm not here right now, but you can leave a message, and I'll get back to you as soon as possible." A prompt beep followed his businesslike tone.

"Max! I had to walk home. Kane and Asaron got kidnapped by the Romans. They left me by the river and I don't know where they are. I lost your horse, I'm so sorry." She was rambling now, and crying, but couldn't seem to stop. "I don't know where Dad or Mama are, I don't know what to do." The phone cord stretched long when Toria slid down the wall into a heap on the floor. In a whisper, she repeated, "I don't know what to do."

With no energy to stand and hang up the phone, she let it drop into her lap. The voice mail registered the silence and started giving her options, but Toria just stared at the phone.

The cool of the tile floor beneath her seeped into her body. After tugging off her boots, she began to feel a little better. She should get some water, take a shower, go to bed, wait for her parents to come home.

In a minute. She could rest for a minute.

A stiff back and tongue tasting like a dust rag were the first things Victory noticed upon waking. But the familiar fingers running through her long hair soothed her. She hummed a sound of bliss in the back of her throat.

She raised her head from the edge of Mikelos' bed. Her back let loose a loud protest when she sat straight up. "Ouch." The room was dim, so she switched on the bedside lamp.

"I can't believe you fell asleep like that." Mikelos' good hand dropped back onto his stomach.

"I've slept through worse, believe me." His eyes were brighter now, a definite improvement, but he still looked pale. "How are you feeling, love?"

"Okay," he said. "What time is it?"

"I have no idea." Max had sat with her for a while after Daliana left, then helped her scrounge the hall for spare blankets to hang over the window. A faint glow of sunlight shone through the edges of the blanket and showed the day had almost passed. She pulled herself out of the wretched plastic chair and stretched, arching her arms above her head and then out to the sides. Her back complained one more time before settling back into its normal alignment. She checked the clock above the door. "A little before nine. You've slept for over sixteen hours. I think I passed out around seven this morning. The nurses were probably glad. I was getting snippy."

"I'm sure you were." Despite the new energy in his eyes, his voice was still soft and listless, bereft of its usual musical lilt.

She wanted her old Mikelos back. "Are you hungry?" Don't ask about the violin, she prayed. I can't deal with that right now. Neither can you.

"Starved."

"I'll be right back, then." It took a few minutes to wave down a passing orderly and demand Mikelos be fed. The man was eager to assist her; she'd earned herself a bit of a reputation that morning when she'd told off a nurse for trying to take the blankets off the window. If she didn't know better, she'd have thought they were trying to kill her just to get her out of their way. She remembered doctors from her past. Maybe they were. This time, the thoughts amused her.

The orderly returned with the meal cart half an hour later, along with the cup of coffee and daily paper Victory had slipped him some cash for. After they maneuvered Mikelos into the least painful sitting position, he fell on the meal with gusto. He must be hungry if the stuff the hospital called food appealed to him. Victory shoved the horrid chair into the far corner of the room and settled herself cross-legged at the end of the bed.

Coffee made the world seem more manageable. Later she would call the blood donation office and ask for a proper breakfast to be sent up, but this would do for now. Victory spread the paper over the lump of Mikelos' cast.

"Ah, hell."

Mikelos looked up from his dinner, his spoon of soup hovering inches from his mouth. "What?"

"There's nothing in here about the attacks last night."

"Attacks? Plural?"

Victory sketched out what Daliana had shared the night before. She had tried to find the other victims before dawn and get more information about their attackers, but there was only so much she could do in the middle of the night. Come of think of it, maybe that was why the nurses weren't fond of her. "We're pretty sure they were attacked by these 'Humanists' like you were," she said.

"But why me?" Mikelos stared at her coffee until she relented and handed the cup over. "I understand the elf and wolves, but I'm closer to human."

"Because they're stupid, but not that stupid," Victory said. "An elven girl doesn't look like much. And enough humans can take out a werewolf, at least one of the younger ones. An elder wolf would rip them to shreds. But no one in their right mind would go after me."

She stole her coffee back and studied the paper spread in front of her. "Werewolves, and the panthers, have that ancient reputation of stealing livestock. The elves steal human children and leave changelings, but they've managed to twist the legends in their favor, reminding the public that they only steal children destined for horrible lives." Like the life Toria would have had, left to grow up in the middle of nowhere at the edge of the Wasteland. "But the chosen prey of vampires has always been healthy humans. And if they're so convinced I'm evil, then these Humanists are going to assume that I'll eat them if they go after me."

Mikelos laughed at her look of distaste, then put his hand to his ribs and groaned. He gasped a mixture of laughter and pain. "Okay, don't make me do that. Please." He shifted in the bed again. "So what are we going to do about these Humanists?"

"I have no idea, yet. We have to find a way to implicate them directly in the attacks," Victory said. "Max said he would head back to the police station and get an update after he got some sleep. He'll call me." She traded her coffee again for a bite of applesauce. "Ugh. I'm sneaking you in some proper food."

"I don't think so." Dr. Preston entered the hospital room and flicked on the overhead light. "And I hope that's not coffee."

Mikelos handed the cup back to Victory. "Of course not, doc."

Victory slid off the bed to give Dr. Preston room to examine Mikelos. She flipped through the newspaper, hoping to find any mention of the attacks. If they weren't on the front page, maybe they'd been buried in the back. Nothing. The biggest news story was how the university sailing team had defeated a college up in the British Colonies. At least now she knew what side of this political mess the local media was on.

"I heard you had quite a morning, Victory," Dr. Preston said. "My nurses started complaining the second I got in this evening."

She resisted the urge to snap at him—with words or teeth. Irritating the man in charge of Mikelos' health seemed like a bad idea. "I had a rough night."

"If you were one of my patients," Dr. Preston said, "I would insist that you go home and get some proper rest."

"I'm fine." He could baby Mikelos all he wanted—that was his job. But she was a grown woman, and she could take care of herself.

Okay, maybe she needed some sleep in her comfortable bed, not hunched over Mikelos'.

Mikelos covered his laughter with more soup. He knew her too well, and she could see the amusement playing out in his eyes.

The doctor ignored her. "Well, everything looks good here. It's looking like the ACL surgery won't be necessary after all." He made notes on Mikelos' chart. "How are you feeling? Need any more pain medication?"

"Not yet. I'll ring for a nurse if I change my mind."

"Good, see that you do. No need to suffer right now, there'll be plenty of time for that later once we start you on some physical therapy."

His joke fell flat. "Right," Mikelos said.

"I'm off on rounds, then. I'll try to drop in on you before I leave later." With a nod of acknowledgement to Victory, Dr. Preston left the hospital room.

"I don't think I like him very much," Victory said. "Maybe he's one of the Humanists." She didn't mean it. Really.

"Now you're being paranoid. Though I have the feeling he doesn't like you much, either. He's right, you do need sleep." Mikelos interrupted himself with a yawn. "Me, too."

She placed a hand on Mikelos' cheek. "Then be sure to get some, love. I'm going to try to poke around some more. I'll check on you before I leave at sundown." Different nurses were on duty now, and she might be able to speak with the other attack victims. She hoped the morning shift hadn't given them too much warning. Victory removed the meal tray from Mikelos' lap and helped him lay flat again. She gave him a goodnight kiss before pulling up his covers. He neared sleep by the time she left the room.

Getting thrown out of a hospital by a nurse had to be almost as humiliating as getting thrown out of a bar by a bouncer.

Nope, more so.

And Victory had been thrown out of a lot of bars in her long life, for one reason or another. Once or twice she had even deserved it.

Thanks to gossip overheard in her slow meander by the nurses' station after she left Mikelos' room, she knew the two werewolves were still in intensive care. They had chased her out of that unit once already that morning, and she didn't look forward to a second attempt.

The elven girl had been transferred from the emergency room to a recovery ward. Either she'd escaped with light wounds, or her healing ability was quite strong. Victory hoped general nurses would be less neurotic than the intensive care ones.

None of the nurses, doctors, aides, or other evening visitors paid attention to Victory wandering down the third-floor hallway, admiring the bland hospital art decorating the pastel yellow walls. Watercolor landscapes seemed to be the rule of the day, though she did see a few random pieces consisting of strange geometric shapes. The majority of patients in this unit were human, but she caught the earthy scent of a werepanther halfway down the hall. Not her primary target, but now she was suspicious of any injury to a nonhuman.

After a gentle tap on the doorjamb, she slipped into the room. The young panther slept with his cast-covered leg held above the bed in traction. Victory stared at the contraption for a few moments, thanking whoever or whatever listened that Mikelos hadn't been injured so much.

The teenager mumbled a bit in his sleep. When he didn't wake at her presence, she crossed the room and picked up the chart hanging from the end of the bed.

A quick flip through showed he had been the victim of a soccer accident during afternoon practice. A werepanther had the innate speed and grace of an excellent goalie, but that hadn't saved him from a bad tangle with a teammate. Poor kid. She hoped he'd be able to play again.

So not another Humanist attack. At least at first glance. But she couldn't dismiss anything out of hand, regardless of the age of the victim or apparent circumstance. For all she knew, the younger nonhumans might be a more tempting target for the Humanists. Victory would interview him later when he woke.

"Can I help you?"

Victory slipped the chart back into its holder, then turned to face the nurse who'd entered the room. "Nope, I'm good, thanks."

The nurse narrowed her eyes at Victory. "This is a private room. Do you know the patient?"

"Yes, of course," Victory said. The nurse didn't mention Victory's perusal of the chart, but it couldn't have escaped her notice. How did they manage to look so intimidating in purple pants and pink shirts decorated with cartoon cats? "Tyrone is a friend of my daughter. I was in the hospital on business so I thought I'd see how he was doing."

The nurse held the door open wider and gave Victory an expectant look. Not wanting to press her luck yet, Victory took the unspoken invitation and exited the boy's room. The nurse shut the door right on her heels.

"Sheesh." Victory stopped in the middle of the hallway and eyed the closed door. Part of her wanted to make sure the kid would be okay, but she squashed down that sudden bout of paranoia. Okay, so maybe these nurses were worse than the ones in the intensive care unit. This might be more difficult than she had first thought. Victory surveyed the hall, but things were still quiet. So she continued to saunter in her original direction.

Past the nurses' station on one side, two more rooms containing human patients on the other. Then she caught what she had been looking for: the light scent of Other, the smell of fresh-cut grass and tangible sunlight that always said "elf" to Victory's vampiric senses. It was a relief from the harsh antiseptic smell permeating the hospital.

And it was quite obvious this patient was not asleep.

"No fucking way! I said I'm fine!"

With her senses still tuned to their highest notch, Victory resisted the urge to cover her ears at the high-pitched yell emanating from the hospital room. The girl had a set of lungs on her. She peeked around the corner into the room.

Three harried nurses stood around the hospital bed, one holding a glass of water and cup of pills out to the elven girl. "But you'll feel so much better," she said. "If you take the painkillers then you'll be able to eat. You need to keep your energy up so you can heal."

"Yeah, I need to eat real food! Not mess up my head with your crazy drugs." The girl slouched forward and pouted, and Victory caught the flinch of pain the girl almost hid. A possible injury to her ribs, to accompany the butterfly bandages holding together a long cut on her left cheek and temple. "That shit is not food. And your so-called medicine already made me puke once. Fuck that."

Victory stifled a laugh. She had never known an elf to be so loose with her language. This girl would horrify Daliana.

The nurse set the items on the bedside table by the untouched tray of hospital food, slowing her movement just in time to avoid slamming it down and scattering the contents. "Fine. Do what you will. Let's go, ladies."

Victory ducked back out of the room and studied more art, hoping she retained her look of inconspicuousness. It must have worked—when the three nurses left, they passed her without notice, heading straight for the nurses' station. Then Victory slipped into the hospital room.

"I *told* you—oh," the girl said, cutting off her attitude midsentence. "You're not one of those vultures."

"Nope," Victory said. "Mind if I have a seat and talk with you for a bit?" She gestured in the direction of the chair in the corner.

"Can I bribe you to get me real food from the cafeteria?" The girl released her arms from across her chest, relief visible on her face.

Taking that for a yes, Victory pushed the door just short of closed before dragging the chair closer to the bed. "You don't even have to bribe me. I know how bad the patient food is here." Different style of chair, even more uncomfortable. What was it about hospitals? "I'd like to ask you a few questions, and then I'll go pick up whatever you want."

"Deal. You're my hero for the evening."

Victory held out her hand. "I'm Victory, by the way."

"I know who you are. Vampires aren't exactly common in Limani." They exchanged handshakes. "I'm Syrisinia, Syri. Sorry I'm grumpy. I've had a crappy couple of days."

"I don't blame you," Victory said. "My daywalker is in the hospital, too, and he's not the greatest patient either."

Syri sat straight up in the bed. "Shit. They got him, too?"

All of Victory's attention now hung on Syri's every word. "Tell me what you know." If her version of events was anything like Mikelos', she would have serious evidence against the Humanists.

"I don't know much. I danced with Mikelos at the Twilight Mists last night before we got kicked out of the club with the wolves," Syri said. "I wanted to go back in, and the wolves were gonna back me up, but Mikelos convinced us not to, said you were taking care of things in council. Then he headed off."

Victory answered her unspoken question. "He was attacked by the bouncer who kicked you guys out. Right in front of the council hall."

"While council was in session? Bloody idiot."

"Indeed. Not the brightest idea," Victory said. "So where did you go after Mikelos left?"

Syri started to shrug, thought better of it when a wave of pain creased her forehead, and relaxed her shoulders again. "The wolves left to go do whatever werewolves do," she said. "I stuck around for a bit, tempted to sneak back in. Two other elves came up to the club, and I ended up warning them off. I might be stubborn, but I wasn't going to let them get into trouble, too." She eyed the tray of food next to her, but dismissed it with a wrinkle of her nose. "Then I heard the shouting start a couple blocks away. When I heard the howl, I figured it was the wolves in trouble. So I ran to the rescue."

Victory hadn't heard anything so ridiculous since the last time Toria declared her serious intention to figure out how to make a flying carpet. She studied the girl. Since she looked Toria's age, Syri was still not more than a child by the standards of elves, who could live thousands of years. And despite whatever magic she possessed, the girl was built like a twig, and not a sturdy one.

"Don't give me that look," Syri said. "I may be stupid, but I'm stronger than I look. Sort of."

Victory laughed at Syri's admission. "So did you rescue them?"

"Hey, they're in the intensive care unit, and I'm not." Syri's smug voice matched her look. "What do you think?"

"I think that I'm suitably impressed and one day I'd like to know how you managed to pull that off," Victory said.

"I ain't going anywhere," Syri said. Her voice lost its bantering tone when she continued. "There were six humans, all men, and they'd cornered Mal and Gregory in an alley. They had guns. I can't remember the last time I saw a person in this city with a gun."

"Silver bullets," Victory said, realization dawning. She couldn't get anyone to tell her the extent of the two werewolves' injuries, and Daliana had cited patient confidentiality.

"Gregory had already been shot in the stomach, still in human form. I could tell it wasn't steel since he was sitting on the ground, dazed. And Mal hadn't bothered to shift to wolf-form, he was just next to him growling at them instead of attacking back."

"If it'd been a regular bullet, it wouldn't have fazed him," Victory said. "They're weird like that."

"Yeah, they are. So…I kinda jumped into the fray," Syri said. "I got knocked around with the wooden clubs a few of them had before the cops showed up and they ran off. Hence the forehead and cracked rib."

"Syri, I should tell you something," Victory said, forcing her voice calm. "Silver-tipped bullets are just that—silver-tipped. There's still plenty of iron in the rest of them. Pure silver isn't strong enough to be fired well from a gun."

The blood drained out of the girl's already pale elven skin. Her voice catching, Syri said, "Are you serious?"

"Did anyone ever tell you I used to be a mercenary?" Victory said, keeping her tone light. Time to calm the girl down before she had a belated panic attack over her inadvertent close call. Iron was poison to elves, as silver was to the werecreatures and vampires.

"I think so," Syri said. "Before you came to Limani? But that was a long time ago. I know you've been here since before I was born."

"Yes," Victory said. "And I occasionally do temporary work if I feel the situation calls for it, to keep my hand in. Time moves differently for you and I. But I've kept the skills up. Weapons have changed, and sometimes your elders forget that." She took Syri's hand, and the girl gripped it tight. "When I was young, the world was different. I saw the empires move from swords, to guns, to missiles, to nuclear weapons. After the war that created the Wasteland, your people forced us to go back, returning to a world of blades."

"But isn't that still all we have?" Syri said.

"Sort of," Victory said. "There are antique firearms still floating around, pistols and rifles. My sire told me that he's run into a few old automatic machine guns. But there are always going to be those who want a better gun, one that will shoot farther and make bigger holes, even despite the world-altering spell. So elves and werecreatures and even vampires have to remember we're still vulnerable to what the humans can create. The world isn't safe anymore for those like you and I. Immortality can only take us so far. We've lost our edge, and now they can kill us as easily as they kill each other." Had Syri learned anything about the Humanists? One way to find out. "And it looks like they've started again."

"What is going on in here?" a voice snapped.

Victory twisted in her lumpy chair to see one of the ever-present nurses glowering from the entrance to the room, and a male orderly hulking behind her. "Can I help you, ma'am?" Victory said. Talk about terrible timing.

"You are disturbing my patient," the nurse said, sneering. "What's wrong with you? Filling a girl's head with such ideas when she's already hurt."

"I'm old enough to be your grandmother, lady—" Syri cut off this newest rant when Victory squeezed her hand in warning.

After checking the nurse's nametag, Victory again said, "Can I help you, Ms. Sjolander?" No point in being indignant over the fact that the woman had been spying on them.

"Visiting hours are over," the nurse said. "Sully will escort you from the hospital now so Syri can get her rest."

"Well, I couldn't very well come during regular visiting hours, could I?" Victory said. Reasoning with the woman was a long shot, but it never hurt to try. "Since they're during daylight hours. I'm almost done speaking with Syri, I'll be happy to leave right after."

Syri piped up with her own opinion. "Yeah, she's fine. It's not like I sleep much. Victory can stay as long as she wants."

Ms. Sjolander tensed at the mention of Victory's name. So that's what this was all about. How long had the nurse been spying on them?

"You're the vampire?" Ms. Sjolander's hands clenched at her sides.

Victory rose to her feet. She was still shorter than the nurse by a few inches, but it made her feel better. "Yes, I am."

Without a word, the nurse spun on her heel, grabbing the elbow of the confused orderly on her way out.

"What the hell was that about?"

Victory resumed her seat next to Syri. "Hell if I know." The elven girl's language was catching. "But now we have to talk fast. Where were we?"

"You said something about someone starting again," Syri said.

"Right," Victory said. "The reason you and the others were kicked out of the club? And why you were all attacked? There's a group forming, the Humanists, who—"

She heard heavy footsteps in the hall, and caught a voice saying, "She's in room 302." Damn, that was fast.

Syri also perked up, her pointed elven ears even more sensitive than Victory's. "I'm room 302."

Victory shot out of her chair and whirled around in time to see three hospital security guards appear in the doorway.

"Ms. Victory," the lead guard said, "you need to come with us."

Starting a fight in the middle of Syri's hospital room would not be a smart idea, even though Victory's hands itched for a nonexistent weapon. "I'm not finished talking to my friend yet."

"Hospital policy is that only immediate family may visit outside of visiting hours." The guard took a step forward. "You can either return to Mr. Connor's room or leave the hospital."

Ms. Sjolander appeared behind the security guards. "I think she needs to leave the hospital. She has been harassing the patients and staff since last night."

"It's true, sir," the youngest guard said. "There've been lots of complaints."

What complaints? She'd gotten chewed out by the one intensive care nurse that morning, but no one called security on her. Victory straightened further, drawing on the poise acquired over centuries. "Syri, I'll call you tomorrow."

"I'll be here," she said. "Have a good night. And get some sleep."

That settled it. Victory must look tired if even Syri could comment on it. Though it pained her sense of independence, she played nice. "So would one of you nice young men like to escort me to my car?" She smiled at the trio, slipping in a hint of fang. If they wanted to throw her out for being a vampire, they got the full treatment.

"Ellis, Wim, go with her," the leader said. And they were even paranoid enough to send her with two of them.

"Thank you so much," Victory said, brushing past them toward the exit. The guards hastened to fall in place on either side of her. Then she paused and looked over her shoulder at the head guard, confusing the two young men even more when they walked right past her. "It's probably best if I leave now," she said. "I haven't eaten in hours."

Now she left the hospital room, on her own terms. To Ms. Sjolander's sputtering, the guards' pale faces, and Syri's hysterical laughter.

Victory left her town-car on the drive in front of the house, not bothering to park it in its spot in the barn. She didn't intend to be home more than a few hours before returning to the hospital to see Mikelos again and check on Syri.

Despite her levity while the guards escorted her out of the hospital, a lump in her throat had formed the second she got in the town-car and grew larger the entire drive home. She feared that if she stopped moving, she would burst into tears and be worthless to everyone. Better to stay active, put in calls to Max and Daliana and the other nonhuman councilmembers. Then back to the hospital, and this time she would try to make it home again before dawn. She could sleep then.

Victory kicked off her sandals in the foyer, then headed into the kitchen. She flicked on the overhead lights and saw the telephone off its hook, hanging down the wall by the cord behind the kitchen island.

Huh. She hadn't touched the kitchen phone in a few days, at least. Maybe one of the others forgot to hang it up before leaving last night—Asaron, perhaps, since he and technology did not mix well. Victory walked around the island to return the phone to its rightful spot, hoping no one had called while she was stuck at the hospital all day.

She was tired, more than she'd admit to herself. So she didn't realize the significance of Toria curling up on the kitchen floor right away, beyond wondering why her daughter chose that particular spot for a nap.

Then it hit her. "Toria!" Victory crouched next to her daughter, placing a hand on her shoulder. She saw no obvious signs of injury, nor did she smell the telltale tang of blood. "Wake up, sweetie."

Toria groaned in response, the same groan Victory received every morning she woke her daughter through elementary and middle school. She had been glad to shove the job onto Kane when he moved into the manor in high school. Before Victory resorted to more drastic measures, Toria's eyes popped open, then changed to slits against the bright kitchen lights.

"Mom?" Toria reached for her mother's hand, and Victory pulled her into a sitting position. She stared around the kitchen. "Oh, man, I didn't mean to pass out here." Her voice sounded cracked and dry.

Victory recognized that tone. She stood, hanging up the phone before fetching a glass from the cupboard and filling it with water from the refrigerator. Toria took it in two shaking hands with a look of utter gratitude.

"Are you okay?" Victory kneeled next to her again while Toria drank. "What happened?" She took in Toria's grimy and sweat-stained sports bra and jeans, her shirt and duster lying in a pile on the counter above them. "Where are the guys? I didn't expect you back until tomorrow at the earliest." The news couldn't be good, and she dreaded to hear it. She dreaded sharing her own much more.

Setting the empty glass down on the floor next to her, Toria scrubbed her face with her hands. "We weren't supposed to be. Things got bad, Mama, really fast."

Victory clasped her daughter's hand in her own. "Where are Kane and Asaron?" She braced for the worst. But wouldn't she feel Asaron die? He was her sire, linked by blood even tighter than Mikelos.

Toria breathed deep, staring into space over Victory's shoulder. "We ran into a Roman patrol right after the guys crossed the Agios River. I was still trying to get my horse to cross, probably all that saved me. I focused my power to Kane to help him fight them off, but a backlash knocked me out." With obvious effort, she brought her eyes to Victory's nose, her daughter's equivalent of looking at her straight on. Toria's face was ashen, and a single tear trailed down one cheek. "When I came to, they were gone. So was my horse, and the patrol had searched me."

Mikelos lying in front of the council hall—unconscious, bleeding—had been a blow to the stomach. The news of her captured sire and foster son was almost a stake to the heart. A sharp pain bit her palm and she jumped before she realized the nails of her empty hand were digging into her skin. She unclenched the hand before she could draw blood. "But why—"

"I don't know why they left me," Toria said. "Maybe they didn't have room for another prisoner. They should have taken me."

"No!" Victory lowered her voice and said, "More likely you were left in warning."

"For who?" Toria laughed without humor, staring up at the white ceiling. "It's the army of the Roman fucking Empire. They declared hostile intent when they took Kane and Asaron. Limani doesn't stand a chance."

"For someone with such a grasp on tactics, it's a wonder that you're so terrible at chess." Victory's joke fell flat. Mother and daughter shared a look of despair.

"How can you joke about this, Mama?"

Because if she didn't, she was going to put a fist through the wall. "I'm sorry. But Asaron has been in worse situations over the years. He'll take care of Kane."

With a noncommittal nod, Toria braced a hand on the floor and pushed herself to her feet. "Hey, where's Dad?"

This time Victory avoided her daughter's eyes while she also rose. "He's in the hospital."

"What! Why?"

"He was attacked," Victory said. "The Roman Army's not the only thing we have to deal with right now. The Humanists have also made their move."

Victory needed to time her announcements better.

Toria had let go of the counter. At Victory's news, she staggered to one side, catching herself on the island in the middle of the kitchen. Victory grabbed her elbow before she could fall.

"Gah, Mom," Toria said. "Don't do that. Is Dad okay?"

Pain and fear filled the look Toria gave her. The fear for her family was obvious, but the pain concerned Victory more. Ignoring her daughter's question, she instead said, "When you were knocked out last night, what exactly happened?"

"Mama. Is Dad okay?"

"He'll be fine, he just hurt his knee and ribs." She wouldn't mention the hand. Victory grabbed Toria's chin and peered into her eyes. She didn't know quite what doctors looked for when they did that, but she didn't see anything out of the ordinary. But Toria's storm-gray eyes seemed large for her pale face. "Now what happened to you? How did you get hurt if the Romans were across the river?"

"It's just power backlash," Toria said, pulling out of Victory's grasp. "I've never had one this bad before, but using a river for power is kind of a rush. Can't expect anything less."

"You need to see someone about this," Victory said.

"Who? A doctor?" Using the counter for balance, she headed for the entrance to the family room in halting steps. "This isn't anything physical. I just need some sleep."

Victory started forward to help Toria when the phone rang. Her daughter waved her off, and with reluctance Victory darted past her for the cordless phone in the family room. Switching it on, she stuck it between her cheek and shoulder, freeing her hands to once again help Toria collapse on the couch. "Hello?"

"Toria! I just got your message. What's going on?" Max's concerned voice poured out of the phone, his volume piercing.

Victory pulled the phone a few inches away from her ear, but not fast enough. "I don't sound that much like my daughter, do I?"

"Sorry," Max said. "But have you seen her? She left a panicked message on my private line a few hours ago."

"I just got home, and she's here. Had quite an adventure, too." Victory tried to hand the phone over to her daughter, but Toria grabbed a pillow and curled around it on her side. So Victory settled next to her and related the events of Toria's past day and night to Max. "She's passing out here on the couch next to me. I want to pass out with her, but we have work to do. I just got home and was about to give you a call."

"Thank gods she's okay," Max said. "If no one answered the phone I was about to tear over there."

The relief in his voice was a nice change from the earlier panic. Victory returned the phone to her ear once she was sure he wasn't going to blow her eardrums again. "So, we need to figure out what we're going to do."

"On two fronts, now," Max said. "Both with these idiots here, and now with an army. Toria's sure Kane and Asaron are okay?"

"Her link with Kane was still strong, but that doesn't tell her anything about Asaron," Victory said. Toria wasn't asleep—she grunted in affirmation, and Victory rubbed her shoulder.

"Can you tell whether he's okay? He is your sire."

"Sorry, Max," Victory said. "I wish it worked like that."

"Worth a shot," he said. "So. Meeting?"

"Meeting. With whom?" She wished for a better way to get things done, but that was her mercenary days speaking, when she could grab a sword and fix things her own way. But now too many lives were at stake. And she wasn't about to try to take on an army by herself. Contrary to Asaron's stories of her wild youth, she had never been quite that stupid.

"The usual suspects," Max said. "Daliana, Tristan, Genevieve, Lorus."

"And Lena." Her hand stilled on Toria's shoulder, her complete attention on Max. "Did you know that one of the wolves attacked last night was Tristan's Second in the werewolf pack? This is a pack matter now, not just a problem for the council to deal with."

"It became a pack matter when they got kicked out of the Twilight Mists with Mikelos," Max said. "I haven't spoken with Tristan, but I'm sure he's furious."

"Fun, fun."

"What was that?" Max said. "You mean you don't want to deal with an enraged werewolf? I hear they're almost as obnoxious as enraged vampires."

"Shush," Victory said. "Hopefully he's calmed down a little since last night. We do want this to be a productive meeting."

"One can only hope. So, you get your ass over here. Since this is going to be on my territory, I'll make the calls."

"No problem." Victory studied her daughter. "I'm bringing Toria. Do you have any other mages in the Guild right now?"

Silence from the other end of the line for a few seconds. "Victory, why do you think I want your pair so badly?"

"There's no one?"

"Aside from those two, there are maybe a dozen mages in Limani," Max said. "And none of them come close to matching our two for power. Why, what's wrong?"

"Toria suffered some sort of power backlash last night—"

"I'm fine," Toria said, not even opening her eyes.

"—and I wanted someone to take a look at her," Victory continued over her daughter.

"I can ask Daliana whether she knows of any elves who have experience with mages when I call her," Max said. "Other than that, I've got nothing."

"Good idea. See you in a few."

"Take care."

She switched off the phone before dropping it to the cushion next to her. "Let's go, sweetie."

"I'm staying here and sleeping." The pillow muffled her words. "Tell me how it goes in the morning."

"No way. I'm getting you checked out," Victory said. "Come on."

She'd managed to achieve the tone of voice that made Toria do what she said. It didn't happen often. With a groan, her daughter pushed herself up. She eyed Victory with irritation. "Can I at least get a shower first? I feel gross."

"You look gross. I can't believe I let you on my couch," Victory said. That got a rise out of Toria, who swatted at her. "Promise not to pass out in the shower?"

"I'll be fast." She held out her hands, and Victory stood to pull her off the couch. "But bang on the door after five minutes, just in case."

Victory slung Toria's arm across her shoulders and supported her around the waist, walking her out of the family room and back through the kitchen. "I'll even pick out clothes for you. You can sleep in the car, and I'll bet Max will let you crash on one of the couches in his office."

"Like he'll have much choice."

Victory helped Toria up the walk toward the front entrance to the Hall, lit up more than usual for this late at night. People must already be here.

"I can walk, Mama." When they neared the front steps, Toria pulled away from the arm around her waist.

But Victory held her daughter tight. Earlier, she'd rescued Toria from almost falling down the stairs at home, and now she wasn't taking any chances. Relief washed over Victory when Max opened the front door to greet them.

"Here, let me take her," he said, coming forward. "Give your mum a rest." With one swift movement, he hooked his arms behind Toria and swept her up like a baby. "I'm glad you're okay, girl."

Toria gave a quiet laugh, then relaxed her head against Max's shoulder. "Thanks."

That proved more than exhaustion was plaguing Toria. Standard operating procedure was to contradict all comments Max or anyone else made about her age or general level of experience. Victory held the door for Max while he carried Toria inside. "Have you heard from Daliana?"

"I did," Max said. "She's on her way over with someone who may be able to help. Do you want one of the guestrooms on the third floor or a couch in my office?"

"Couch," came the muffled reply from Max's shirt. "Better than those things you call beds."

"I'll take you up, then," Max said. He tilted his head toward the common room to the left. "Meet you in a few, Victory. Genevieve and Tristan are already here. Lorus brought a friend. And the coffee's on."

Victory pressed a kiss to Toria's cheek. "I love you. Rest."

"Love you, too." Max whisked her up the stairs and away.

Victory could not help watching to make sure Max got up the stairs with her daughter in one piece. She also admired the ease with which Max ascended the stairs. Toria stood three inches taller than Victory, and her muscles were real compared to the strength Victory derived from her vampirism. Maybe it was his elven heritage. Or maybe Max was just that strong.

Once he disappeared around the corner at the top landing, Victory felt able to head for the gathering room, drawn by the sound of talking and aroma of fresh-brewed coffee. She pushed open one of the frosted glass doors to see a handful of people clustered on the room's four couches drawn together into a lopsided square.

"—is why they will ultimately fail," was the first clear phrase to reach Victory's ears. The speaker looked up at Victory's arrival, then dismissed the vampire to return to her conversation. "Fabbri doesn't have the charisma needed to lead this kind of revolution. She has the drive, but no finesse."

Victory lurked by the entrance, identifying the other guests before making her own presence official. Lorus stood by the coffeepots, spooning sugar into a mug. The other two werecreature representatives shared one couch. But who was the elderly woman perched on another sofa lecturing them on revolutionary theory?

Lorus waved Victory over to hand her a mug. "Black, right?"

Victory accepted the drink and took a long sip, savoring the harsh burn of the liquid that would have scalded anyone else. The coffee might be useless to her, but it did make her feel better. Feeling the unnatural warmth soak into her, she said, "Thanks, Lorus."

"My pleasure," he said. "Max told us what he knew. How's Toria?"

She was touched. Victory wasn't aware Lorus even knew her daughter except by reputation. "Not sure. She seems fine on the outside, if tired. But I think something went wrong magically. Toria's trying to brush it off, but I can tell she's not herself."

"Mother's intuition," Lorus said.

"Something like that, I guess," Victory said. "Daliana's bringing in someone to check her out." She curled both hands around the warm mug. "Question for you, though. Who's the woman I don't believe I've ever seen before?"

Lorus looked pained. "Oh. Yes." He took a deep breath. "The other werecreatures of Limani don't have a proper hierarchy like the wolves and panthers. You know I'm only on council because I'm the only one willing to take the job. Since I don't have a proper Second, I brought Bethany." One hand held his coffee mug steady, but the other traced nervous patterns on the side of his pants leg.

"I'm sensing regret here."

"Well, I thought it would be a good idea," Lorus said. "I figure any plan we get her to agree with should get the support of the rest of the other weres. But I always forget that she's kind of cranky. And she's gotten worse with age."

Almost on cue, Bethany's voice rose against a response from Genevieve. "I don't care what right Fabbri has! She's acting like an upstart little cub with this group of hers. I say we go in and clean them all out."

Victory studied the woman more closely, noting the gray-streaked black hair, the plain clothing, the slight plumpness around the waist. "She doesn't look terribly intimidating. More like someone's old aunt. What type of creature is she?"

"A badger," Lorus said.

"They make werebadgers?"

Lorus flicked his tongue at her, a disturbing reptilian sight from a human face. "They make weresnakes."

"Point taken."

"Shall we sit?" Lorus gestured toward an empty couch. The seat in the room farthest away from Bethany.

Repressing a smile, Victory said, "Let's." She curled up in the corner of the couch with a pillow in her lap. Had Lorus heard about Kane and Asaron or just that Toria was injured? "Do you—"

The doors to the room opened and Max escorted Daliana and Lena in. "Good, everyone's here," he said. "Have a seat, ladies. I'll be right back, and we can get started."

Daliana settled herself between Victory and Lorus. "Zerandan is one of our more powerful mages. He's talking with Toria now."

Victory quashed the automatic fears accompanying the thought of Toria alone with a strange man. If Daliana trusted him, that was enough for her.

Perhaps sensing Victory's hesitation, Daliana said, "He's my grandfather."

Well. In that case. "Thank you," Victory said.

"What is she doing here?" Tristan glared at Lena.

Genevieve put a hand on his arm, but Lorus spoke up first. "She's on the council with us. One of the nonelected members. Isn't that status the problem Fabbri has with us?"

"But she's a human. And we're dealing with the Humanist problem."

Victory was ready to leap to her friend's defense along with Lorus, but Lena was faster. "Perhaps you don't know this," she said, the politeness in her voice blade-sharp, "but I was thrown out of Fabbri's restaurant right beside Victory. I may be a pureblood human, but I've thrown my lot in with the monsters and that makes me even worse. So I'm here."

"Monsters?" Genevieve said, a note of challenge in her voice.

"I wandered around the farmers' market this morning," Lena said. "The Humanists were recruiting. 'Monster' was one of the nicer terms I heard."

"Then we are glad to have you on our side," Genevieve said.

Tristan slumped in his seat, and Victory noted the unshaven chin and rumpled clothing. He must worry for his Second, Gregory, the same way she did for Mikelos. Her aggravation at him drained away. He was in the same situation.

The conversation halted when Max reentered the room, and Victory got the uncanny feeling her daughter once described to her—teacher was back in the classroom, so the troublemakers faded into the background. Well, this was Max's territory, and werecreatures respected territory and dominance more than anything else.

Max took the empty seat next to Bethany, a notebook and pen in hand. "So. The situation. Victory's daywalker Mikelos is in the hospital, along with an elf and two werewolves." He held up the crumpled flier Daliana showed them the night before. "The Humanists have declared themselves an active organization and are not likely to stop with these attacks. On top of it all, the Roman Army is camped outside our borders and the vampire Asaron and warrior-mage Kane Nalamas have been taken prisoner. For reasons unknown, they left behind the warrior-mage Toria Connor, but she might be suffering from some kind of magical attack."

Genevieve interrupted when Max paused for breath. "Poor Victory. Your family has come out the worst from all this."

"Might that be intentional?" Lena now studied the Humanist flier. She passed it to Lorus and looked up at Victory. "It wouldn't be the first time grand events have been orchestrated to enact personal revenge against you."

"I don't think so," Victory said, "but I can't say for certain. It would be more likely for Asaron to have major enemies. Besides, they might not have even known who they were capturing."

"But who with a grudge against Asaron would try to take on the whole city?" Genevieve said. "He's not even a permanent resident."

"The Humanists can't have predicted Mikelos would try to go dancing," Victory said. "And the Romans can't have known Max would send anyone on recon so soon."

"So we take it all at face value for right now," Max said. "Humanists on one side, Romans on the other, and Victory stuck in the middle out of sheer coincidence." He consulted his notebook. "First question—how the hell are we going to deal with all this?"

Since she'd already read the flier and felt no urge to see the dried bloodstains a second time, Victory passed it right to Daliana, who also handed it to Tristan without reading it.

"Shouldn't the Roman Army be a problem of the complete city council?" Daliana said.

"Right now the council doesn't have the solidarity to fight its way out of a paper bag," Lorus said.

"And I'd still like to know how Emily Fabbri knew about them at the meeting last night," Max said. "We can't assume that there's no connection between these problems."

He had something there. Another thought occurred to Victory, almost lost in the madness of the night before. "That would be too much of a coincidence," she said. "Remember, Fabbri wanted to use the army to distract us from moving to impeach her."

The Humanist flier reached Bethany, and the woman spoke up in outrage. "Easy solution, then, to at least one of the problems. We don't have time to fuck around. We know exactly where these Humanists are going to be and when. We go in and wipe them out. Then we deal with the Romans without any of this internal nonsense."

Everyone in the room gaped at her. Next to her, Lorus sank into the couch.

"Sure, that's brilliant," Genevieve said. "If we want a civil war, allowing the Romans to waltz in and kill everyone while we're too busy fighting each other."

"But isn't that the point?" Max said. "The Romans are camped out on our border. The easiest invasion is when you can walk in and take over. Victory?"

He needed agreement from the one person in the room ever involved in a large-scale war. Victory was more than happy to provide one. "It's true. I've been on both ends, and even if the city shows no resistance, it's not pretty. Keep in mind that all of us are automatically marked for death because we're political figures. And this is Limani. Even if the council surrenders, the city's not going to go peacefully."

"Rioting in the streets, then looting and rape when the Romans pour in," Max said.

Victory forced her eyes to remain open. If she closed them, the memories of scenes Max described would be all too vivid.

"So maybe the Humanists aren't that much of a coincidence," Lorus said. "Does Emily Fabbri have any Roman blood in her?"

"Fabbri is a Roman name," Lena said. "And Emily is a derivative of Emilia. Evidence points to it."

"No," Victory said. She had lived in this city for a hundred years. Even after brushing aside those memories of battle, the enormous weight of her age still settled on her shoulders. "Let's not go down that road, condemning people because of their heritage. Especially not based on such a flimsy excuse as a name. Limani has been open to settlers from either empire for hundreds of years, and the families are so intermingled it would be pointless. We're not going to start discriminating now."

"Regardless of the fact that's exactly what they're doing to us?" Tristan said.

"There's a difference between taking the higher moral ground and getting anything done," Max said. "Much as I'd like for both to be possible."

"So we need to figure out how far we're willing to go," Victory said.

Lorus toasted the room with his coffee mug. "And how far we'll have to push everyone else along with us."

Toria's decision to stay in Max's office instead of taking a bed in one of the Hall's guestrooms might have been the wrong one. The couch might be comfortable enough for sitting or lounging on, but any real sleep would be impossible.

Then she remembered the lumpy mattresses in the guestrooms. She once accused Max of getting them from a trash bin, and he never did argue the point with her.

But tonight Max gave her a pillow and tucked her under a warm blanket with orders to yell if she needed anything. The level of his concern almost shocked her, but she and Kane were Limani's treasured warrior-mage pair. Max had been itching to declare them official mercenaries since high school, but Victory forbade it, claiming they needed more experience first. But maybe he didn't have any ulterior motives—in his own way, he did care for them.

Toria reached out with her mind to touch Kane's presence. But she couldn't do more than verify that his spark of life still burned before the wave of black washed across her field of view and spikes of pain jolted through her brain.

She squeezed her eyes shut against the pain and pressed her face into the pillow, riding out the throbbing in her head. When it receded, she made the conscious effort to relax her tensed muscles and lay breathing hard. "Damn it all to hell," she said into her pillow.

"That's no way for a lady to speak."

Toria popped her eyes open to see an elderly gentleman standing in the open doorway of Max's office, hands in front of him resting on the head of a cane. He dressed like he came straight from the stage, in old-fashioned black breeches and a dark emerald tunic over a shirt of a lighter green. He radiated age and power, but the face was unlined. She didn't know why she had thought he was old, unless it was just the cane that threw her off.

The man gestured toward the couch on the opposite side of Toria. "May I come in?"

"Yeah, please." The pale hand with long tapered fingers sparked recognition and she knew this man was an elf, though the first she'd seen with such short hair. He kept it cropped close to his head, covering the ears that would have otherwise given him right away. "Sorry, I'm not usually this rude."

Toria braced an arm beneath her and made to rise, but the man said, "Please, remain comfortable. I understand that you've been through quite an ordeal." Before taking a seat, he held his hand out to her. "I am Zerandan. My granddaughter Daliana asked me to meet with you."

If Daliana was his granddaughter, Zerandan was one of the oldest elves Toria had ever met. That made her previous rudeness even more inexcusable. She dredged her elven manners out of the back of her brain, where she stored them next to her old piano lessons and how to write in cursive. While she shook his hand, she said, "It is my pleasure to meet you, Zerandan, grandfather of Daliana, friend of my mother. I am Torialanthas Connor, daughter of Victory, friend of your granddaughter." She was lucky the connection was so simple. Anything more would have been tough to wade through right now.

A glint of humor flashed in his green eyes. "Nicely done, child," he said, settling into his seat across from her. "You go by Toria, I believe?"

"Yes, sir," she said.

"Ah yes, the foundling child of the Wasteland," Zerandan said. "Your adoption was quite the scandal, you know. That was fifteen years ago?"

"Yes, sir," Toria said again. "Something like that." She hoped he hadn't come to reminisce about a past she had just sketchy memories of. She sensed magic around him, almost leaking out of his pores. But when she opened her senses to investigate further, the spikes were there again, driving through her head.

When she managed to open her eyes after this latest wave of pain passed, she found Zerandan's eyes mere inches from her own. He knelt on the ground by her couch, cane discarded, two of his fingers resting feather-light on her upraised cheek. "Don't do that again." The humor left Zerandan's voice, replaced by concern. "At least not until I tell you to."

This time she couldn't even manage a "Yes, sir." Toria nodded once. She rubbed away the tracks of tears leading from her eyes to the pillow.

"How often does this happen?"

He was all business now, the paternal figure replaced with a mage who must equal Asaron in experience of years. Maybe more. "Every time I try to use magic. No, every time I even try to actively sense magic."

"And which were you doing just now?"

His fingers remained on her cheek, and she felt his power pressing against her own. She shied away from it but didn't try to block him out. "You felt like magic. It's habit to check. One of those things you do."

"One of those things." Zerandan closed his eyes, but humor was still evident in his voice. "Yes, I see. So. Tell me exactly what you were doing when this feeling first occurred."

Toria sketched out the events of the brief battle with the Roman soldiers, concluding with feeling the backlash of the power she'd poured into Kane and passing out on the riverbank. "But I don't think this is a backlash headache. I thought it was, but now I'm not so sure. I've had them before, and this is different, somehow."

"You tried to harness the power of a river, child." His eyes opened again, the amusement back in place. "You thought this would be a normal backlash headache?"

"But those are usually constant pain for a few hours," Toria said. "Like when I woke up, I had a bad headache, but then it passed. Right now I'm fine unless I actually try to do something."

"Like contact your partner?"

"Exactly." Wait a second. "How did you know I've been trying to do that?"

"I could see it." Without bothering to explain his particular insight any further, Zerandan continued, "I have had some experience with warrior-mage pairs over the years. They don't do well apart."

"We manage okay," Toria said.

"Since you've bonded, what's the longest the two of you have been separated? By both distance and time."

Zerandan's eyes bored into her, and Toria avoided his stare by looking up at Max's office ceiling. It was an old building—there was some water damage in one of the corners. "Three days? Well, a weekend, I guess, when I went camping with Dad, and Kane couldn't miss play rehearsal. We did almost break the partnership in high school, but we were still in school together all day, so the distance bit doesn't really count."

"Do you know what happens when warrior-mages are separated for too long?" Zerandan removed his fingers and retrieved his cane. His eyes never left her while he pushed himself to his feet.

That didn't sound good. "It's never been a problem for us. And there haven't been any warrior-mages in Limani in so long. The only other person I know who's met a pair is Mama, and she never mentioned anything bad to me," Toria said. "So I don't know, sir." She braced herself for bad news.

"Neither do I, as a matter of fact," Zerandan said, dropping down onto the couch behind him. "Nothing bad, I hope."

Toria released the breath she'd been holding. Age must make you crazy. This reminded her of the pranks Asaron played. "Well, do you know what's wrong with me?"

"Not yet," he said. "I've scanned you lightly, but I wanted to warn you before I went any deeper. This might not be a purely internal problem."

Magical theory was Kane's department, but Toria could still put the pieces together. "You think I might have been cursed?"

"You said you didn't know why the Romans left you behind?"

"Mama thinks it was a warning," Toria said. "Rome is a really patriarchal society. It makes sense they would leave behind the useless girl and take the two men who are more valuable hostages, who they might get ransom for."

"Were any of the group who attacked you mages?" Zerandan said.

"I don't know," Toria said. She thought back, feeling the breeze of the arrow brushing past her once more. "They shot at me and were fighting Kane and Asaron with swords and hand-to-hand. Wouldn't any mages have used magic against us? Especially since they were the attackers and would have had time to plan spells or effects against us."

"This is a moot point," Zerandan said. "There's no way to know for sure. The real question becomes, will the proximity of someone else's magic give you the same pain?"

"Well, unless I've suddenly developed an allergy to magic, I guess that would be a pretty good test of whether I've been cursed or whether this really is some insanely strong form of backlash headache."

"Will you allow me to do a deeper scan of your magic?" Zerandan balanced the cane against the couch, resting his elbows on his knees. "It can be a personal experience for the person at the receiving end. You'll have to completely lower your shields for me."

She couldn't even remember the last time she'd done that. Could she even bring herself to do it for a strange mage, even if he was an elf and Daliana's grandfather?

But she needed to find out what was wrong with her. It might not be an easy fix, but the sooner she found out what was going on, the better. "Let's do it."

"I still vote to be rid of the Humanists." Bethany raised her chin in defiance to those around her. "Get free of one problem so we can focus on what might, I don't know, wipe us all out."

Victory saw that Genevieve looked ready to launch herself out of her seat, inching to the edge of the couch but restrained by Tristan's gentle touch on her arm. Both of them seemed to be taking turns being the silent voice of reason. Better than either of them starting an actual fight. "I cannot believe you would advocate such a thing, lady."

Bethany opened her mouth to retort, but Lorus beat her to it, waving her silent with a slice of his hand. "Bethany, I did not invite you here so you could tell us to kill people."

This needed to stop before everyone got too wired. It looked like Victory wasn't alone in her lack of sleep. "The problem," she said, "is that Bethany's idea is sound. It's her method that's flawed."

"What are you talking about?" Tristan said. "The woman's crazy." He'd managed to pull Genevieve back onto the couch, and now both of them sat with hands gripped tight. Victory would have thought it charming except for the white knuckles indicating the death grip each had on the other.

"Question." Max's turn to head off an outburst from Bethany. "How many of us here have actual military experience?"

Victory raised her hand, along with Max. To her surprise, Lorus did, too.

Lorus shrugged when everyone looked at him askance. "Well, it depends on what you consider military experience. It was a long time ago, before I immigrated to Limani. A short time in the British Air Corp out of Eire. I never saw combat."

"But you were still trained, and you must know the basic goal behind every fight," Max said. "Victory, you're in a swordfight. What do you watch? Your opponent's blade?"

"Their eyes." She'd never been much for formal fencing since the masks interfered with the specific part of Asaron's training so ingrained in her. "A sword can feint in any direction. The eyes never lie."

"Good." Max entered full teaching mode. "So what do we need to do to the Humanists?"

Tristan gave a grin full of pure feral hunger. "Cut out their eyes?"

"Something like that," Max said. "We need subtlety here. Can't let them know we're on to them, despite the fact that they haven't exactly hidden their intent."

"We can't let them hold this meeting," said Lena. "We can't afford to let them become any more organized than they already are."

"Find an excuse to close down the Twilight Mists," Genevieve said.

"And every other major gathering place in Limani? The theater, the high school auditorium?" Lorus shook his head. "I don't think so. Perhaps cutting off the head instead of removing the eyes might be a better allegory."

"We need to find Emily Fabbri," Victory said. "Find her, get her under control."

"Our control," Tristan said. "Preferably somewhere the other Humanists won't go looking for her."

"I'll deal with that once we track her down," Daliana said. "They can search the city all they want, but they're not going to think of looking on another plane of existence, in the elfhames. And I don't trust her safety anywhere else." Her eyes did not leave Bethany.

"Excellent plan," Max said. "She's been implicated in the attacks last night, and the police are already looking for her. I can set the mercenaries on the chase in the morning."

"Consider my panthers at your disposal," Genevieve said.

"The wolves are already on the hunt," Tristan said. "After this is over, I'll put out the word that they're not allowed to kill her if they find her." He didn't look happy about the idea, but Victory knew he would bow to the wishes of the council majority. At least this part of the council.

"We should still do something about a few of the meeting places," Victory said. This was one area she had plenty of ideas about. "I can manufacture a reason to shut down the Twilight Mists. It's easy enough to find an old file in my library I never turned over to the new owners with information about hazardous insulation."

"And everywhere else?" Bethany said. Her voice dared Victory to come up with such a large plan.

Lorus spoke first. "The owner of the movie theatre is a werebear. He certainly won't let them hold a meeting there."

"And I can talk to the principal of the high school," Lena said. "Convince him not to let them move there. If he argues, I can get Sethri to order him not to since the school is public property and under the command of this council. They're not going to get the auditorium at the university while I have anything to say about it. Those are the first places they'll try to arrange, so that will delay them at least a day or two."

Max made a few notes on his pad. "Speaking of Sethri, you really think he's solidly on our side? The only reason I didn't invite him tonight was because I wasn't sure how you all would feel about it. His is an elected position."

"I've known the man for decades," Lena said. "He firmly believes in the tenets Limani was founded on, of freedom and justice."

Victory had also known Alexander Sethri since he was first elected to the council almost forty years ago. He had been there the longest after her. "I'll second that."

"I'll be sure to invite him next time, then," Max said. "That takes care of the preliminary problem the blasted Humanists have presented us with, that stupid meeting. Now what are we going to do about the Romans?"

Toria dragged one of the couch cushions onto the ground, wrapping the blanket around her shoulders to sit against the couch. Zerandan sat cross-legged on the carpet a few feet in front of her with his cane resting on his lap. Something told her it wasn't just a simple cane—maybe it was the emerald orb that appeared, replacing the original wooden handle. A neat trick, one she filed away under the mental folder labeled "Things to experiment with later."

"Are you comfortable, child?" Zerandan rubbed his hands together and rolled up his shirt cuffs.

"I was more concerned for you, sir," Toria said, pulling the warm blanket tighter around her shoulders.

"I'm not so old that I can't sit on a floor," he said. "I've barely topped two thousand!"

She wasn't going to give him the reward of shock. "That would surprise me more except that you're about the same age as my grandfather. Sorry."

"Ah, the cynicism of youth," Zerandan said. "Let's get started, shall we? I'll shield around us both, and you can drop yours underneath. If it's magic itself you've acquired an allergy to, at least you'll only sense mine." He surveyed Max's study. "You know our host better than I. Is there anything in particular nearby that I should be worried about?"

Toria pointed to the bookcases on either side of the larger window overlooking the training room. "There are some magic books there, and a few charms and talismans in the box on the second shelf. Everything really powerful is in a safe that's already warded and shielded under the desk, but I don't think those will be a problem."

"I suppose I'll have to take your word on that," Zerandan said.

"You have to," Toria said. "I helped to shield and ward it."

"A good reason indeed." Zerandan rolled the cane over his knees, wrapping his fingers around the emerald orb. "Ready, child? Give me to the count of ten heartbeats after I drop my hand, then release your shields."

This was it. "Okay."

Zerandan closed his eyes and lifted his right hand, reminding Toria of her father pretending to direct orchestras from the stereo. Like a conductor, his hand dropped, and Toria counted.

At four heartbeats, she almost jolted out of her concentration by the white shimmer that began to distort the room around them. By seven, it encased them in a wide dome Toria knew continued into a full sphere below the floor of Max's office.

Eight brought Toria back on task, and she laid a mental finger on the invisible button in her head she hadn't used in years, the one that brought all of her protections down in one fell swoop. Kane was the only other person with access to that switch, and he helped her craft many of the protections around it.

At nine, she braced herself.

On ten, she pressed the cartoon red button labeled "Off" in her head.

The light from the shimmering white shield exploded around her, and Toria closed her eyes against the double brilliance of the physical and magical sight of Zerandan's power. Her shields protected her from every spark of magic in the world being visible to her sensitive mind, and she no longer had that shelter to hide behind.

She risked a peek, keeping her eyelids cracked to prevent the light of the shield from blinding her. To her shock, she could even see echoes of other colors from the bookshelves behind Zerandan's shields, the magical items it contained shining through.

It all paled in comparison to the brilliant aura surrounding Zerandan. She thought that Kane's aura of earthen magic was powerful. It was nothing compared to the ancient viridian power flowing across and under Zerandan's skin.

Her own prismatic purple shields were gone, but motes of electric energy still danced around her. Her eyes adjusted to the brilliance, and she let the sparks entrance her, keeping her distracted from the eerie "rummaging" feeling going on in her head. Zerandan's touch was light, but she could still feel his power tracing through her, searching out the problem.

After no more than a minute, the touch receded and Zerandan gestured with his hand again. Taking that for the signal to bring her shields back up, she waited a few more seconds to be sure he was gone before rebuilding. First came the walls around her mind itself, and the blinding lights around her began to pale. Then she reconstructed her familiar crystalline shields.

Her mind once again her own, protected in mind and body from the onslaught of the world of magic around her, Toria slouched against the couch. She now realized how tense she had become. "Anything?"

"I'm sorry, child." Zerandan's calm had never faltered, but his eyes filled with regret. "You felt no pain just now? I kept my probe purely mental, but I was worried my shield or other items in the room might have an adverse effect on you."

"Nope. I'm still tired, but nothing actually hurt." She tried to look on the bright side. "So at least I'm not allergic to other magic. And I still have control over my shields."

"Shielding is not technically active magic, because over the years it has become an innate part of you," Zerandan said. "Like you can still feel the link between yourself and your partner."

"Then we know the limits to all this," Toria said. "Active attempts at magic equal horrible headaches. Got it."

"And since you are still able to manipulate your passive magic," Zerandan said, "then I think we can safely say you've been cursed."

"You know, the Romans haven't contacted us," Lena said. "Did we ever really establish that this was indeed an invading force?"

"I think the attack and kidnapping made it pretty clear," Victory said. They were going around in circles again. If possible, she thought this half of the council might be more ineffectual than the whole at making a decision on such a grand scale. Now that they had a temporary plan of action against the Humanist problem, everyone seemed reluctant to make any further commitments. She drained the last vestiges of her coffee, then set the empty mug on the floor by her feet.

"But has anyone tried to actually talk to them?" Bethany said. She caught everyone's attention with her wild suggestion. "What if they just wanted to expand their border to the river, and they took the two because they invaded their territory. They left Toria because she never actually crossed the river."

"What, and ransacked all of her possessions and stole her horse for the hell of it?" Genevieve said.

Victory smothered her impulse to second Genevieve's retort. But Bethany did have an idea there. Pulling herself a few mental feet away from the emotional situation, she acknowledged it was a sound theory when looked at with a more rational and experienced mindset.

"Soldiers are soldiers," Lorus said, speaking aloud her unvoiced thoughts.

His voice stony, Max said, "We're lucky they didn't do worse to Toria."

Victory tried not to think about what a horrible experience her daughter escaped with the narrowest of margins. Soldiers were soldiers, but her daughter told her that while they took the gear from her belt, no evidence pointed to anything worse occurring while she was unconscious. Victory breathed another huge mental sigh of relief for that.

"Perhaps we should speak with the Romans?" Daliana said. "Approach them as a diplomatic group instead of potential spies?"

"At this point, it's probably our only option," Victory said. "Anyone else we send across the river risks the same fate as Kane and Asaron."

"Any volunteers?" Lorus said.

Victory shot her hand up, with Max's following immediately after hers. While what the Romans were doing across the river concerned her, the opportunity to find the location of the rest of her family interested her more. It was a good bet Max had the same idea.

"No surprises there," Lorus said. "And you're our best fighters if everything goes bad and you have to get out in a hurry. This should probably stay a small group."

"We have to take Sethri with us," Max said. "It's only right, since he's the real head of the council. We are representing the city. If it was just Victory and me, they would have to assume we're a rescue mission in disguise."

Which they might still end up being. Victory couldn't dismiss the option until they knew more about the whole situation. She checked her watch. Already past midnight, and she still needed real sleep at some point. "We'll go tomorrow night, then. Leave right at sundown."

"Armed? Unarmed?" Max deferred to Victory's experience.

"And risk being taken along with the others? Armed, of course," she said. "But not too blatantly. We are trying to be polite."

"They're the ones invading our territory," Bethany said. "We have every right to go drive them off."

"We've always been outnumbered by our neighbors," Tristan said. "Despite the treaty nonsense about a neutral zone, we're here on their sufferance."

"We'll have to see what they want and hope for the best," Max said. "I guess that's it for tonight."

Victory remained curled in her corner of the couch, wrapping her arms around the pillow in her lap, while the others filed out of the room. She would rest here a few minutes while Max showed everyone out, then she could work out the details of tomorrow night's excursion with him.

She jolted out of a light doze when a weight settled next to her on the couch. She looked forward to home and bed. It was highly unlikely she would make it back to the hospital tonight to see Mikelos. "Everyone gone?"

"Yep," Max said. "You really think this is going to work?"

"Which part?" Victory stretched her arms above her head, feeling the pull of muscles not exercised in almost two days. "Controlling the Humanists or having a rational discussion with the Romans?"

"Right now I'm not laying bets on either," Max said.

"Why don't we call the British to our aid?" Victory said. "Tristan was right, Limani is the neutral zone. They're not going to be happy about the Romans taking us over."

"You talk like our doom is inevitable," Max said. "No, I hadn't thought about calling the Brits."

Victory could already see the wheels spinning behind his eyes. "On the one hand, offering aid to us might be seen as breaking the treaty. On the other, they might do it so we can stay neutral, their own personal buffer zone."

"Damned if we do, damned if we don't," Max said. "They help us, the Romans attack for the violation of the treaty. They stay out, the Romans attack anyway, and we get taken over or wiped out."

"The only silver lining we have right now is that this can't turn into another Wasteland," Victory said. "Not with the world-spell still in place."

"But we won't be around to appreciate it if they do invade," Max said. "We're the government. Even if they take over the city with minimum bloodshed, we can't be allowed to live."

This was getting ridiculous. The new power-hungry Roman Caesar didn't have enough to deal with on his continent, so he had to be greedy with hers. "What a mess. Fabbri couldn't have picked a better time to stir up trouble."

"On the positive side, she can be executed with the rest of us when we lose," Max said.

"Fatalist. So. Pick me up tomorrow right at sundown with Sethri?"

"And we'll head south toward the river," Max said. "We can even use a truck instead of taking horses from the stable. Ride in style."

"Sounds like a plan," Victory said. "Want to go grab Toria for me? I need to take her home so both of us can get some real sleep."

Max did not hide his appraisal of her, and she wondered how deep the bags under her eyes were. Coffee couldn't cure all.

"Yes, that you should," he said. "I'll be right back."

Victory laid her head back against the side of the couch for a few seconds, then hauled herself to her own feet. They all needed rest, and the real work had only just begun.

There wasn't much Zerandan and Toria could do after figuring out that only Toria attempting to use magic caused her pain. There was no additional affect when Zerandan cast a glamour over her or briefly levitated her over the couch. But he stayed with her, investigating the books on Max's shelves, while Toria dozed on the couch. He did promise to research and make a few calls when he got home to try to figure out how to reverse whatever the Romans had done to her.

But that didn't prevent her feelings of helplessness. Her sword was gone— again—and now she couldn't even use her magic. Some warrior-mage she was. This made the rescue harder, but at least Victory had plenty of spare weapons back at the house. None could replace her rapier, but she could still be lethal against the Roman bastards who took her partner.

With her thoughts running in circles, she drifted on the verge of sleep. She came awake right away when Max entered his office. "The meeting over already?" She struggled to push herself up. She had been comfortable and warm after Zerandan tucked her blanket back around her.

"More or less," Max said. "Ready to head home?"

"Oh, yes." A real bed that she could pass out in without worrying about her mother dragging her anywhere else. She wouldn't even try to get Victory to take her back to her place. Her mother would feel better with her close, and she didn't think she could face the apartment with Kane's absence haunting her.

"Then I shall be off," Zerandan said, snapping closed the book he held. The old man act returned, and he placed more weight on his cane than Toria suspected he needed to when he rose. "I will contact you when I learn anything, my dear."

"Thanks, Zerandan," she said. She nodded her head in respect to the elder elf, who gave her a slight bow before wishing Max goodnight and exiting the office.

"Let's get you downstairs," Max said. "Victory's waiting, and she needs to get you back to the manor before she passes out herself."

"One second," Toria said. She remained in her seat, cross-legged on the couch with the blanket wrapped around her shoulders. She wasn't about to move yet. She wasn't even certain she could. She would figure that out when she came to it. "I need a favor."

Max grabbed the book Zerandan left on the other couch and searched for its correct place on his bookshelves. "And that would be?"

"In the morning, you have to come with me to rescue Kane and Asaron." She held her breath. He had to say yes. If nothing else, leaving Kane in the hands of the Romans for any longer than necessary risked the survival of his treasured warrior-mage pair. She couldn't offer a better bribe.

Max found the book's correct home and slid it into place. After a few seconds of silence, he said, "Absolutely not."

"You have to!" Why was he being an idiot? "Do you want Kane to die?"

"He's still alive right now, is he not?"

Toria checked again, grateful this small act didn't fall under the category of giving her searing pain in her skull and making bright painful lights explode behind her eyes. "Yeah, for now."

"If they didn't kill him right away, he'll probably stay alive for the foreseeable future." But then he sat next to her on the couch and wrapped a comforting arm about her shoulders.

Not wanting to, and still cranky, she couldn't resist the hug. It had been a hard day, and she did need the comfort. That still didn't mean he wasn't being a bastard.

His voice softened. "I want to get Kane back, too," he said. "I've had friends captured before. I know what you're going through."

She knew she was being petulant, but she couldn't hold the words in. No one had been part of his soul the way Kane was for her. "No, you don't."

His shoulders moved in a silent sigh. "Toria, you're in no shape to go running off. You could barely walk into the building, and I know you wouldn't have been able to make it up the stairs."

"I'll give you that much," she said. She could compromise. "I'll go home and sleep for a few hours. We can leave after dawn—I'll be okay by then. Then Mama can't even stop me." A huge yawn welled up inside of her. She knew it hurt her case to let it out, but she couldn't stop herself in time.

"I can't go with you anyway," Max said. "I'm leaving at sundown with Victory and Sethri for a diplomatic meeting with the Romans. An attempt at a diplomatic meeting, at least. We're already planning to demand their release. You can't go running off on your own after them."

It was clear, then. She was on her own. She let her shoulders slump. "Okay," she said, letting a twinge of relief swim into her voice. Let Max believe she would be a good little girl. "Promise you'll ask after him?"

"Of course, Toria," Max said. "We'll do everything we can to get him back." He squeezed her shoulders one more time. "Now let's get you home. Can you stand?" He held his hands down to her.

"Let's find out," Toria said. She gripped both of Max's hands, and he hauled her up. The blanket slid off her shoulders into a heap on the couch. He let go, and the world tilted around her while a strange darkness encroached on her peripheral vision.

"Whoa, girl!" Max grabbed her shoulders to prevent her from falling any farther to the side. "Okay, up you go." He swept her up into his arms like before. "Home for you, now."

"Sounds good." She couldn't prevent another yawn, relaxing into his arms while he carried her out of the office and down the stairs.

Toria would sleep, for at least a couple of hours. She acknowledged how futile a rescue attempt in her current state would be.

But when dawn arrived, she would be up and preparing to go. Was the saber between the ballroom windows sharpened? What horse could she finagle from the Hall's stables?

She would get Kane back.

Toria's alarm clock beeped away, never knowing how close it came to flight across the bedroom. Her mental deal with herself the night before admitted waking up at dawn would be too painful, but seven seemed a reasonable compromise.

Seven o'clock was no less agonizing when she squinted in the bright sunlight streaming through the windows into her corner bedroom at the manor. More than anything, she wanted to burrow her head underneath the comforter and sleep until Kane dragged her out of bed for breakfast and a workout.

But Kane wasn't getting her up this morning. With that cold reminder, Toria shoved aside the blankets. At the change in elevation when she sat up, her head came alive in fiery pain. The tap dancers were back for a second run of their performance. Groaning, Toria collapsed back onto her pillows. She remained still until the pain receded to a manageable level, then rose with more care. She stretched out legs protesting her harsh treatment of them the day before, an interesting counterpoint to the headache.

She had more important things to do than bemoan the early hour, so Toria rolled out of bed—careful not to revive the headache with sudden movements. The six solid hours of sleep renewed much of her energy, though she knew she didn't have any reserves to speak of. Adrenaline would carry her today.

She dressed in a clean shirt and pair of jeans, then opened a window to beat the dust from her long coat. After running a brush through her hair and tying it back, she headed downstairs for a much-needed high-energy breakfast.

While water for her oatmeal warmed in a pan on the stove, Toria walked down the hall to the ballroom to rearm herself for the upcoming trip. She surveyed the weaponry displayed around the room. But she had been right in her first decision the night before, and she crossed the room to grasp the hilt of the old saber hanging between two of the windows by a rapier and scimitar. She looked in longing at the rapier, but knew attempting to wield it with any success would be hopeless. The charm that lightened her own rapier was the sole reason she used it with any degree of skill. Her wrists couldn't take it, otherwise.

She considered the Roman gladius displayed on the other side of the room. It would be appropriate to take out Kane's kidnappers with a weapon of their own design. But she took into account its size in relation to the blades she was used to. She didn't have time to adjust to the gladius' shorter reach.

The saber it was. She gave a few practice swings in the middle of the ballroom on her way out. She hunted down its proper scabbard from a chest to the side of the room, along with collecting extra knives and a small pistol from the locked cupboard in the corner. She eschewed firearms as a general rule, but now all the stops were out. She would get Kane back no matter what it took.

Toria stared at the kitchen phone while she sat at the counter to inhale her oatmeal. Was bringing backup even possible? Max had already turned her down, and any of her fellow mercenaries might let their Guildmaster know their plans. Certainly none of her school friends had the requisite martial training for such an excursion. Looked like she was on her own.

By seven-thirty, Toria headed out of the manor. She didn't make a huge effort to be quiet. Mama must have been more tired than she let on while they drove home from the Hall. Let her have her sleep.

She tossed her pack into the back seat before climbing in the town-car, glad Dad insisted each vehicle have at least two spare sets of keys. With one last look at the silent manor house, she started the engine and headed back into Limani city-proper.

Toria drove toward the Hall, but passed the building and instead pulled into the rear parking lot of the high school campus. She took a far corner spot, leaving the town-car in the shade of a large oak's branches. Since classes were out for the summer, with any luck no one would notice her town-car for a day or two. She planned to be long gone in a few minutes anyway.

Slinging the backpack over her shoulder, Toria locked up and shoved the keys into the outside pocket of her bag. Since the keys didn't seem any safer on her person, she felt no reason to suffer through them digging into the side of her leg through her jeans pocket while she rode.

Between the high school campus and the grounds owned by the Mercenary Guild stood a small copse of trees. She left the backpack in the crook of two tree branches, then continued through the woods toward the stable behind the Hall. She climbed the split rail fence and cut across one empty paddock, crossing mental fingers Max wasn't up this early, and that if he was, he didn't look out his office window right this second.

"Toria!" David, the Guild's resident Master of Horses, rose from behind his desk when she entered the small office attached to the main stable. "You've come to check on Greenstar?"

Toria stopped in front of the desk, jolted out of her meticulous plans by David's question. "Greenstar?" She hoped she didn't have a look of stupidity on her face to match the way she felt.

"Yeah, all three horses made it back home on their own yesterday!" David pointed a thumb over his shoulder down the hall leading from his musty office into the spotless stable. "Isn't that wonderful?"

That's right, Greenstar was the name of the horse she had borrowed from the Guild. She might not feel it in her body, but her exhaustion slowed mental reactions. "Great!" she said. "In fact, that's why I'm here. To find out whether they came home okay." Good save, girl.

But David's concern was only for his beloved horses, and he continued to chatter while she followed him past the rows of stalls. "It's quite amazing, actually," he said. "All three of them still had their tack. Whatever the Romans wanted with your friends, they obviously didn't have interest in much else." He gave her a sideways look. "Good for you, I guess."

David followed a more traditional school of soldier mentality. So she did not make a retort about her value compared with Kane and Asaron's. "So, do you mind if I take Greenstar out for her exercise this morning? To make up for her misadventure the other night?"

"That would be right sweet of you, girl." David beamed.

Toria expected to have to talk the Horsemaster into lending her a horse. Short of that, she was prepared to "borrow" one. This worked out better than she hoped. "It's no problem," Toria said. "She's a good horse, a joy to ride." Yep, keep talking up the horse.

David ate it up. "I have a fresh pot of coffee made in the office," he said. "Why don't you go relax and help yourself to a cup while I saddle her for you."

"Thanks, I'd love some coffee." Maybe it would even help her headache. She allowed him to shoo her back in the direction of the office.

Brilliant. That couldn't have worked out better if she had planned it.

The sun was high in the sky three hours later and proved to be even hotter than the day before. Toria twisted in the saddle to dig her bandana out of the backpack strapped behind her. After wiping the sweat from her face and neck, she tied it over her head. It would keep her humidity-induced frizzy hair out of her face and the sweat dripping down her forehead from going straight into her eyes. But she couldn't complain. Compared with yesterday, today bordered on luxurious.

She regretting forgetting her sunglasses on her dresser, though. And her sore feet did not appreciate being returned to her boots.

She stopped at a crossroads in the wooded trail to check the map again. Taking the same road Asaron led them down the first time seemed like a bad idea, but she wasn't as familiar with this backwoods route, having been down it just once on a camping trip with Kane back in high school. According to the map, the river crossing was a handful of miles away. She also chose this particular route because an old bridge still spanned the river, built from sturdy concrete. Toria hoped Greenstar had fewer issues about going over water than through it.

David must have realized ages ago that Toria never meant to take Greenstar out for a short jaunt. She'd be in for hell when she got home. But Max hadn't come with her, so he could blame himself. By the time David figured out she was gone for good, Toria had ridden too far down the trail to worry about pursuit. And with any luck, she would have Kane and Asaron with her when she got back, and they'd be too happy to berate her for horse theft.

Toria stuffed the map in the outer pocket of her backpack, exchanging it for a granola bar. She needed to keep her energy up, knowing this adrenaline came from nerves and excitement alone and she could crash any time. So despite her lack of hunger, she forced herself to eat every bite of the snack, ignoring the cardboard taste.

On the plus side, Greenstar didn't seem to connect her misadventure two nights ago with her current rider. So at least Toria didn't have any problems with the horse and had even given the mare her head so she could relax in the saddle while Greenstar plodded along through the trees. "Good girl." She patted the mare on the neck and trusted this particular brand of luck would hold out once they sighted the river.

While the sun rose higher in the sky, warming the back of her neck even further in sporadic beams of light through the overhanging tree branches, Toria resisted the urge to hook a knee around the saddle horn and nap. The one cup of coffee at the stable wasn't enough. She would have brewed a cup before leaving the house, but the smell was certain to wake her mother when nothing else would. And since this time she headed into enemy territory, she couldn't sing to amuse herself. She resorted to identifying the different species of plants on the side of the road, dredging up old memories from Intro to Botany two semesters ago. She remembered a lot more than she'd thought from the required biology class, a nice surprise. It even made up for the resentment she'd felt at being forced to take the course when she'd much rather have kept going with her chemistry studies. But just a little.

She avoided thinking about the immediate problem about her magic, which hung over her head like a boulder. Better to plan how to steal her family back from the Romans. She must rely on her own physical skills and prowess rather than the magical tricks up her sleeves. Figuring out ideas that didn't rely on magic were good thought problems in and of themselves. It made her glad Mama and Max often barred her and Kane from using their magical ability while passing various tests in their training—Victory never hesitated to tell them stories about foolish mages who fell into the trap of believing that magic could solve all the world's problems.

She jolted back to the present when a gunshot echoed through the trees and her violet shields flared to life around her. Greenstar jumped in fright, and Toria had her hands full keeping the mare from bolting.

Her mind raced while she calmed the horse. An item coming toward her at high speed had activated the physical shields that lay dormant around her until needed. With a thought, she pulled them up again, settling the comforting amethyst prisms around herself. Greenstar protested at the shell of light forming around her, but otherwise did not act up. Maybe because it wasn't made of water.

With that glib thought echoing in her head, she pulled the saber from the scabbard at her waist, sparing one more wish for her familiar rapier. Her brief inspection found no one, and a second attack did not follow on the heels of the first. So, a warning shot, and perhaps they weren't out to kill her. She was five miles from the city at this point, enough distance that nearby Roman activity did not surprise her.

"Come out, come out, wherever you are!" Toria wheeled Greenstar around a slow circle in the middle of the path. She refused to be frightened off by one hidden soldier. It might not even be an enemy soldier, just a local hunter who'd thought she was game. Larger than usual game, but she could give them the benefit of the doubt.

No one emerged from the underbrush at her summons. She knew she made a menacing sight with sword brandished and shields glinting around her. They were smart, whoever they were.

Her shields flared again, deflecting the bullet that hit one of the fractal edges. The echoes of a gunshot reverberated in the woods around her, unmistakable in the silence of the forest. This time Greenstar wouldn't stand for the excitement. Toria managed to keep herself in the saddle with sword still in hand when the mare took off at full charge. It might have been intimidating if Toria hadn't been so concerned about not falling off and impaling herself on the way down.

She grabbed the reins in her free hand, resisting the urge to jerk them back. "Stupid horse!" Greenstar took Toria farther down the path, straight in the direction of who knew how many more enemies. "Slow the hell down!"

But the horse ignored her pleas, and the mad dash had one side bonus: her complete surprise of the mysterious attacker. No more gunshots barked behind them, and Greenstar soon followed a bend in the path that took them out of sight, and thus safe from more gunshots for the immediate future.

Once out from the direct line of fire, Toria calmed the mare down enough to come to a restless stop. Toria let her have her nervous whickers. It was preferable to her bolting again.

Silence reigned from the trees around them, aside from the sound of some birds in the far distance. Like Greenstar, the gunshot frightened away the rest of the local wildlife. Smart animals. Stupid horse. Toria sheathed her sword in favor of the pistol holstered at the small of her back, sparing a brief wish for the shotgun still locked up at home.

Even more than the shotgun, Toria wished for her magic. It was quite a change, having to rely on her normal eyesight to scope out danger instead of switching on her magesight and scanning for human—or werecreature or elven— auras among the emerald glow of the trees. And bolts of lightning were much more effective than tiny bullets.

Instead, nothing. "Okay, Greenstar." Wait, was that movement? No, a robin fluttering to a different branch. "What do we want to do now?"

The mare swiveled an ear back toward the sound of her rider's mutterings but did not deign to comment. Now that they were out of direct danger, the horse seemed bored.

"Well, we can't go back the way we came or we'll get shot at again." With a gentle touch, lest she set off another mind-boggling headache, Toria tested the strength of her shields. The attacker was a lousy shot if he'd been trying to take her out. Both blows had glanced, and she just needed to tighten a few corners, whereas direct hits would have required major rebuilding.

Slouching back in the saddle, Toria continued talking. "Maybe they were warning shots?" She was too used to having Kane around if she'd resorted to conversing with her horse. "Either way, we might have just screwed ourselves since you decided to run even farther into the direction they probably didn't want us to go."

The snap of a branch made Toria whirl around in the saddle and bring up the gun. A Roman legionnaire in half battle armor emerged from the woods a handful of paces behind her. Toria did not appreciate the full-blown smirk on his face. "You got that right, kid." He couldn't have been the shooter from earlier, but he did have his own pistol at his waist to accompany the standard-issue gladius. It must have been an accomplice, urging her into this trap. But two soldiers with guns? These were no ordinary foot soldiers, to be trusted with such valuable equipment.

The dig at her age did nothing to help Toria's anger. "You're in Limani territory, sir," she said, in the most level voice she could manage. "State your name and business."

"Julius Octavian at your service, miss," the soldier said. "Scout for the Eighth Legion, investigating the state of this road."

"And why the hell would you need to know a thing like that?" Toria said. With the gun stilled aimed at Octavian, her other hand drifted toward the hilt of her saber. She wasn't messing around.

He was too relaxed. So much for the famed Roman chivalry, but Toria gave him credit for not being stupid enough to bow and take his eyes off her. "Scoping out possible supply routes," Octavian said. "Or escape routes."

"And why would you need either?" This veneer of civility was wearing thin. Toria searched for signs of rank on his uniform, but nothing stood out from his camouflage. Asaron's lessons on foreign rank had been a long time ago. But Octavian looked to be in his mid-forties, much too old for a simple recruit.

"One never knows what one will need," Octavian said.

No rank, too old, and way too comfortable in her gun sight. Plus the hints of long-healed scarring creeping up the side of his neck above his gear. So. Special ops, then, or something close to it. The first shiver of real fear trickled a clammy path down the sweat on Toria's back. "Well, you seem to have gotten lost in your search." Her own poise in the face of an experienced fighter amazed her. This guy was no Max. "Will you kindly allow me to escort you out of Limani territory?"

Octavian took a small step forward, and Toria fought to keep the gun from wavering in her grip. Now he wasn't relaxed, but instead held himself with a purpose unclear behind his calm. "What a noble offer from a woman of such status," he said. "Whatever have I done to warrant the regard of the daughter of the vampire Victory?"

Toria froze, a litany of curses flowing through her mind. Only one way he could know her identity. "You have Kane and Asaron."

Octavian gave a single nod that spoke volumes. "The vampire Asaron and the warrior-mage Kane Nalamas are with the Eighth Legion, yes. And it would be my honor to have Toria Connor join them." He took another step toward Greenstar.

Toria realized her gun hand had drifted down and snapped it onto Octavian again. "What the hell have you done with them?"

"They are our honored guests." Octavian's smile, while attempting to be disarming, made Toria's skin crawl. "And what a pleasure it would be to have a pair of warrior-mages gracing our camp on the eve of battle."

What? The startling confirmation of the worst threw her for a loop. "Eve of battle—?"

That single second of mental distraction was all Octavian needed. He slipped under her gun and wrapped strong fingers around her wrist, jerking it away from him with a snap. A sudden wrench of pain seared Toria's arm and she cried out, giving Octavian all the time he needed to grab her shoulder with his other arm and pull her from the saddle.

Her instinctual attempt to surge electricity through her shields backfired, instead burning a sharp path through the center of her skull. She lay dazed on the ground, not quite sure when she'd landed. When her vision cleared, the sight of Octavian mere inches away from her face prompted her to lash out in a more controlled manner. She brought up the elbow of her right arm, aiming for a fierce blow to his jaw.

But he snagged both of her wrists and pinned her to the ground. With practiced ease, he transferred her wrists to one large hand, digging them into the ground above her head. He straddled her chest, centering enough weight on her to make breathing difficult. His free hand circled her neck, and she froze when he began to squeeze, knowing it wouldn't take much to make her pass out from the combination of forces upon her body.

He shouldn't have managed to take her out so fast. Her reflexes were shot thanks to yesterday's insults. Time to reconsider her strategy.

To his credit, he lessened his grip when she stopped struggling. "Good girl," Octavian said. "Now, here's what you're going to do." His hand remained where it was, ready to tighten around her throat again.

Toria couldn't move without risking strangulation, but that didn't mean she would lay back and take whatever he gave her. Behind teeth gritted in fear, she said, "Bite me." Oh, for the power to call lightning from the sky straight on this guy.

Octavian loomed even closer, putting his mouth to her ear. "Don't tempt me, girl."

His breath tickled her cheek, and she twisted her face away from him. Octavian blew again, this time on her neck, and she could not prevent the terrified shivers racking her body. She couldn't move, and she almost couldn't breathe. This was not good.

Octavian laughed, pulling his head back once more. "Paying attention now? Good." His long blond hair was pulling loose from the small club at the base of his neck. He blew a few stray strands away out of the corner of his mouth, an incongruous gesture in the midst of such a threatening act. "Now, technically we're still in Limani territory," he said, his conversational tone belying the harsh glint in his dark eyes. "So I can't do what I ordinarily would in these circumstances."

"Juggle and hunt for unicorns?"

His hand twitched around her throat. She took the hint and shut up.

Her captor knew that if he wanted her in any position to talk, he couldn't cut off her air for a long period of time. But he could squeeze her wrists together, pushing them into the ground and digging his nails into the tender skin. Even blunt nails hurt with enough pressure. "Unicorns wouldn't come within a hundred feet of me," Octavian said.

She forced down the immediate retort that sprang to mind. Baiting him in her position wasn't the best of the past few days' bad ideas, but she wasn't one to lie back and take whatever he dished out. But she still couldn't inhale enough to fill her lungs. Never mind his grip on her neck, the guy was heavy! So she kept quiet this time. Maybe letting him explain what the hell he was doing on this side of the river was a better idea.

His hand left her neck, though the grip on her wrists was still firm, and he ran it down the side of her body in parody of a gentle caress. Toria never took her eyes from his, but she could feel his disturbing touch through her coat and shirt. Then the touch grew harsh, and he gripped her breast and gave it a sharp twist.

Toria couldn't prevent her yelp of pain, and she didn't like the hungry expression that passed over Octavian. But the pain was secondary to her anger. "So do whatever you're going to do to me and get the hell out of here," she said.

That might have taken things a bit too far. She steeled herself for the inevitable. When first discussing her potential future with the Mercenary Guild, Victory hadn't shied away from discussing the realities of female mercenary life with her daughter. Toria knew what Octavian was threatening. But if he did try anything, she would risk the most painful headache in the universe to incinerate him where he knelt.

He smirked. "Alas, we are still in Limani territory. That would be breaking more treaties than I intend to just yet." His harsh grip on her breast loosened, but his hand remained where it was. "But remember. I could take what I wanted from you, right here, right now." He drew closer again, and this time she did not turn away. "What makes you think I haven't taken what I want from your partner yet? Unlike you, he is not protected by Limani land. And he has only himself to blame for that."

The pronouncement was designed to scare her, but it only made her more irritated with him. Unless the Romans cursed Kane too, there was no way he would allow this man within ten feet of him against his will. This would be an

119

appropriate place for Toria to spit in Octavian's face, but the angle was all wrong and she didn't want to end up drooling on herself. Not quite the intended effect. "What happened to 'honored guests'?"

"Everything's relative," Octavian said. His hand stayed on her breast. "Since I cannot do what I wish to such an impertinent brat, regardless of how helpless you are right now, you'll have to serve some other purpose."

His hand squeezed again, and Toria hoped her expression of disgust was quite evident to him. Not that it would have much effect, since he seemed to get off on that sort of thing. "And what's that?"

"Messenger," he said. "I want you to tell the vampire Victory that the Roman Emperor has decreed an expansion to his colonial borders across the ocean. Since we have already expanded south to the Peninsula of Leon and west to the Wasteland, there is only one logical direction in which to go. And Limani stands in our way."

Mama was right. The new kid ruling the Romans was an idiot. She couldn't help it—the words came spilling out. "You do realize that on the other side of Limani are the British, right? And even if the Brits don't give a shit about us, they're really not going to appreciate you sitting right on their border?" Toria fixed him with an imitation of Max's best imperious gaze, the one he used when she was up to her worst mischief.

Her head snapped to the side with the force of the stinging blow across her cheek. Too far, Toria. Time to shut up again.

"Be careful," Octavian said. "You wouldn't want me to take out my anger on your friends. Leave Kane with a few of my more degenerate officers. Forget to bring Asaron in come dawn."

He brought his lips close to her own, and for a panicky breath, Toria thought he would kiss her. Molesting her through her clothes she could deal with, but a kiss might break the wall holding tears at bay.

But he stopped before contact. "Are you capable of delivering such a message? Or do I need to beat more sense into you?"

Clenching her teeth, Toria nodded. Maybe now he would let her go, leave her alone.

"Good," Octavian said, a look of satisfaction on his sharp features. "Perhaps I won't give Asaron the opportunity for that suntan after all."

He sat back, pulling Toria's wrists up with him. The relief that came with the sudden ability to take a real breath of air cost her the precious second she had to act. Octavian's free arm pulled back, and Toria had time for one thought before his fist connected with her head.

Not again.

Slimy stuff dripped on her face. Kane had better not be playing another one of his crazy jokes on her. She hadn't pranked him in ages, so she wasn't currently owed any retaliation. Or did she? And what was wrong with her bed?

Toria opened her eyes, prepared to tell him off. But instead of Kane's devious face, she met the chocolate-brown eye Greenstar aimed at her. A drooling Greenstar, which explained the wetness on her face.

Toria wiped off the gunk with the fabric on her shoulder. "Damn horse. At least you didn't run off and leave me this time." With caution, she probed for another headache. But aside from the familiar pain of a head blow—she hoped she didn't have a concussion on top of everything else—and one small tap dancer doing a solo behind her left eye, there was nothing like the other night's blinding agony. Octavian had a hell of a punch, but he hadn't inflicted any more magical injuries on her.

Make that General Octavian. She didn't know why the commander of an army was wandering Limani's woods. Maybe he didn't trust his own scouts. Maybe he was bored. This was not her current priority. Toria pushed herself up on her elbows. Greenstar wandered away to munch at the vegetation on the side of the path. She hoped the mare hadn't gorged herself while she'd been out.

She started to check her watch, remembered the soldiers stole it days ago, and instead peered up into the sky. The sun had coasted over noon and almost dropped into evening while she was out. Another whole day wasted. She was surprised Greenstar hadn't wandered home again.

Toria climbed to her feet and took stock of this new situation. The solo tap dance changed into a quartet. She looked for her sword and pistol, discarded when Octavian hauled her out of the saddle, but found nothing. Two lost swords in two days. That had to be a record.

To be fair, it was a nice saber. Mama said it was an antique.

But he'd left Greenstar alone, and Toria dug out a water bottle and another granola bar. Once again, she was in the same situation, despite the added benefits of still having a few of her supplies. Without weaponry, without her magic, her hopes of a grand rescue were dashed.

"Dammit," she said. Greenstar flicked an ear toward her, but Toria ignored the horse.

Well, if Octavian wanted her to play messenger, it looked like her only real option. She would tell Victory what happened—or at least an edited version of it—and her mother would have to help with a rescue, now that Octavian threatened both Kane and Asaron with real harm.

She pulled herself into the saddle. "Let's go home, Greenstar. Time to call the cavalry." Toria snorted. She was still talking to her horse. She hoped the bastard hadn't hit her harder than she thought. "Maybe this time they'll answer."

Toria didn't bother riding back to the stables and picking up her town-car. It was a shorter trip to the manor house. After leaving Greenstar with her reins looped around the porch railing, Toria ran inside screaming.

"Mama! Mom!"

She pounded up the stairs to the third floor and burst into the suite of rooms Victory shared with Mikelos, giving a perfunctory knock on the double doors leading into the bedroom. Toria blinked in the dimness of the room shrouded with heavy drapes.

Her mother sat up in the large four-poster bed, a study in confusion surrounded by a tangled mass of hair. "What? Are you okay?" Victory switched on the bedside lamp. "You've been out."

Her jeans were caked with mud after the tussle with Octavian, but that wasn't important right now. After catching her breath, the words rushed out. "The Romans are invading."

"Right now?"

"No, but they're definitely planning on it."

Victory rubbed the palms of her hands over her face. "Okay, love. Go get changed, let me get dressed, and I'll meet you in the kitchen. Then we'll talk."

"Okay," Toria said before heading back down to her old room on the second floor. She knew not to feel put off. Unless a life was in immediate danger, Victory took a few minutes to become a rational thinker upon waking.

After throwing on clean clothes, she washed the grime off her face in the bathroom shared with Kane's old room. She could still feel Octavian's hands on her, could still see the scratches his nails left in her wrists. She felt in desperate need of a shower, but there wasn't time. In the mirror, the side of her face had swelled and begun to blossom spectacular shades of purple.

Toria beat Victory to the kitchen, and started the coffee machine. Victory strolled in a few minutes later, dressed in a bathrobe and hair pulled back. She settled herself at the kitchen table while Toria exorcised her nervous energy preparing their coffee.

When she held a steaming mug in front of her, Victory took a long sip before looking up at Toria. "Okay. Sit down and tell me what I'm pretty sure I already know you did. Then convince me why I shouldn't be incredibly angry with you right now."

Toria placed her own mug on the table and sank into her chair. "I went to rescue Kane and Asaron since I couldn't get any help."

"Yes, that I figured out already," Victory said, her tone dry. "Skip to the part where you tangled with the Romans."

"One Roman," Toria said. The rest of the story took a short time to tell. Looking back, Toria realized she had been in Octavian's grip for less than five minutes. It felt much, much longer. "So we're pretty much screwed, huh?"

Victory wrapped her hands around her mug. She looked down into her cup and didn't speak.

Oh boy. Even if Limani wasn't screwed, Toria was. It took a lot to make Victory angry, but Toria had managed it more than once in her life. And she knew how to recognize the calm before the storm.

Releasing the coffee mug, Victory placed her hands flat on the table. She leveled her steady gaze on her daughter. Toria met her eyes, but the prickle at the back of her neck screaming *Prey!* under a vampire's stare forced her to look away.

"Here's what you're going to do. You're going to go take care of that poor horse. You're going to go get a shower and clean yourself up. By—" Victory noted the time on the microwave clock. "—seven, you'll go to the hospital and keep your father company for a few hours. At sundown, Max and Sethri are picking me up. You are not coming with us or following us. You're not even going to think about coming with us or following us. And I hope to gods you haven't screwed up what we're trying to do to save the city."

With that last admonishment ringing in Toria's ears, Victory stood from the table, deposited her empty mug in the sink, and left the kitchen. Toria could do nothing more than stare after her. She'd just been told to run to Daddy like a good little girl and leave the grown-up stuff to the adults.

She wanted to go after her mother and scream at her. Scream that while they played around with diplomatic nonsense, Kane and Asaron could be killed. Remind Victory what Octavian threatened to do. Point out what Octavian could have done to her.

But all at once, her anger deflated. She sagged in her seat, taking a deep breath to regain a bit of equilibrium.

Victory's daywalker was in the hospital. Her sire and adopted son had been kidnapped. And her daughter was being an idiot of the biggest sort. Toria was lucky she hadn't been locked in her room like a child.

That shower sounded good, just the thing she needed to wash the memory of Octavian's hands off her. Then she would go visit Dad. And she would wait for this diplomatic mission to come back before she tried anything else.

Just because she couldn't go with them now didn't mean she wouldn't have plans ready to go into action when they got back.

"I do not know what to do with that girl."

Victory paced in the large bathroom off her suite of rooms, phone clutched in her hand like a lifeline. She'd meant to get a shower, but she needed to talk things over with Mikelos before Toria showed up at the hospital. Maybe he could talk sense into his wayward daughter if she wouldn't listen to her own mother, the one with centuries' worth of experience. She pulled her robe tighter around her, shaking in a combination of anger and—fear? Yes, fear, for what could have happened to her beloved girl. The twit.

"It's okay, love." Mikelos still sounded tired, but much better than the day before. "Send her over, and I'll keep her occupied until you leave. And probably give her a piece of my own mind, but that's beside the point."

"Toria's a smart girl. What the hell was she thinking, staging a rescue on her own? She could have gotten killed!" Victory sank down on the edge of the bathtub. "She's already cursed!"

"And how rational are you when I'm in danger?" True to form, her daywalker was the voice of reason. "Toria loves her grandpa. And Kane is even more a part of her than I am of you," Mikelos said. "How can you fault her for doing everything in her power to get them back?"

"I can't fault that," Victory said. "But I can fault her for being an idiot about it."

"Then go tonight," Mikelos said. "Find out what's going on. And when you figure out what to do about it, make Toria a part of the plans. She's already accomplished this much. You're going into this tonight with the knowledge that the Romans definitely want the city. You have to give her credit for that."

"But that doesn't mean I have to like her methods."

"No, her methods need work," Mikelos said. "But that's the type of thing that comes with time. For all the power and knowledge she has, she's still a kid. I almost don't want to think of the mayhem Kane and Asaron have put the Romans through in the past two days. You know they can't be quiet hostages."

A small spark of cheer entered Victory's heart. "You're right. Maybe this Octavian will hand them back as not worth the effort when we show up tonight."

"I'll keep my fingers crossed." Muffled voices came from Mikelos' end of the phone, and when he spoke again, he said, "I have to go, the nurse is being adamant about dinner. Thinks I'm too skinny. I'll expect Toria by seven?"

"Yes," Victory said. "She has to return that horse, and then she'll drive to the hospital. If she's not there by seven-thirty, send out the search parties."

"And I won't let her out of my sight until after sundown. Promise," Mikelos said. "I love you. Take care tonight. Don't let Max do anything stupid."

"I love you, too," Victory said. "And I'll see you soon."

She turned off the phone and let it dangle in her hands, staring down at the tiled floor. Max was due to pick her up soon after sundown.

Switching the phone back on, she dialed Max's personal line. "Max? It's Victory. Get everyone over here. We have more problems."

Victory pushed open the library's last window and paused to inhale a deep breath of fresh air. The one room in the manor house big enough to hold them all still felt unbearable when they all started yelling at each other.

Steeling herself, she confronted the room again. "You were wise to take this spot, Sethri," she said to the lone figure in this back corner. "I'm inclined to stay out of this group's way myself."

The human head of Limani's council patted the hand she placed on the back of the oversized armchair. He had claimed the room's far corner upon realizing this informal meeting consisted of unelected councilmembers. "I'm making sure I retain a little plausible deniability. Max never warned me what I was walking into when he picked me up."

"I should confess, then, that I'm the one who called this meeting," Victory said.

"Then go, give them your rational voice," Sethri said. "They need it."

After slipping between the bookshelf-lined wall and couch holding Lena, Daliana, and Genevieve, Victory retook her seat. She perched on the edge of her desk next to Max, trying to imitate his stony calm.

"We no longer have the option of wasting time." While Victory had opened the windows, Tristan left his own chair and now stood before the group, fists balled at his side. "We need to find Fabbri and take her out, get rid of that problem. Then we need to call up the Mercenary Guild forces and march on the Romans."

Bethany laughed, harsh and unamused. She'd shown up with Lorus again. "Isn't that what I've been saying the whole time? Now the pup listens."

Lorus hissed low in his throat. "I didn't bring you here to instigate foolishness, woman. But Tristan, that's still the worst plan we could have."

Tristan snarled back. "I didn't hear you come up with anything better, snake."

Victory realized the werewolf's eyes had changed from chocolate brown to the lighter caramel of his wolf-form. When Lorus made to rise, it was time to step in. "Gentlemen!" Her cutting voice drew both glares. She stared down Tristan, and after he looked away, Lorus. Humans might be a vampire's chosen prey, but blood was blood. Sethri was right, it was time to assert control. When it came down to it, she was the stronger predator, and they would bow to her dominant will.

Lowering her voice, Victory spoke again. "Gentlemen. This is not the time to charge ahead with ill-thought-out plans. Lorus, do you have a better suggestion?"

With an almost imperceptible movement, Lorus shook his head.

Victory transferred her stare to the other aggressor. "Tristan?"

He also remained silent, but did sit down again. She would take that much.

And last, to head off future antagonism. "Bethany?"

The werebadger looked startled to be called upon. Not moving from her slump on the second couch next to Lorus, she said, "What do I know? Not all of us have your fancy military training."

That wasn't an argument she wanted to have right now. To Victory's relief, Max took over.

"And I'm sorry to say, but that's what it's come down to. A military operation. We can't dick around with the Romans like we can with the Humanists. The Humanists might be violent, but even they don't want Limani wiped off the face of the planet." He picked a glass paperweight off Victory's desk, spinning it between his fingers. "Based on Toria Connor's report," Max said, "the Romans might not have such compunctions."

126

Victory plucked the paperweight from Max's hand and set it on the desk. "From the threats Toria said were directed toward their prisoners, I would hesitate to believe any of us are safe when the Romans invade."

"'When?' What's this 'when' stuff?" Bethany sat up straight. "You haven't even talked to the Romans yet. Your daughter went against your wishes when she was attacked. How do we know she didn't make that up to get us to do what she wanted?"

"Get a clue, old woman." Genevieve saved Victory from the need to argue.

"The girl might be impetuous," Lena said, "but she's not manipulative. And again, military training plays into this—"

Max finished Lena's argument. "Toria knows reporting the truth is imperative under these circumstances. Lying, or even exaggerating, provides false information that could lead to unnecessary deaths."

"There, we are agreed that Toria is not lying," Daliana said. "A Roman invasion is imminent. We have also agreed that attacking first is a bad idea. Why?"

"How strong a force can we call up on short notice, Max?" Victory said.

He stared into space, then stole a blank paper from Victory's desk. "Can we count on you and Toria?"

Victory handed him a pen. She, of course. But Toria? Operating under the assumed immortality of youth, her daughter would never forgive her if left out of the action. Praying she wouldn't regret it later, Victory said, "Yes."

Max made a notation on his sheet. "Tristan, Genevieve, and Lorus, how many fighters could you call from your clans?"

She had only been asking about the Guild, but this worked, too.

Without hesitation, Tristan said, "Worked that one out two nights ago. I had over fifty volunteers, and I would count on thirty-seven."

Bethany snorted. "Thirty-seven? You think the others wouldn't step up?"

Tristan leveled his golden gaze at her. "I think the others are either too old or too inexperienced, but volunteered anyway."

"The panthers also met last night," Genevieve said. "And by that same vein, we can add thirty-three hunters. I had to weed out my own fair share of overeager kittens."

"Lorus?" Max said.

"Long as this fight isn't happening within the next few hours," Lorus said, "that gives me time to call Tersuigel's pack in from the bush. That would put us at nineteen or twenty, depending on whether she deems her youngest kit ready yet."

"The hyenas?" Genevieve sniffed in disdain. "Scavengers."

"Scavengers that have been known to take down live prey when provoked," Lorus said. "And Tersuigel herself is a former trained mercenary. So, including me, we'll play it safe and say twenty."

"Twenty-one," Bethany said, her voice low.

While everyone else looked at her with various expressions of surprise, Lorus said, "Oh, don't fret. You were already added. Think I would leave you out of the fun?"

Victory could make nothing of Max's chicken scratches over his shoulder, but when he finished his calculations, he cleared his throat. "So. Total comes to one hundred and seventy-three."

"Victory, can I borrow your phone to start calling in my clan?" Genevieve said.

"And I need to head out to call in Tersuigel and start rounding everyone else up," Lorus said.

"Wait a second," Max said. "I'm still taking Sethri and Victory out to meet with the Romans tonight."

"We can't afford to lose you three," Tristan said. "You two make up the most experienced military personnel we have, not to mention the official political head of the city."

Max shoved the scrap of notepaper in his back pocket. "While I should blush at being compared to the esteemed Victory here, where I'm concerned, the plan hasn't changed."

"I'll second that." Moving forward into the circle of conversation, Sethri settled himself on the couch arm next to Daliana. "Thought I'd better participate now, since it's my life being discussed."

"What are you going to do, go in under a white flag?" Bethany said. "I thought we were taking the threats against your two friends seriously. You want to burn like your sire, Victory?"

Bethany had gone too far, but Max grabbed Victory's arm before she could snap back. He dug his fingers into her skin until she relaxed. "Nobody is going to burn," he said. "We will ride in and ask to meet with this Octavian. They're not going to kill three people alone on a diplomatic mission."

"I still disagree that this is the best option," Tristan said.

"Enough!" Victory had reached the end of her rope. "Disagree all you want. This is a council session, right? We should put it to a vote. Second?"

"I'll second," Lena said.

"It's your house, Victory," Max said.

"Fine," she said. "Sethri and Bethany, I want you two in on this." Shock appeared on faces around the room, including human and werebadger, but no one dared to argue. "All in favor of a preliminary diplomatic mission to the Romans, say aye."

Missing the meeting at her own house bugged Toria to no end. She should be there, giving her input and helping Mama keep control of the situation. Share information she alone had as the one person to have direct contact with any of the Romans.

She loved her father with all her heart, but she did not want to be stuck at the hospital tonight.

From where he lay half-asleep on his hospital bed, Mikelos said, "I can hear you brooding from here. You sound like your mother."

Toria jumped up from the chair by the window and began to pace. "Brooding doesn't make noise, Dad."

"Do me a favor then, will you?" Mikelos lifted his head from the pillow, but Toria darted to his side so he could relax again.

"Of course, Dad, what do you need?" She was supposed to be there so he could keep an eye on her and make sure she didn't do anything else stupid. Instead, she prevented him from getting his much needed rest. Too bad Mama didn't see it that way.

"Food here is terrible," he said. "Run to the cafeteria and grab a sandwich for me? And salad for a friend?"

"Sure," Toria said. "Whatever you want."

After pressing a quick kiss to her father's cheek, she headed down to the cafeteria. She took the long way around once she got to the main floor, not anxious to pass right by the main security station. They might not recognize Victory's daughter on sight, but there was no reason to press the issue.

The bright cafeteria bustled with evening business—worried relatives and tired doctors who nonetheless had the energy to demand their sandwich be made just-so. The harried cashier still took her sweet time puzzling over how to bill the ham-egg-tomato-mushroom sandwich Toria ordered for her father. She overheard two nurses conversing behind her in line.

"—can't wait until the doc discharges that girl," one said. "Been a thorn in my side ever since she got here."

"The poor dear's been through a lot." The second nurse picked through the selection of coffee creamers next to the register. "Hasn't even had anyone to visit her."

"Just that vampire-woman who got thrown out——"

"Seven dollars and thirty-five cents!" The cashier thrust her hand under Toria's nose.

Toria fumbled in her wallet for the correct amount, then grabbed the bag and her coffee and escaped the cafeteria. She had a good idea who the salad was for now.

A few minutes later proved her right. After dropping the sandwich off with Mikelos, he sent her to room 302 with the other meal. She knocked on the semi-open door.

"What, a knock? I'm bloody honored." The sarcasm jarred the otherwise melodic feminine voice.

Assuming permission to enter had been given, Toria walked in. "Hey," she said. "Brought you a real dinner." The hospital bed held a young elven girl, prompting a note of familiarity in Toria's mind. "You're Syri, right? I've seen you at the Mists."

"That's right," Syri said. "Victory's daughter?"

Toria handed over the boxed salad, then dug the accompanying fork out of her purse. "The same. Torialanthas Connor, Toria. My dad asked me to bring you the salad."

"Syrisinia, Syri."

Informal elven introductions were so much simpler. Toria felt better than she had earlier, but she still didn't have the energy for formal elven mental aerobics.

Syri dug into the greens with gusto, pausing between bites to say, "Have a seat. Yeah, your mum owed me food in exchange for talking to her last night. Got kicked out before she could bring it to me."

Halting before moving the proffered chair, Toria straightened. "Am I gonna get in trouble for being here, too? I can't afford that now."

"Nah, you'll be fine." Syri waved a dismissive hand, and Toria dragged the chair closer to the bed. "I'm feeling better, so I was gonna ditch this place tonight anyway. You can help me sneak out." She gave Toria a conspiratorial smile, waggling her corn silk eyebrows.

"No freaking way," Toria said, taking both a seat and a much-needed sip of coffee. "If the hospital staff doesn't kill me, Mama will."

After placing the fork in her salad, Syri folded her hands in front of her to give Toria a prim look. "Nobody is going to kill you. And besides, I can help you find Kane."

Toria almost bolted out of the chair. "What? What are you talking about?"

"Kane is your partner's name, yes?" Syri resumed her meal.

Toria relaxed again. "Yes, it is. How do you know he's missing?"

"Simple," Syri said around a mouthful of cucumber. "There's mayhem about to explode in the world outside, and you're here without him. So he must be gone. And since you didn't burst in here all happy that the bitch indirectly responsible for my current condition had been found, I also assume she must still be on the loose."

"Yeah, pretty much," Toria said. "Why would you be willing to help me?"

Syri's impish grin vanished. "All the fucking mayhem, remember? We may not know each other, but we know of each other well enough. And I know we need you two as a working pair to defeat what's to come with these damn Humanists. So where is he?"

"You haven't heard about the Romans?" Toria feared bursting the girl's gung-ho bubble.

"Imperial industrialists fucking up good land down south and chasing the elves out?" Syri shrugged. "What about them?"

Catching Syri's complete attention, Toria said, "They've declared war on us." She waited for a torrent of curses to flow over her.

They didn't come. Instead, Syri let the laden fork drop back into the box. "What?"

Toria leaned forward. "Let me tell you all you've missed while stuck in here."

While Syri changed into her street clothes, Toria poked her head out to survey the hall. The dinner rush had ended an hour before, so all the patients were tucked away in their rooms for the night. Two nurses manned the station in the middle of the hall, both busy with paperwork. No one else was in sight. Room 302 sat next to a stairwell, and Toria planned to take advantage of that in their escape.

"Ready?" Toria pulled her head back into the dark room. "Where did you go?"

There was a slight hint of movement in the shadows next to her, and then Syri stepped back into view.

"Neat trick," Toria said. "Teach me?"

"If you're good," Syri said. "But it won't work in that bloody over-lit hallway, so don't count on it." A wave of pain darkened her face when she stuck one arm in her leather jacket.

"Careful," Toria said, remembering her companion's injuries. "It's warm out, you won't even need that." She realized now that Syri didn't even come up to her chin. The elven girl looked like a punked-out china doll.

Syri finished pulling it on. "I always need it." Without elaborating further, Syri took her own sneak peek out into the hall. "So, shield us, and we'll make a break for it."

"Minor problem," Toria said. "No magic, remember?" Syri had been suitably sympathetic over Toria's current dilemma, as only another magic user could be.

Pulling back into the room, Syri gave her a hard look. "I've got to do everything myself tonight, don't I?"

The beginnings of a beautiful relationship. Kane would put up with her a lot better. But if this girl could help Toria find Kane, she could put up with more. She held still while Syri gave her another hard look, lips moving with no sound emerging.

"Okay, let's go," Syri said. She strolled into the hall, seeming without a care in the world.

Toria held up her hands, but neither noticed nor felt any change. Trusting the girl, she followed Syri out of the hospital room and down the stairs. She relaxed when no demands to stop erupted behind them.

First, a quick stop in Mikelos' room to leave her sleeping father a note: *Taking Syri home with me. I promise she'll keep me out of trouble.* She propped it against the vase of flowers on the bedside table.

Once Toria arranged it to her satisfaction, Syri snagged the paper to include her own addendum: *Or Toria will keep me out of trouble. Get well soon, daywalker.*

Toria replaced the note once more before leading Syri back out of the room. They passed nurses, doctors, and even one security guard on their way out of the hospital to the parking lot, and no one gave them a second look.

Once they settled in Toria's town-car, she said, "You'd better take off the spell now."

"It's not a spell," said Syri. "And why?"

"Because I've already had one run-in with the police this week, and I don't feel like explaining why the car appears to be driving itself if we get pulled over."

Syri studied her, head tilted to the side. "Good point."

Toria waited. "I don't feel any different."

"Because it's not a spell!" Syri laid her head against the back of the seat and heaved a melodramatic sigh. She waved her fingers at Toria. "There, it's gone. Better? Or you want me to recite a bloody limerick, too?"

Toria started the ignition, and they began the drive in silence.

"You know," Toria said at a red light, "I had an elven teacher in high school. And what you do is not elven magic."

"You want me to help find Kane or not?" Syri kept her eyes straight ahead on the road, refusing to meet Toria's sideways glances.

Victory shut the door behind the departing councilmembers, letting the gentle thud lift a tremendous weight from her shoulders.

"Time for action?"

She twisted the deadbolt home, resisting the urge to rest her head against the wall. Instead, she squared her shoulders and turned around. Max still stood where he had said his own goodbyes to the council, and Sethri lurked behind him.

"You mean be productive instead of all this endless talking in circles?" Victory joined the two men. This time she did not resist the urge to rest her head, choosing Max's shoulder for a convenient pillow. "Yes, please! Anything!"

"At least we got them to agree with us," Max said.

"It was too close."

Max gave her a quick hug. "But they still came through."

"Then I believe it's time to hit the road," Sethri said. "Max stowed our gear in his truck. Do you still need to get ready?"

"Just to change my clothes and grab my pack upstairs," Victory said. "And leave a note for Toria. Let me make you guys a snack from the kitchen before we go."

After fixing them each a sandwich, Victory stood at the kitchen island, chewing the end of a pen between her teeth. How to convey everything she wanted to tell her daughter in a few simple words? Toria must still be angry with her, a thought that never sat well with Victory. The girl could be headstrong and impulsive, but she was also one of the bravest women she had ever met. A feeling of pride blossomed whenever she thought she might be the influence.

Toria,

Leaving with Max and Sethri now. Goal is to be back by dawn, so I'll see you in the morning. Hope you've still got good ideas of how to deal with all this, because I want to hear them. Be good. Love you.

She attached the note to the refrigerator with a handmade magnet. Tracing a finger over the glazed blue and purple clay an eight-year-old Toria had claimed was a cat, she steeled herself for what was to come.

Drifting out of the kitchen, Victory found herself bypassing her original destination of the stairs and wandering into Mikelos' studio. He must know the fate of his violin by now, but he had yet to talk to her about it. She ran a finger down the curve of the antique violin displayed on the fireplace mantle. Good thing Mikelos refused to take this one out of the house. It matched the cello in the corner, and these were two of the few remnants Mikelos had of his life before her. Connor had given him the broken violin, but it had been a practice instrument. This piece was his pride and joy.

Every once in a while, she found herself jealous of his music. Jealous of the history it meant and the peace it gave him. Her own history bled violence and warfare.

So she clung to her life in Limani with passion. She had found her peace. It was Mikelos and Toria. And Kane, Max, Daliana—the list of friends she cherished was long and loved.

An upstart emperor on another continent would not ruin that.

Max's voice echoed down the hall from the kitchen. "You ready yet?"

He hadn't needed to shout, she could hear him fine. Habits of human nature, she supposed. "Just a minute!" With one last caress of the violin's smooth wood, Victory left the studio.

She bounded up the stairs to her third-floor suite of rooms. After making sure her pack did not lack any essential supplies—she couldn't be too prepared after the boat misadventure—Victory stripped off her jeans and tank top, replacing them with gear she'd laid across her bed, already dug out of its chest earlier that afternoon.

First the supple buckskin pants, a gift from her friend Sir Justiniusal, an elven knight, after his return from an expedition across the Wasteland to the western coast. She left the matching vest in favor of a simple black knit top. When the summer night was warm to her, she knew it must be unbearable to those who felt the temperature. She ducked into the bathroom long enough to grab two hair ties. She pulled back her mass of dark hair, braided it, and tied off the bottom, letting the thick tail swing loose against her back.

She sat on the bed to pull on her boots and picked up her utility belt from the nightstand. After double-checking the pistol holster and ammunition clips, she finished clasping her broadsword scabbard to the belt. She buckled it around her waist, settling it around her hips to check the balance.

Footsteps on the stairs, then down her hallway. She unsheathed her sword in one smooth motion and fell into a defensive stance. She held the familiar leather-wrapped hilt in both hands next to her head, pointing the tip of the blade at an invisible enemy's forehead. She'd owned this sword for almost five hundred years, and it was an extension of herself. She knew where every inch of the blade was at all times, along with the weak points of her entire surroundings. This was her music.

"You're dropping your point."

Flashing forward with an attack to remove an enemy's head in one smooth slice, Victory whirled around and ended with her blade aimed at Max's chest. Good thing her large room had a high ceiling. "Still could kill you."

Max didn't budge. "You wouldn't dare. You don't know where I keep my keys." She noticed he'd changed from his jeans into standard Guild-issue leather-armored pants, but wore a loose shirt of plain linen above. She bet herself a beer he kept the keys in one of his belt pouches.

"Oh, do grow up." Victory resheathed the sword at her side. "You ready?" She strapped one knife around her right ankle and the stiletto to her left forearm.

Max picked up her leather trench coat from over the armchair in the corner and held it up for her to slip into it. "Waiting on you, milady. Don't know how you can wear that in this weather."

"Thanks." Settling the coat into place, she slung her pack over her shoulder. "And what weather?"

"You're unbelievable," Max said, following her out of the room.

"No, I'm undead." Victory led the way down the stairs. "You're welcome to join me. I'll even share all the perks."

Sethri awaited them in the foyer, grasping his briefcase in front of him. Unlike his traveling companions' martial attire, he wore an impeccable business suit. His shiny green tie reminded Victory of elven eyes. "Are you threatening to kill my Guildmaster, Victory?"

"That's nothing new." Max pulled open the front door, digging his keys out of the pouch on his belt. He dangled them in front of Victory, who gave them a halfhearted swipe. She should have made that bet. "No, you can't drive my truck. You never let me drive your convertible."

"That's because the last time anyone other than me drove it, it was almost totaled." Gesturing for Sethri to take the front passenger seat, Victory tossed her pack into the back seat and climbed in after it.

Max settled behind the wheel and started the ignition. "I'm a much better driver than Toria, I'm sure."

"Is the entire trip going to be like this?" Sethri cast Victory a withering look over his shoulder.

"Yes," Max said, at the same time Victory declared, "No." Sethri didn't hang out with mercs enough. They got punchy when a fight was coming. She and Max understood each other.

"Oh, dear," Sethri said.

Max solved the problem by shoving a disc into the dashboard stereo. He pulled off the manor drive and onto the main road while strains of music flowed around them. Mikelos would be able to identify each of the instruments, but Victory sat back and enjoyed, letting the breeze from the open windows rustle loose strands of her hair.

She drifted to the music and motion of the truck during the half-hour drive. Time to clear her head of everything the world had dumped on her in so short a time. There would be more trouble to come when they met the Romans, but right now Victory needed the peace.

The last time she had been this stressed, she and Max had confronted an entire pack of werepanthers on their own. And Toria killed a vampire to protect Mikelos and Kane.

No way would she let her daughter be in such danger again. Not that Toria would ever give her the choice.

"Victory?"

Her eyes snapped open. "Max?" The forest on either side of the road was pitch black, the moonlight invisible in contrast to the truck's headlights. "Why are we slowing down?"

"We're reaching the point where the Romans attacked. Figured I'd check it out first, then head downriver to the bridge if we didn't find a welcoming party." Max pulled the truck to the side of the road before it ended at the river, then cut the engine and headlights.

The world went black for a split second before her sensitive sight adjusted to the moon's scant illumination. "That your way of asking me to take a look around?" She grasped the door latch before he could respond.

"Please?" Max said. "Better night vision and all? Besides, one of us has to stay with Sethri."

"I'm more than capable of taking care of myself—"

Max waved off Sethri's protest. "Humor us. We know what we're doing."

"Sure, send out the immortal. Cover me." Victory stepped out of the truck, twitching her coat clear before lifting the outside handle and easing the door back into place.

"Already done."

Victory heard the unmistakable click of a cylinder being snapped back into a revolver. She walked around the truck to peer into the dense forest. Dappled moonlight cast shadows on the ground between the trees, but the night was still. Most convenient place to hide scouts.

Or snipers.

No heartbeats beside the two back in the truck. Not even a breeze across the water ruffled the omnipresent heat. Sethri must be dying in his suit.

Circling to the other side, Victory took a few steps out into the open area between the trees and the river. She waited for the hair on the back of her neck to prickle, her usual warning of invisible watchers when she was so exposed, but felt nothing. They might have to head for the bridge and leave Limani territory to find the Romans after all. Not her favorite idea in the world, but she had to trust Max's judgment. He might not be so old or experienced, but the merc had seen his share of combat.

At the river's edge, she spun in a slow circle. Still no hint of company. All of her training dictated leaving a guard across the river. Invaders would press whatever advantage they had. On the other side of the river, this road must lead straight into the heart of the Romans' encampment. The dark forest across the water taunted her—the glow of the moonlight off the river prevented her sharp eyes from piercing the darkness. No signs of life reached her ears over the water.

They had to be here. So where were they?

She headed back to Max's truck. The tide had washed away any signs of fighting left on this side of the river, though according to Toria, her daughter hadn't had the chance to make many. She knelt next to a few old horseshoe tracks leading to the water, but saw nothing to give her any information Toria hadn't been able to glean.

"Nothing here!" Victory stood again and continued toward the truck.

Max sagged against the side of the door. "You serious? They have to be here."

"I thought so, too," she said. "Guess we're going to the bridge." She slid back into her seat. When her seatbelt clicked into place, Max restarted the truck and flipped on the headlights. The world shrank back into the area lit by harsh yellow beams.

Sethri stared at them both, head twisting from front to back seat. "And if they're not there?"

"Then I will be very, very confused," Victory said.

They rode in silence while Max turned the truck around and got back on the road. After about a mile, he took the cutoff toward the ancient bridge.

"This worries me," Max said. His grip on the steering wheel turned his knuckles white.

She sat forward on the seat to squeeze his shoulder. "Me, too."

Sethri cast her another nervous look. "How so?"

"Because they're not worried," Victory said. "If they were worried about Limani launching an offensive attack, the river would have been crawling with soldiers."

"They must know we're in no position to do such a thing," Max said. "Either that, or—"

"Or they outnumber us so badly they don't need to be worried." Even saying the words, Victory did not want to acknowledge them. This wasn't the first time she had been outmanned and outgunned. That didn't mean she liked it.

They were less than ten minutes away from the bridge, but that didn't stop Victory from resting her head against the back of the seat and tuning out the rest of the world once more. Let Max have his plans about what to do when they met the Romans. She needed to start figuring out what to do if they didn't.

If the Romans weren't camping on their border, how had Fabbri known of the potential invasion? And if the other councilmembers were right, and the Humanists' timing was too much of a coincidence, then what did Fabbri stand to gain from all this?

It was hard not to feel blindsided, and Victory kicked herself for becoming so complacent. The Greeks founded Limani on peace, and even though they fell to the Romans on the mainland soon thereafter, their colony still stood two and a half centuries later. Victory had been fighting for the British in Thuringia at the time, though Asaron had been hired by the Greeks as a "consultant."

She never could figure out why the Romans let him set foot anywhere near their lands after that.

Limani forgot they always risked the same fate that befell their founders. But then the Last War happened, and no one bothered with such a small territory. And for the past fifty years, the Roman emperor had lived by the tenets of peace. It was this new kid stirring up trouble.

"What's that?"

Sethri's question broke Victory from her musings. She scooted forward on her seat, peering out the front windshield. "What's what?"

Max started slowing the truck. "Flash of light," he said. "Looked like a lantern being put out after we turned the curve."

"So someone's up there," Victory said. "I'll give you two guesses who."

"But I just need one."

Max finished the old joke offhand, but she didn't blame him. Now came the hard part. This had better not be an ambush—she wasn't in the mood.

Keeping the truck to a crawl, Max eased toward where the light had been. "See anything?"

Victory strained further, but saw nothing except the road and more trees. By her estimate, they should almost be to the second river crossing.

"Shit!" Max jerked the steering wheel to the left, throwing them all hard against their seatbelts. The truck avoided striking the lone soldier who stepped into the middle of the road by a narrow margin. Max hit the brakes before the truck could end up in the shallow ditch to the left of the road.

One by one, Victory released her fingers from their death grip on the back of Max's seat. She hadn't seen the soldier until he appeared right in front of them. Vampire? She heard no heartbeat, but she might not have been able to over the harsh pounding emanating from her companions.

Max rolled down his window to poke his head out. "What the hell is wrong with you, kid? I could have killed you!"

Oh, Max. Victory almost shut her eyes in dismay. What a way to make an entrance.

The young soldier sported the standard Roman foot soldier's uniform, not the more extensive gear Toria said Octavian had worn. However, he grasped the hilt of the gladius at his side. Victory poised to release her stiletto. Not much use inside the vehicle, but it was habit.

The soldier, young enough to have not been shaving long, was nevertheless unintimidated by Max's rebuke. "Please step out of the truck, sir."

Sethri placed a hand on Max's shoulder, and Max allowed himself to be moved away from the window so Sethri could speak with the soldier. "Good evening," he said, his tone calmer. "My name is Alexander Sethri, head of Limani's city council. Escorting me are Maximilian Asher and Victory, also members of the council. We're here on a diplomatic mission, and we wish to speak with General Julius Octavian."

At his words, five more soldiers stepped out of the woods to surround the truck. Each of them carried either a sword or longbow aimed at the truck. The first soldier drew his own blade.

"Step out of the truck," he said again, still calm. "Now."

Where is that stupid thing? Toria dug through another kitchen drawer, searching for the lighter that had to be there. She hadn't needed anything other than her mind to light a candle since middle school. This curse thing took some getting used to. But one of Kane's ex-boyfriends had smoked—part of the reason he was an ex—and left cheap lighters everywhere. She remembered tossing one in a drawer somewhere.

"Ah ha!" Toria retrieved it from the back of the drawer, where it had been hidden under a pile of bobby pins. She shoved the drawer closed with her hip and turned around. Syri stood in the middle of the apartment, eyeing the homey clutter with vague disdain. "What's wrong?" Toria asked.

"Huh?" Syri brought herself back from wherever her mind had been. "Nothing. Admiring the décor. Do you even have a proper workroom?"

"It's under the carpet you're standing on. Just needs to be rolled back." Toria picked up a box of chalk from the counter and threw it to Syri, who caught it with one deft hand. "The circle and cardinal points are painted on the floor and already enchanted. Do whatever else you need to do. How many candles did you need?"

"Chalk," Syri said, examining the box. "How quaint." She tossed it back to Toria unopened. "Five candles, please. No specific type or colors, though I imagine you might want one you feel most comfortable with." She knelt to roll up a corner of carpet to reveal the lines painted on the hardwood floors. "Wow, you are never getting your security deposit back."

"We lost that the first time I set the kitchen on fire," Toria said. "Kane's primary is earth, he can restore the wood before we move out." While she propped the rolled-up carpet in a corner, Syri began drawing glyphs on the floor with lines of white light from her fingertip.

Ten minutes later, Toria sat in the center of the glowing circle on her living room floor, facing Syri to the northeast. A faint bit of starlight shone through the skylights in the apartment ceiling, but the rest of the room's warm glow came from the candle Toria held and the four others placed at the main cardinal points of the circle. The halfway points between the main cardinals shined with unfamiliar glowing symbols. She hoped Syri knew what she was doing.

"Do you know what happens when a warrior-mage pair gets separated?" Syri matched Toria's cross-legged pose, shimmering hands resting on her knees.

Toria did not respond, fighting down the chill that crossed her in the warm room at the uncanny echo of Zerandan's rhetorical question the night before.

"For too long, I mean," Syri said. Her eyes caught Toria's and held them, her cat-slit pupils large in the flickering flames.

"The elf Zerandan didn't know." And if he didn't know, there wasn't an icicle's chance in summer Syri did.

"Zerandan's my great-great-uncle," Syri said. "You were in good hands with him. And it's true. Nobody knows. And I don't imagine you're in any hurry to find out."

"Do you really know how to get me in contact with Kane?" Toria could not resist looking over her shoulder to the southern point of the compass, where Kane would sit during a formal working like this. That's the direction she was used to facing, and this whole situation felt odder by the minute. His absence was an aching wound in the back of her mind. Just the fact that she was certain to feel it if he died kept her from succumbing to true panic.

"I'm damn well going to try." Syri raised her shimmering hands from her knees and placed them flat on the ground in front of her within the circle. "Deep breath. Relax. Leave the hard stuff to me."

Like Toria could argue. Even the shields for this were all up to Syri. Despite Zerandan's claims that shields were passive magic, she was pretty sure attempting to mesh shields with not one, but two, unfamiliar magic systems qualified as active. Ending up with a splitting headache would put a hitch in Syri's plans and might ruin them altogether.

Syri did not move, leaving her hands braced against the floor. The room around them began to lighten, and out of the corners of her eyes, Toria caught glimmers of a curtain of translucent light. It followed the lines of the circle around them, arching into a dome above their heads. The four candle stubs around the circle gleamed brighter, and the four unfamiliar symbols followed suit. Toria felt drawn to the one on her left, admiring the glitter of unfamiliar magic. The scientist in her stirred, and she began listing questions for Syri on her mental clipboard.

Her voice a harsh whisper, Syri said, "Either look at me or look at your candle. You don't think I know what I'm doing?"

Toria whipped her head back to the other girl. "Sorry."

"Don't care. Just don't fucking move."

So she sat still, thumb and forefinger from each hand wrapped around the base of the new taper of purple wax resting on the ground in front of her. A trickle of strange power wound its way up her spine, and she repressed the urge to meet the power with a tendril of her own, investigating it and how it worked. Instead, she stared into the small flame before her.

The tendril traced up the back of her neck and up to her head, making the roots of her hair tingle and feel like they stood on end. Now Syri was in her brain. Where Zerandan's link had felt like an archaeologist gently sifting through sand, Syri unwound a tangled skein of glowing silken threads.

Syri picked at every knot until she knew what it was—Toria's skill with a sword here, her talent for baking there. Even the knowledge gleaned from her recent history class.

Then Syri found the magic. Seeing her crafted physical shields rise around her, fluctuate larger and smaller, and then drop again was an odd experience, as if Toria's own hand moved without her control.

Syri couldn't contact Kane on her own. At most, they might have held a polite conversation in passing at the Twilight Mists. And that was an optimistic guess. On her own, Syri would have no way to sense Kane from here to the Roman encampment, not without knowing Kane's magical signature the intimate way Toria did.

So Syri would use Toria's magic to find Kane. A sneaky way of getting around the curse, but it worked. Toria opened her mind even more, letting Syri explore what it meant to be a warrior-mage. Elven magic was dissimilar from human magic. She couldn't compare the two. They might not even fall on the same spectrum. Double-edged blade. A nudge in one direction, and Syri would have access to every iota of talent and knowledge Toria possessed. A slip in the other direction, and Syri could crush Toria's mind, overwhelming it with her own power.

Or Syri could fall all the way in, leaving her body an empty husk while Toria gained an unwilling second personality.

No wonder Syri had snapped at her to remain still. Toria wouldn't want to share a brain with herself either.

"Whoa!" After cutting the truck's engine, Max put both hands in the air, and Sethri followed suit. He left the headlights on to keep the surrounding soldiers illuminated. "What's the big idea? We're just here to talk."

After slipping the stiletto beneath her sleeve, Victory raised her hands in the air, too. "Tell Octavian that Toria Connor sent us," she said, pitching her voice to carry out Max's window. "He should be expecting us."

The first soldier traded a look with the other standing beside him, who was armed with a longbow. "The general told us to expect tricks," he said, his gladius steady.

Victory bit her tongue. What tricks? They were the ones who took her sire and adopted son. They were the ones who hurt her daughter.

With his smooth voice made even more soothing, Sethri tried again. "My name is Alexander Sethri. I represent Limani's ruling council. We have come to discuss recent events in hopes of coming to a diplomatic solution. I can assure you that we travel alone, armed for personal defense."

He was good, Victory gave him that. If this party had consisted of only her and Max, the mayhem would have already begun. She appreciated his steady presence.

"We'll have to disarm you if you want to talk to the general." The gladius lowered a handful of inches.

"That is to be expected," Max said. "I'm sure the general and I can understand each other."

At a gesture from his partner, the second soldier lowered his bow and took off at a jog through the darkness. "Now will you get out of the truck?"

Max looked back over his shoulder. Oh, now he wanted her to decide? "Might as well," she said. "How else are we going to talk to Octavian?"

Taking the lead, she switched the lock and pushed the door open. If they changed their minds and shot her, the odds of them piercing her heart directly were slim. She'd get back up again. She stepped out with her hands in front of her, slamming the door shut again with a small hip bump. The two soldiers who covered her resheathed their swords when she got out—a good sign. "I have a knife at my right wrist and my sword at my waist," she said. She would neglect to tell them of the ankle dagger unless it looked like they might perform a physical search.

"May we have those, then?" Good, it looked like they planned to take the polite route. One of her new friends held out his hands, and she snapped the stiletto into her palm. After handing the knife over, she unbuckled the scabbard from her waist. His partner took that, and she managed to relinquish it with just slight hesitation. Unlike Toria's magical attachment to her rapier, Asaron taught Victory to treat her sword like a tool, nothing more. But centuries of use created a certain amount of fondness. She hoped she would see it again.

If things went to hell, she would need it.

Max also stepped out of the vehicle to relinquish his own small arsenal to the waiting soldiers. "Careful with that, now," he said, handing over his entire belt to the young man who first stopped them.

"I think we know how to handle weapons," he said, looping the belt around his arm and holding the bottom of the sword for balance. "We are trained soldiers, mercenary."

Victory waited for the explosion. Max might be a laid-back guy most of the time, but the value of mercenary work versus formal soldiering was one of his more touchy points.

From the other side of the truck, Sethri called out a warning. "Max..." The soldiers around them tensed, and hands drifted once again toward weapons.

But Max laughed, clapping the soldier in front of him on the shoulder. "So you are, kid. One pointer though: next time a potential foe hands over his weapons, walk a few steps away so he can't take them right back from you."

The soldier's eyes widened, and he ducked from under Max's hand to follow his suggestion. Tension broken, the surrounding soldiers chuckled at their fellow's expense. Things would be fine. Max knew soldiers. He had been a Guild trainer in New Angouleme before relocating to Limani. Victory was too out of touch with that world these days. With any luck, they would avert this whole mess, and she could keep things that way.

Another soldier escorted Sethri around to their side of the truck, and he stood between Max and Victory. Smart man. Even sans physical weapons, they were still lethal. One soldier rifled through Sethri's briefcase, but returned it to him after assuring himself it contained no weapons.

The runner returned, emerging from the darkness behind the bobbing beam of a flashlight. After regaining a bit of breath, he said, "The general has agreed to see you. His pavilion is just over the bridge. If the three of you will follow me?"

Max reached through the truck window to switch off the headlights. Save for the flashlight, the surrounding area descended into darkness. If this had been a hostile mission, it would have been Victory's cue to act. For a few seconds, she had the advantage over all present.

But this wasn't a hostile mission. Victory placed her hand into the crook of Sethri's elbow, quietly alerting Max that she would take responsibility for the civilian. Max stepped behind the soldier and gestured for him to lead the way.

The remaining men fell in loose formation around them while they walked down the road. Around a bend, and the river spread in front of them. The water here was wider and deeper, the current stronger. An ancient metal and concrete bridge spanned the river, remnant of the time before the Last War. Now it was the sole physical link between Limani and Roman territory.

And they planned to use it for their invasion.

"Are you *that* Victory?" A solder next to her broke the silence.

The man behind them shushed him, but Victory said, "Yes, I imagine I am."

"My great-grandfather fought with you in Castille during the Battle of the Straits." He gave her a lopsided shrug. "He would always end the story by telling us how beautiful you were. He is right."

That twist left her a bit speechless, but Max took up the slack. "Oh yes, she's quite lovely with a sword in her hand. It's the dresses you have to watch out for."

J.L. Gribble

"Says the man who takes his own sword out on more dates than he does women." More of the soldiers around them attempted to hide snorts of mirth.

She took a good look at the soldier next to her, noting the dusky skin and almond eyes marking those descended from the southern portion of Hispania. She looked similar, but her now pale skin took more of an olive tint—Asaron had found her in Aragonia, the northern part of the peninsula.

The Castillans lost the Battle of the Straits, almost a hundred years ago. It led to the eventual absorption of both it and Aragonia into the Roman Empire.

It was the final straw before she fled to the New Continent and Limani. It was a miracle that this soldier had a great-grandfather live to tell such stories after that battle. Had she been human, she would have died any number of times in that long fight.

When they approached the bridge, more armed Romans came into view stationed around its base. She wouldn't be surprised if they had also wired it with explosives. That was how the Romans fought. Octavian proved things hadn't changed when he attacked Toria this afternoon.

Victory brushed those thoughts from her mind when they stepped from dirt and sand onto concrete. No time to get riled up over past bloodshed. And while Octavian threatened Toria and prevented her from following him, he'd done no lasting harm. Who knew, maybe the curse she seemed to be suffering under was nothing more than a side effect of her separation from Kane. Nobody knew exactly how the warrior-mage bond worked, least of all her.

She crossed the bridge holding her head high. From this vantage point, she could see the numerous campfires spread through the woods on the opposite side of the river. Those trees held the missing members of her family.

"Hey." She touched the soldier next to her on the arm, capturing his full attention. In a low voice, she said, "Maybe you can help me out."

"Depends on what it is," he said.

"Two of my friends are being held here," she said. "We're worried about them."

"Yeah, the kid and the other vampire. I saw them yesterday."

"And?"

Giving his fellows darting looks, the soldier stepped closer to her. "I didn't get to talk to them or anything, but they looked okay. Quiet, mostly."

Waves of relief washed across her. Toria would be even more ecstatic. Now they knew the prisoners were held here and hadn't been transported farther south. Excellent news.

He pulled away, returning to marching attention. They'd reached the end of the bridge. This side was in much worse shape, having lost its gentle slope up from the land and instead ending in a sheer drop. The group dispersed into a single line to climb down the rickety wooden ramp.

A handful of floodlights came on all at once, lighting the base of the bridge in fluorescent brilliance. Victory shielded her eyes with a gasp, and Sethri caught her elbow before she lost her balance. But she recovered quickly, blinking away the afterglow.

These Romans moved fast. Military efficiency had improved over the past hundred years. Soldiers scurried about, setting up tables and chairs under an open-sided pavilion at the tree line.

The party stopped and waited until preparations were complete. Victory tried to catch her new friend's attention, but he'd found himself a place on the other side of the group. That was okay. She had the information she'd been hoping for. Digging for more might cause trouble.

On an unspoken signal, the setup crew faded back into the trees, and the soldiers escorted them forward to the pavilion. Sethri took the seat in the middle of the three arrayed on one side of the long table. Victory took her cue from Max, and he solved the problem by taking the seat on the right. She placed herself on Sethri's left, flipping aside her long coat to sit, and the three settled in.

With little fanfare, an older soldier approached the pavilion, emerging from the dark trees flanked by two bodyguards. He wore a fancier uniform than the various styles of fatigues and forest garb his subordinates sported, but little in the way of medals or ribbons. Victory recognized the single immediate sign of rank: the small bronze eagles pinned to his collar. A general, though not the highest rank she'd ever seen. He still might be the most experienced in the colonies, evidenced by his blond hair silvering at the temples, despite his apparent age. About the same age as Max, she guessed.

So this was the man who assaulted and threatened her daughter. Not much to look at. She could take him, but alas, now was not the time.

Sethri stood when Octavian reached them, though neither she nor Max followed suit. Both men clasped hands over the table, but it didn't look like either sank to the level of trying to best grips. She already knew Sethri was too professional for such a thing, though it raised Octavian's status in her mind. But not by much.

"Welcome. I'm General Julius Octavian. Please, have a seat." Both men did so, and another officer sat next to Octavian.

He gave Victory a small nod, and she returned it with no more than a thin smile. Let Sethri play at making friends. She was too busy not lunging across the table and ripping Octavian's throat out.

"A pleasure to meet you," Sethri said. "I'm Head Councilman Alexander Sethri, representing the interests of the city Limani and its denizens. With me are Mercenary Guildmaster Maximilian Asher and Master of the City Victory."

Ah, her pointless title, when the majority of the time she was the sole vampire living in Limani. She'd never felt default counted. Sethri was pulling out the big guns tonight. It worried her that he felt he needed them.

Now Octavian smiled, a big grin filled with warmth. Victory didn't buy it for a second. "An honor. Your reputations precede you."

"Yes, we are quite fond of our more famous residents," Sethri said. "But they've accompanied me as fellow councilmembers. I believe we have much to discuss tonight."

"I completely agree," Octavian said. "For instance, the attack staged against my men two nights ago."

"Attack?" Sethri traded looks with Max and Victory, but she had no idea what Octavian was talking about either. "Are you referring to the incident that resulted in two Limani citizens being taken prisoner by your men?"

"I am." Octavian took the slip of paper his aide handed to him. "Mr. Asaron and Mr. Nalamas trespassed on Roman territory. They are also responsible for killing one of my men and severely injuring two more."

A surge of pride filled Victory. Toria hadn't known how much damage they caused, but she knew her guys wouldn't go down without a fight.

"Since when has crossing the Agios River constituted trespass?" Sethri lifted his briefcase onto the table and withdrew a sheaf of papers. "According to the trade agreements established in 2094, passage between lands was unrestricted to travelers by foot, horseback, or small vehicle with no goods intended for sale. I've marked the passage here."

He began to hand it to Octavian, but the general brushed it away. "Thank you. We have our own copies."

"So what has changed?" Sethri set the papers on the table. "And what can we do to reach a peaceful solution to whatever problem there is?"

"Let me give it to you straight," Octavian said. "You are aware of the change in command in Roma?"

"The Emperor is dead, yes," Sethri said. "And that the new Emperor is not one the senators approve of."

Now Asaron's inside information from down south would come in handy. Victory awaited Octavian's response to that one. They would see where the man fell in the political game, and then they would have more influence over the situation. Sethri might be the expert, but she'd been around longer.

"The new Emperor is the old one's nephew, yes," Octavian said. "Benedictus is...an interesting character."

Considering the Emperor was the official head of the Roman military, it made sense for Octavian not to speak out against him. But Victory perked up when the general did not jump to his immediate defense.

"Tell me, one soldier to another," she said. "How much military experience does this Benedictus have, anyway?"

"He is a decorated admiral in the Roman Navy," Octavian's aide said. "And graduated from the Venetian Military Academy in the top third of his class."

"We all know the royals get commissions when they're barely out of diapers," Max said. "Titles and medals don't tell us how much experience he has."

While the aide looked pained, Octavian relented. "The new Emperor is nineteen years old. To my knowledge, his stints aboard a warship have been nothing more than pleasure cruises."

Now they were making progress. "I understand that," Victory said. "Especially since military experience has never been a prerequisite for emperorship like it is for the prime minister position in Britannia."

"But that still doesn't explain why all of a sudden he seems to want Limani," Sethri said.

Now Octavian clammed up. Stalemate. Victory's turn again.

"The latest rumors from Fort Caroline," she said, "were that your new emperor needs to prove his worth and make a name for himself."

The aide's expression grew icy, but Octavian remained aloof. "The emperor merely has plans for expansion."

His own voice cold to match, Sethri said, "Have the British been consulted regarding these plans? One of the major clauses of the Revised Treaty of 2072 insists Limani remain an independent city-state."

"I feel it only fair that we know what the Romans have ceded to the British in return for our lands," Max said.

"The Empire of Roma has ceded nothing," Octavian said. "To my knowledge, the British have not been consulted."

Time to break out her knowledge of the Roman political structure. "What does the Senate have to say about the emperor's actions?" Victory said. "Don't they have to approve major military offensives?"

"To my knowledge," Octavian said again, his voice more hesitant now, "the Senate has approved all of the Emperor's plans currently being enacted."

More than anything else she had encountered or heard in the past few days, that statement chilled Victory's already cool blood. A truism that had held solid for centuries stated that if you wanted a good plan to be destroyed without bloodshed, give it to the Roman Senate to pick over. She caught Max's eye behind Sethri's head. She read his visible shock and imagined she looked much the same.

The Senate hadn't even wanted this emperor. Why would they all of a sudden let him ride roughshod over established treaties and policies? While she was usually happy that an ocean separated the New Continent from Europa, now she lamented the fact. The soldier earlier had brought up old memories of a war long lost. If she'd been in Castille or Aragonia or even Britannia, it would have been child's play to travel to Roma to find out what the hell was going on. But now they knew next to nothing, with no time to send an operative overseas to remedy their lack of information.

Through it all, Sethri seemed unfazed. "Then I hope you will not find it amiss if I take steps to inform the British of your plans? In fact, any information you can give me regarding those plans, such as a tentative timeline, would be greatly appreciated."

"I'm afraid that would be impossible," Octavian said.

Now the smarmy smile that'd made Toria's skin crawl appeared, and Victory didn't blame her daughter for getting the creeps.

"Fair enough," Sethri said. "It is understandable that such plans might still be in the fluid stage."

Max sat up straight in his chair, and Victory found her hand drifting to the place where her sword hilt belonged. Sethri remained calm. She would have been over the table in a second had she still been armed and not surrounded by dozens of Roman soldiers.

"Returning to the subject of your prisoners, then," Sethri said. "What sort of ransom were you expecting?"

"Ransom?" Octavian settled back in his chair, the relaxed air returning. The smile became less nasty and more confident. "I believe you are mistaken."

"You are holding a vampire with almost two thousand years of combat experience and master Mercenary Guild status as well as one half of a warrior-mage pair with journeyman status," Sethri said. "We are prepared to offer a substantial sum for their returns."

Whatever it was, Victory would pay it without question. But she had a feeling this solution would be too easy.

Proving her right, Octavian said, "While your offer is both heartfelt and expected, I'm afraid I cannot negotiate their return. Their presence would be more advantageous to you at this time than your money would be to us."

"As the Guildmaster for Limani," Max said, "I must remind you that refusing to accept ransom for Guildmembers can incur the Roman Army a substantial fine."

Slamming a hand down on this pile of papers, the aide said, "The Roman army does not hire mercenaries. We employ honest soldiers."

The Mercenary Guild of the New Continent had stricter policies than did the old-fashioned Guild system still used in Europa. If this aide was not a native, his prejudices were understandable. Victory had seen the best and worst the occupation had to offer over the centuries. "No one is disputing the integrity of the Roman army," she said. "However, the men you hold are not enemy soldiers. Whether you like it or not, if you're going to fight Limani, you're going to have to deal with mercenaries."

"And that requires you abide by Guild rules," Sethri said. He opened the briefcase again to remove a different set of papers. "Here are the Guild's ransom protocols to be used when the opposing sides are countries, instead of individuals or business organizations." He handed them across the table to the aide, who plucked them from Sethri's hand as if expecting the paperwork to bite him.

Octavian took the papers and scanned down the first page. "While I'm sure there are established procedures for such situations, I'm still afraid I can't ransom my prisoners." He placed the sheaf on the table and looked back at them.

Stalemate, once again. This was going nowhere, fast. Victory thought even faster. "You realize how few options this leaves us."

Octavian nodded, once. "I do."

"Then tell us this," Max said. "Is Rome planning to invade Limani?"

The aide looked about to grab Octavian's arm, but he held back. Ignoring him, Octavian said, "Yes."

And that was their cue to get the hell out while the going was good. Victory stood, followed immediately by Max. "Then we thank you for your hospitality and will take our leave now," she said. "Sethri?"

Securing his briefcase, Sethri rose to his feet. The aide laughed, saying, "You think we're going to let you three walk out of here? Guards!"

"No," Octavian said, remaining in his seat. "They came in peace. We will let them go in peace." He gestured to the guards the aide had summoned to join them. "Please escort our guests back to their vehicle and return their weapons."

Victory exchanged bemused looks with Max. And here she'd expected to take on the entire force to make it back out. They might stand a chance of getting home yet.

She looked over her shoulder once while they walked back toward the bridge. Octavian stood watching them leave. She caught his eyes, forcing him to look away.

Stillness reigned in the apartment. The candle flames held a hint of flicker, and the magical sigils burned with steady light. Toria couldn't tell whether Syri even breathed.

The elven girl's exploratory presence in her mind stabilized. Her brain no longer felt like a ransacked room, but rather the subject of a scientific and methodical search. If she hadn't spent the last ten years of her life preparing for long workings like this one, Toria's back and rear end would be screaming in agony. Instead, she compartmentalized the discomfort in an area Syri had already passed over, dismissing it from her mind.

But while she could ignore the physical discomfort, her impatience and anticipation were another story. She understood the necessity of Syri getting this just right. That didn't mean she could stay calm about it. When would she get to talk to Kane?

Soon. Syri's lips didn't move, but she picked up on Toria's thoughts and responded to them. *Wait, never mind. Now.*

With little ceremony, the room around Toria winked out of existence. Blackness engulfed her. Before she had time to panic, the image of a different location altogether swam into view. But now she looked with another's sight.

The world lay tilted, and she saw the inside of a canvas structure from the perspective of one lying on their side. Backlit silhouettes patterned the canvas of a small, enclosed pavilion. A second cot sat on the other side of the tiny space, this one empty except for a few rumpled blankets.

More silhouettes passed outside the tent, human-sized ones. Now volume faded in, the distinct sounds Toria knew accompanied an encampment full of military personnel with no immediate plans and under no direct threat.

The head she looked out of shifted, the body rolling on its side to crumple a pillow in its arms and rest its face in the crook of an elbow. Even from this perspective, she knew that sprawl anywhere. Syri had done it!

Kane?

The body jerked, and a wave of seasickness passed through Toria's own body when Kane surged to his feet, giving every corner of the pavilion a wild survey.

Don't do that. Slow is good. Please.

"Toria?"

Kane's frantic searching halted, and her stomach calmed. In a lower voice, he repeated, "Toria?" With a thump that threatened to collapse the cot, he sat back down. *You're in my head?*

It would seem so.

How?

Syrisinia. Elven girl. You know her? She sent a mental image of Syri as Kane might have known her, sinuous movements in the middle of the Twilight Mist's dance floor.

Waves of love and worry and happiness and sorrow crashed over her, and she sagged under the weight. *Kane! It's okay. Calm down, love.*

Sorry. It's just...it's been tough the past few days.

Are you hurt? Where's Asaron?

Silence. The room blacked out again, and Toria worried she'd lost connection. But then another wave of love rolled over her, and she realized Kane had shut his eyes. When he opened them again, he stared down at his bare upper body. No, his left wrist, encircled by the loose fingers of his other hand and resting on his crossed legs. Strips of pale cloth that contrasted with his dark skin wound around his wrist. Even in the dim light, Toria could see the red stains soaking through.

They won't give him anything other than pig's blood, or cow's blood. He can't survive on that. But we're doing the best we can.

No one knew how many millennia ago vampires had evolved to be humanity's natural predator. For all their versatility, they were still a very specific breed of creature. They could exist on the blood of another animal in a pinch, but not for long. Human blood alone contained all the essential nutrients needed to make a happy vampire.

Brilliant, in a twisted way. The Romans kept the vampire underfed, who then kept the mage weak—otherwise impossible without a powerful magic user of their own.

Where is he now?

They let him outside for a few hours during the night. They do the same for me every morning.

A flash of memory that wasn't hers unfolded in her mind through the link. Kane stood in the center of the ring, blocking a hailstorm of twigs and small stones with his arms. Now she noticed the masses of small bruises and cuts decorating his skin.

If I try to escape, they kill Asaron. If he tries to escape, they kill me. If he tries to eat anyone, they'll cut off all blood and he'll have only me to feed from. If I try to use magic, Asaron isn't brought back inside at dawn.

Despite the even tone in which Kane recited the rules he now lived under, the horror of their situation dawned on Toria. She cursed Max for not helping her. She could have saved them from this nightmare.

Don't be mad at Max.

Why the hell not? I wouldn't have failed today if he'd come with me.

Why? What happened today?

With another transfer of memory, Toria imparted all she had been through in the past few days. Waking by the river to discover her partner gone, Zerandan's diagnosis, her second failed rescue attempt, and her meeting with Octavian. She glossed over the more difficult parts, but she never could hide anything from Kane.

He fixated on the mental image of Octavian over Toria, grabbing her and touching her. Threatening Kane, in worse ways than he faced now. *I'll fucking kill him. He comes to check on us once a day. I can take him out.* His imagination had always been better than hers. The images of a broken and bloodied Octavian lying at Kane's feet startled her, despite her longing to exact the same form of vengeance.

I hate to be the voice of reason, but what about Asaron? You just said he'd die if you used magic. She could feel the frustration welling up in Kane. Despite the jolts it gave her insides, she did not complain when he stood to pace the length of the pavilion. *Mama and Max and the head of the council should be there now. They went to meet with Octavian to try and get you guys out.*

Too bad they won't give us up.

You're both members of the Guild. The Romans have to let Mama ransom you.

But we know too much.

What, the location of the camp? We know that anyway. Numbers? Armaments? Those aren't good excuses to deny ransom. She was pretty sure she shouldn't be reminding Kane of these facts. He'd always paid better attention to Max's lectures unless they involved direct combat.

A shadowy image overlaid Kane's immediate surroundings. *This.*

A cylindrical object perhaps half the length of Toria's town-car and as wide around as the trunk of a horse lay on the canvas flooring. Despite the fuzziness of its details, Toria noted the metallic shimmer of its surface and the small keypad and computer screen set in the top.

Clearer image? All of his other memories had been picture-perfect.

Best I can do. They blindfolded me before they brought me to wherever it's being kept. But it radiates power. Awful, disgusting power. Nauseating. So much that this is what I could see through the scarf.

Magic?

I don't know what it is. Kane sat up once more, swinging his legs up onto the cot. *Not any type of magic I've ever felt before. But I'm the naturalist. You're the techno-junkie.*

I'm sorry. I've never seen anything like it either. But it looks like a machine. Why did they bring you to it?

Octavian wanted me to see whether I could feel anything. I didn't tell the truth. Just that I could feel warmth on my skin from its direction. Which was true, but not all of it.

And that's why he said you could never leave?

That he couldn't risk it, yes.

She could feel Kane's memory of nauseating discomfort returning the more he maintained the image, so she studied it hard. The object's fuzziness didn't help much, but she memorized every possible detail. Was that striping on the metal? No, it looked like a series of numbers or letters printed down one side. One of the cylindrical ends was rounded to a point, while the other remained cut off at the edge. She couldn't make out the symbols on the keyboard, but it looked no larger than the one on her own computer. The screen was small, though, perhaps two hand spans wide and no more than one tall.

Movement on the screen? Despite the straining of her mental vision, it never resolved itself. But she did detect the faint hint of constant change coming from the screen. Like someone typing, but the rate was too regular. Or a...

No. Oh, no. It can't be. They can't. In the real world, her stomach twisted even more than it had during Kane's pacing.

What?

The question came in unison, from both her physical and mental companions. Her fear and tension must be bleeding through the double link with Syri like a waterfall.

Once upon a time, she'd made it her mission to catalog all the books in the manor's library. Jarimis died before she was born, but she felt like she knew the man based on the books he'd collected and done research on. History was his passion, and once upon a time, she'd been determined to follow in his footsteps. So she'd read all sorts of obscure things.

Such as books called *Weapons of the Last War*, and tech manuals for things like nuclear missiles. Toria pulled up a mental schematic, as much as she could remember, and compared it to Kane's hazy memories.

You really think that what I saw was a nuclear weapon, Tor?

What else could it be? I found a treatise by a European mage a few years ago on nuclear power plants, and what you felt matches everything she recorded about her experience with radioactive materials. The heat, the nausea.

Then this isn't good. This is worse than not good. Because I don't think Octavian knows what he has.

Ice gripped Toria's heart, but Syri asked the obvious question. *What the hell do you mean?*

He thinks it's a regular missile. His pet mage isn't too powerful, which is why they called me in.

And if they use that to hit Limani— Syri's mental voice came to an abrupt halt, and Toria could feel her horror seeping through the mental link.

They won't just be destroying the city so they can come in and take it over more easily. Toria forced the next words out, knowing they would be true despite her unwillingness to accept them. *They'll be ruining it. For a long time, longer than anyone except Dad and Mama have. Limani will be gone forever.*

"Admit it—that could have been a lot worse."

The rattling of the window at every rut in the road did nothing for Victory's headache. Perhaps she should remove her head from its current resting place against the pane of glass, but that required movement. "Whatever you say, Max."

"We didn't end up as prisoners," Sethri said.

Not a total failure, but a failure nonetheless. Now Victory rolled her neck to the side and rested her head against the backseat headrest. Better, but not by much.

"We'll rescue them, Victory," Max said.

She noticed his stare in the rearview mirror, but knew the shadows hid her from close examination. "Whatever you say, Max."

"We'll either rescue them," he said, "or they'll bust out on their own. They're not helpless."

"Then why wouldn't they have already?" Sethri craned his neck back and forth between them.

"Because the Romans are smart," she said, gathering the energy to sit forward and rest her chin on the shoulder of Max's seat. "They allow vampires in their territory, and they've got as many mages as any other country. The military knows how to keep such power contained."

Though she did hope their methods had improved over the past two hundred years. Hard to believe at times like these that she had once been a Roman citizen in the mortal life she could not remember. So had her sire and daywalker. Limani herself was a colony of immigrants, with more descendants of Roman and British expatriates than the original Greek settlers.

A week ago, the Romans were amicable neighbors and trade partners. Now their government had gone to hell, they insisted on dragging Limani down with them, and the British were nowhere to be seen.

That reminded her. "Sethri, have you sent—"

Max cut her off when he jerked the steering wheel to the left, slamming her into the seatbelt. "What the hell?" she managed to gasp out after regaining her balance in the backseat.

"Not me! Shit!" Max hit the brakes, hard, flinging Victory forward.

Sethri got the worst of the blow, and two sickening cracks merged together from the impact of his forehead and the fracturing windshield glass.

A second shattering sound, this time right next to her. Had she been sitting all the way back in the seat, the bullet would have hit her temple. Instead, it whisked behind her back, a hair's breadth away from slicing up her favorite coat.

"Incoming!"

She had no idea how Max managed to unbuckle his seatbelt, draw a gun, and get out of the truck in the space of what seemed like less than a second. After a few painful struggles with her own seatbelt, she kicked open the door.

The door hit a solid object, sending it flying away from the truck. Victory drew her sword when her feet touched the ground. She paused a beat, taking stock of the situation.

A situation that, for the moment, seemed to consist of one man with a large branch staggering back from the impact of the truck door, and Max wrestling with a second unknown assailant on the ground, his gun discarded near Victory's feet.

She brought her sword to bear when her own opponent looked ready to charge her again. He halted before acquiring a second mouth below the chin, raising his hands away from his body.

In her peripheral vision, Max had gained the upper hand. She heard more than saw him lay out his adversary with a solid blow to the side of the head. The man went limp, and Max hauled himself to his feet.

"Gun's next to the truck," Victory said, never taking her attention from the man in front of her. Max stooped to retrieve it, checking the weapon and taking up position next to Victory.

She didn't have Toria's innate ability to read people, but she didn't smell anything inhuman about the man. A deep breath confirmed none of the wild scents she associated with werecreatures. Round ears undisguised by his short hair, so elf was out. And he had a heartbeat, so no vampire.

Human. She assumed his friend was, too. Then that raised the question—

"Who the hell are you?" Max brought up the gun to aim at the man's chest. With the adrenaline of the fight still coursing through his body, he looked ready to pull the trigger. Since their other attacker was out cold, that wouldn't do at all.

"Max, go check on Sethri," Victory said, deflecting his attention. "I'll handle this guy." Before the words were all the way out, Max whirled back around to the truck. It took great effort to keep her eyes on the man in front of her and not rush to check on Sethri herself. "Now answer the question. And drop the stick."

He didn't move. Victory took a small step forward and pressed the tip of her sword against his throat. The branch fell from his fingers and landed on the road with a clatter.

"Good," she said. "Talk. Now."

"We're stopping you," he said.

"Congratulations. Stopping us from doing what?" Why couldn't she hear Sethri reassuring Max he was okay? Why couldn't she hear Sethri at all?

"From contacting the Romans."

She lowered her sword, ignoring the drop of blood welling from his neck. Self-control was a wonderful thing honed over the centuries, despite the bloodlust the twit had stirred within her by the attack. "Did you not notice that we are driving *back* to Limani?"

But he even had an answer for that. "Then we're preventing you from bringing news back to your false council."

Who else would send two idiots against a vampire and the head of the Mercenary Guild? "You're a Humanist." Random guys with an antique firearm? These could even be the same people to assault Syri and the werewolves.

He drew himself up straighter. "Yes, vampire."

So, they had a leak in their impromptu council. Victory liked to think none of her fellows had aligned with the Humanists, but she couldn't speak for every elf, every werecreature. A few of the pieces began to find places. Fabbri had known about the Romans before she could give Asaron's news to the council. The Humanists had contact with the invading army. That explained the small force mustered against them, and in time to catch them on their way back. The leak of their diplomatic plans occurred after this evening's meeting, not before.

Stepping forward, Victory rolled her hand over and bashed the iron pommel of her sword into the side of his head. It made a satisfying noise on impact, and he fell to the ground in a heap next to his compatriot.

The entire exchange took place in a matter of seconds, but she started a bit when Max touched her shoulder. "Is Sethri okay?"

She waited for Max to answer while she knelt next to the man to make sure he still had a pulse. She had misjudged her own power before. Not often, but when emotions were high, the bets were off. And humans were such fragile creatures.

Max still hadn't answered her. She tilted her head up, seeking his face against the stars. "Max?"

"Sethri's dead."

Victory didn't move for a few seconds. It wasn't possible. These two jerks didn't get anywhere near the truck.

"Victory, did you hear me?" When she did not respond right away, Max gripped her arms and pulled her back to her feet. He transferred his hold to her biceps, keeping her steady.

"You're joking." Despite the inappropriate timing for such a thing, he had to be. No other explanation.

"No," Max said. "I'm not. He hit his head hard enough on the windshield to do serious damage. I don't know exactly what happened, but he had no pulse when I got back to him."

Victory looked to the two bodies at their feet. "But...how? They never got to his side of the truck."

He shook her, just a bit, before steadying his hands again. "They didn't have to. It was when I swerved. We all got banged around. Sethri got it most."

Victory pulled out of Max's hands and dashed around the truck. Sethri's door was open, and Max had laid him back against the seat. No blatant signs of trauma such as a crushed skull, just a sheet of blood covering half of his face from a point on his forehead. She touched tentative fingers to his cheek, his slick blood coating her fingers.

She moved her fingers down to his neck, checking in vain for the faintest hint of a pulse, despite the heartbeat she didn't hear. There might still be time to get him back home, get him to the hospital or to one of the elven healers.

Max appeared at her shoulder. "Can't you—?"

"No!"

He shrank back when she whirled at him.

Realizing she still had her hand raised, he must have feared she would lash out. Victory paused to collect herself. "No. I can't save him."

"But surely it's not too late," Max said. "Or has enough time passed for brain damage to be a problem?"

"I don't know anything about brain damage," Victory said. She faced Sethri again, this time collecting one of his hands in her own. It still felt warm against her skin. "But that's the point. He's already dead. To turn someone, you don't kill them. You—" The explanation caught in her throat, and she dropped Sethri's hand. The warmth burned. She started over. "You bring them to the brink of death. Sethri is beyond that. If I drained him now, there would be no point." She backed a few feet away from the truck.

Without meeting her eyes, Max said, "I knew that."

"I know," Victory said. It helped to hear it. She'd had this conversation with the bereft many times over the years. Despite her own pain, she could still have it with Max. But right now, they didn't have the time. "We need to get out of here. We don't know if more will show up."

After a small shake of his head, bringing himself out of whatever thoughts immersed him, Max joined Victory away from the truck. "We bringing those two?"

"Damn straight," Victory said. "Got any rope?"

"In the back."

Time to mourn later. Max retrieved a coil of thin rope from the bed of his truck while Victory rearranged the unconscious men. They trussed the two up in a fashion guaranteed to make them miserable upon waking.

Victory couldn't kill the men she held responsible for Sethri's murder, but she could still make them pay in her own fashion. Max wouldn't stop her.

They didn't move Sethri to the backseat. Max seemed shocked when she waved off his suggestion to move the body, but there came a time when logic must prevail over romanticism. Right now, speed was of the essence.

When they retook their seats and Max started the engine again, a surreal curtain descended over Victory. Less than twenty minutes ago, they'd been on their way home. The Romans had been uncooperative, they didn't manage to rescue Kane or Asaron, and war was still imminent.

Victory stared out the back window, avoiding looking anywhere near Sethri's body, propped like a macabre doll in the front seat.

How had things gotten so much worse in the space of so little time?

Toria sat Syri at the kitchen table and fetched a glass of water to accompany the painkillers she'd dug out of the bathroom. The time spent sitting on the floor hadn't been good for the injured elven girl. Her walk was stiff, but she'd waved off Toria's offers of assistance.

Syri took the glass, swallowing the two pills dry before taking a long sip. "Thanks."

"You going to be okay?" Toria dropped into the seat next to Syri, her own body complaining at its earlier unfair treatment.

"Are you?" Syri's measured look bored into Toria's brain. "You haven't had the best couple of days yourself."

If Toria hadn't been sure Syri had shut down the link between them, she'd almost be convinced the girl knew her thoughts. But despite her apparent age and relative immaturity by elven standards, Syri still had a lot more years on her. That had to give her a clearer insight into the range of emotions that ran constant across the various species. "I'll be fine," she said. "But I wasn't the one hospitalized."

The dismissive gesture Syri made before finishing off her glass of water spoke volumes. "My own damn fault," she said. "As your mother has so kindly informed me."

"Dad told me to bring you dinner," Toria said. "I didn't know Mama hunted you down, too."

"Don't worry, she wasn't that bad." Syri made to rise, but Toria plucked the glass out of her hands and refilled it for her. "Trust me, I'm in no hurry for my own mother to find out about this. Good thing she's not in the city." At Toria's inquisitive look, she said, "I live with Zerandan. My mother is traveling with her consort in Britannia. Haven't seen her in about five years. So what's next, boss?"

"Wait, why am I in charge now?"

"Because we've done the easy part, getting in contact with Kane."

"Oh, so once it gets complicated, I have to start making the decisions?"

Syri must have heard the strain in Toria's voice. She set the glass on the table and reached over to gather both of Toria's hands in her own. In the gentlest tones Toria had heard from her yet, Syri said, "For the immediate future, Kane is safe. That is a huge load lifted from your shoulders. Your mother will be back soon with news of the army and report it to the council. Then we'll find her and tell her about the weapon. But we don't know when she'll be back. So what can we do in the meantime?"

Kane. Kane was safe. Not happy, not healthy, but safe. She could feel their link, its strength pulsing within her. The urge to send her love to him almost overwhelmed her, but she resisted it in time to save herself from the blinding pain. However, the thoughts alone steadied Toria.

"The Humanists," she said. "Mama and the council are busy dealing with the big problem, the one that might kill the whole city."

"But that doesn't matter if the fucking Humanists make it self-destruct from within." The old Syri was back. "What about that bitch on the council? She still at large?"

"Far as I know," Toria said. "You want a snack? I'm always starved after a long working." Syri emptied her glass again, and Toria grabbed it from the table before standing.

"That would rock," Syri said. "You cook, we'll talk."

Laughing, Toria began poking around in her cupboards. "Deal. So do you know anything about Emily Fabbri?"

"Other than the fact that she was just elected to council and was behind me getting kicked out of the Twilight Mists the other night with your dad, not much. You?"

Toria related her own personal experiences at Fabbri's restaurant while grating cheese over a plate of flour crisps and popping them into the microwave. She wound down the story as the timer dinged. "She hates me on a bunch of levels," Toria said, removing the hot plate with a dishtowel and setting it in front of Syri. "Because I'm a mage, because I'm a vampire's daughter, and because I probably pissed her off a lot when I called her out on her own territory." Three days ago? Time sure dragged when life was kicking your ass.

"And her influence is corrupting the city," Syri said. "She's like a fucking plague. Find the source, and we can prevent further spread."

At that, both girls dug into the chips, spending a few minutes dealing with hot melted cheese rather than the task ahead of them. When at last they'd scraped the plate clean and licked the last of bits of salt from their fingers, they could face the world again.

"So, we're going to hunt down Fabbri, then?" Syri said, pushing the plate closer to Toria.

"Aren't the elves and werecreatures already doing that?" Toria put the dirty plate in the sink. She'd deal with real life later.

"Well, I can find out where the elves have already searched," Syri said, "but I imagine they'll tell me to stay home like a good little girl. If they don't freak out that I've snuck out of the hospital and drag me back."

"I didn't realize your community was so small," Toria said.

"It sucks being the youngest."

Toria could relate. Youngest mage in Limani, youngest journeyman in this branch of the Mercenary Guild, youngest in her own family. "Yeah, it does. So we're on our own?"

"Looks like."

"Café Lizzette closed an hour ago," Toria said. "I'm sure it's already been searched, but it doesn't hurt to look again. Maybe we'll find some hint of where Fabbri is hiding."

"Can't hurt," Syri said. "Let's go."

Toria and Syri sat in Café Lizzette's parking lot, contemplating the building in front of them. Shadows hid the menacing sign in the front window, but Toria itched to take drastic measures. Like punching through the glass and ripping it to shreds. She would settle for kidnapping the sign's creator and handing the woman over to her mother.

It boggled her mind to think she was contemplating such an action. Yes, she was a member of the Mercenary Guild. Yes, she trained in the arts of warfare. She never envisioned herself using subterfuge and guerilla tactics. Throwing her signature lightning from the battlefield while Kane evacuated the wounded. Confronting an enemy one-on-one with crossed blades. That was the path she had imagined this occupation taking her, at least when she wasn't holed up in a chemistry lab while Kane haunted poetry readings.

"You think anyone's in there?"

Toria squinted through the night into the darkened restaurant windows before answering Syri's question. "Can you, I don't know, sense anyone?"

"Not from this distance," Syri said.

"Well, that sucks," Toria said. "I've got the perfect charm for this occasion. Too bad I can't use it."

"Only one way to find out, then." Syri unbuckled her seatbelt. "Shall we?"

The two girls left the town-car, shutting the doors with gentle clicks behind them. They stalked across the parking lot, lit by two single lampposts at the entrance of the road. This late at night, not even the fluorescent store signs were lit.

Picking the front lock to Fabbri's restaurant proved simple, and Toria gave a silent thanks to Asaron's patient lessons. But when Toria tried to turn the knob, it stuck.

"Damn." She knelt next to the door, but further investigation showed the lock did release. The ends of her fingers tingled when she touched the knob again, and she jerked her hand away.

"Let me see." Syri traded positions with Toria, crouching to place a hand on the knob while Toria kept watch on the silent street. "It's definitely unlocked. But the place is warded."

"What? Warded how?"

"To keep grumpy people like us out, I imagine," Syri said. "It doesn't feel designed to keep things in. It's not elven work though. Got that metallic mage tinge to it."

Warding meant shielded against magic. "Can you get through it?"

"I can try," Syri said. "I might need to pull more power from you."

"Go ahead, it's worthless to me right now." Bracing her back against the wall, Toria held a hand down to Syri, still scanning the street around them.

Syri threaded her fingers through Toria's and once again drew power from her. They must make a sorry sight. The journeyman warrior-mage with no magic and a habit of losing her swords, and the injured elven teenager left doing the jobs by all rights Toria should have.

The emanating power of Syri's manipulations tickled the back of Toria's neck, a sensation rather like spiders crawling up and down her spine. Converting human power must take more out of Syri than she let on, wearing down her own resources.

Let this night end soon.

"Got it." Syri used Toria's arm to haul herself to her feet, at the same time twisting the doorknob.

The door to the restaurant swung open, and Toria poked a head inside. No alarm blared, just the small flash of blue light announcing her entrance, and no one came running. Good signs so far. The dark eatery looked much different than she last remembered, with the chairs up on tables and lack of kitschy music to match the décor. "No second floor to this place. I guess the back?"

"Or the basement." Syri brushed by Toria to stride into the center of the room.

Not bothering to ask how Syri even knew about a basement, Toria caught up to the girl and led the way into the rear. Feeling like a character in a bad espionage movie, she drew the pistol from behind her back and clutched it in both hands, pointed toward the ceiling. The dagger was better for close combat, but Toria wasn't in a hurry to let anyone get near enough for a dagger to be effective. Syri was in no shape for a fight.

Toria pushed open the kitchen door, and did a quick sweep of the room. Dark, save for the emergency light above the back exit, and deserted. Stepping aside to let Syri in, she said, "So, that basement you were talking about?"

"Right. This way."

Toria followed her to the left, toward three doors. The first was marked "Storage" in stenciled letters, and the center door stood open, revealing a cluttered management office. Syri walked straight to the remaining door, and the two paused outside, listening for sounds below.

Syri gestured for her to go first. After giving her a mocking bow, resisting the urge to thank her for the honor, Toria tried the knob. This one wasn't locked, and her fingers didn't tingle with the presence of a ward.

It swung out, and the glow of dim light rose from the bottom of the stairs. Taking cautious steps and keeping the weapon at the ready, Toria crept down with Syri sticking close behind her. The basement spread to the left, but the stairwell walls stretched all the way to the bottom. They were blind until they reached the last few steps.

Toria poked her head around the corner, ready to pull back and make a break for it at any second. Though boxes and crates filled the majority of the large basement, the low light shone from a small lamp in a far corner. There, the boxes had been stacked to partition off a small room, and she could see the edge of a mattress poking out from between them. Now that they weren't moving, Toria could hear small snores emanating from the corner.

Breathing into Toria's ear, Syri said, "It's Fabbri. Pretty smart. She must have come back after she knew this place had been cleared."

Keeping her own voice low, trusting in the sensitivity of elven ears, Toria said, "You sure?"

"I'm sure. Let me handle this."

Feeling like an idiot, but needing to ask anyway, Toria repeated, "You sure?"

Syri patted her on the shoulder and drifted past Toria down the last of the steps, making Toria's earlier stealth sound like a stampede. Ghosting through the maze of stored goods, she rounded the bend protecting the snores.

Toria started at the sound of a muffled *thump*. Then, Syri said, "Got her!"

Gripping the pistol tight, Toria wound her way through the basement until she reached Syri's side. At their feet lay a pajama-clad Emily Fabbri, sprawled on the mattress and covered in quilts. The snores had stopped, at least.

Toria transferred her gaze to Syri. "What did you do?"

"Put her into a deeper sleep," Syri said. "She won't wake up until I tell her to. So now we take her to your mother or whoever can take charge of her."

"This can't have been that easy," Toria said, looking back at the prone body below them. She replaced the pistol in the holster at her back. "But I'm not about to complain after everything else we've been through. C'mon, let's get her over to Daliana's place since I doubt my mom's back yet."

"Sounds like a plan," Syri said. "You get her shoulders."

Daliana collected Fabbri's unconscious body when Toria and Syri showed up on her back steps. "I cannot believe you two," she said, directing the floating body with small finger gestures. It preceded the three women into the house and settled onto a couch.

Fabbri never stirred, not even when her leg fell off the side of the couch and her bare foot hit the hardwood floor with a thud.

"We're just lucky?" Toria collapsed onto the recliner next to the sofa. Syri dropped to the floor at her feet, stretching all the way out on an area rug with a purr of contentment.

Daliana replaced Fabbri's leg and covered her with a quilt. "While I find it amusing that you two did in one evening what twenty of us have been trying to accomplish for days, you do realize your mother is going to be outraged?"

"Nah," Toria said. "She'll be pleased I took the initiative." She hoped. Did the small clock on the mantle really read half past three in the morning? Time did fly when you were breaking into buildings and kidnapping people.

"Despite disobeying every single one of her orders?" The front doorbell chimed, and Daliana retreated with one last shake of her head.

"How long is she supposed to be out?" Toria waited for Syri's answer, closing her eyes and laying her head against the back of the recliner. Her exhaustion was catching up with her, and the chair threatened to lull her straight to sleep.

"Until I say so," Syri said. "Hopefully I didn't misjudge the strength since I was using your power instead of my own."

Oh dear. Toria tried to feel concern, but lacked the necessary energy. "Hope you didn't give her brain damage or anything."

"Give who brain damage?" Max's voice sounded from the hallway.

Toria shot out of the recliner. She collected herself in the middle of the room while Syri struggled to her own feet. "Good evening, Max." Her nonchalance sounded false even to her own ears.

The head of the Mercenary Guild, her boss and mentor, filled the doorway, his gaze shifting from them to the body on the couch and back again. "I'm not even going to ask how you two pulled this one off." He entered the room and stole Toria's seat. "Better warn you, your mother's in the front room with Daliana."

While she felt her skin pale with that bit of news, Toria had more pressing concerns. "Where's Kane?"

Max met her eyes, his gaze steady. "Octavian wouldn't release him to us."

"What?" Toria's nails dug into her palms, a hold on reality to prevent her from collapsing. "Do you have any idea what they're doing to them?"

"We were assured they were safe," Max said. "But being a prisoner of war is no vacation."

Syri placed a hand on Toria's arm, but she ignored the elven girl's look of concern. "They're starving Asaron," she said. "Keeping Kane drained so neither of them is strong enough to escape."

"Damn it." Now Victory's voice came from the entrance to the room. "I knew something like this would happen."

Toria whirled around. Victory strode into the center of the room, and Toria wrapped herself in her mother's cool arms. "I'm sorry, Mama." She buried her face in the crook of Victory's neck, inhaling the familiar vanilla scent of her mother's shampoo.

"Don't be sorry, love," Victory said, murmuring in Toria's ear and squeezing her once. "Daliana told me what you two did. I'm so proud of you."

Lifting her head and taking a short step back, Toria dropped her arms to clutch Victory's hands. "Even though I didn't stay at the hospital with Dad?"

"What's good isn't always right," she said. "Cliché, I know, but still true. I might not be pleased, but I understand when it's easier to ask forgiveness than permission."

"Spoken like a true mercenary," Max said. "And she's not the only proud one, girl."

With that load lifted from her shoulders, Toria broke her more important news. "Syri managed to get me in contact with Kane."

"At least we know for sure they're alive," Victory said. "Octavian wasn't even willing to discuss a ransom. We'll get them soon, though."

That, Toria knew without a doubt. With Asaron being held, Victory must be going through the exact same riot of emotions. Toria considered herself stubborn, but her mother had had centuries to perfect the art. Time to break the bad news. "Ma—"

Daliana brushed past Toria and Victory to stand by Fabbri. She placed two fingertips, which glowed green, on the unconscious woman's forehead. "I called the rest, Victory. They're on their way."

"Good, thank you," Victory said, turning her attention away from Toria. "We'll be meeting in the front room?"

"Yes," Daliana said. "I'll go put the coffee on?"

"Bless you," Max said. His tone belied the fact that he looked dead on his feet.

More political stuff. Toria shared a look of mild resentment with Syri. Time to be sent home again like good little girls, despite all they'd done that evening.

"I'll make up the guest room upstairs first," Daliana said. "The girls can rest while we talk."

Toria waited for her mother to disagree, but Victory surprised her. "Good idea. Okay with you, Toria?"

"Um, sure. That'd be great." Unexpected, but she wasn't about to complain. "Wake us up when you guys make a decision?"

"I wouldn't dream otherwise," Victory said. "You are the heroes of the hour, after all."

Even more unexpected. Victory gave Toria another hug before accompanying Daliana out of the room, Syri trailing behind.

"Wait, Toria." Max reached up to touch her elbow, stopping her from following Syri. "I need to speak with you."

Time for the other shoe to drop. "Yes, sir?"

Max opened his mouth to begin, then paused with a significant look toward the occupied couch.

Toria dismissed Fabbri with a wave. "Don't worry, she's out."

Max's shoulders loosened. "You understand we're vastly outnumbered right now, yes?"

Since that was the exact impression she'd received from Kane, Toria said, "Yep. You have no idea how well I understand that."

"Then you'll understand why you are now the proud owner of a battlefield promotion. Congratulations, Mercenary Torialanthas Connor." Max stumbled over her full name a bit, but it did not detract from the weight of his proclamation.

She was stunned. Even her journeyman status was tenuous until she finished college and could, well, journey around with Kane.

Max softened. "Be happy, but also be wise. We need all the fighters we can get right now. But this still isn't going to be easy."

"I understand," Toria said. "There's another perk, too."

"Yes?"

"If I get kidnapped with Kane, you can charge the full ransom price for me."

Max snorted. "That's my girl. Always looking on the bright side. At least I know you've been paying attention to something other than sword work."

"One more thing." Toria paused, unsure of how to break the news that the situation they faced was even worse than he thought.

He must have sensed the gravity of her attitude, for he sobered at once. "What's wrong?"

"Have you ever heard of a nuclear weapon?"

"And that, ladies and gentlemen, is where we stand." Max finished his speech and resumed his seat on the piano bench in Daliana's formal sitting room.

Victory scooted over a few more inches to make room for him. They had all squeezed in, since no one wanted to leave Fabbri unsupervised. It wasn't like Toria could ward the house in her present state.

"What did you guys do with Sethri's body?" Lorus said. The pain in his voice crept through the weresnake's natural stoicism.

"We dropped him off at the hospital," Max said. "I called in Mason, the physician under contract with the Mercenary Guild. He took charge of the body directly from us and will take care of things on that end. The death of the head of the council isn't something we really want to make public yet."

"And the two men who—" Lorus halted, unable to voice whatever he'd intended to say.

"Locked up in my basement," Daliana said.

Victory brushed a finger over the wood covering the piano keys. She had washed her hands when they'd arrived, but she could still feel Sethri's blood. His murderers would get a fair trial once the city's more immediate problems were taken care of. But they wouldn't be held in comfort. No couches and quilts for them downstairs.

"So, any other questions before we start the next stage of planning?" Max said.

"One, sort of." From her spot on the floor, Genevieve raised a tentative hand. "I, um, don't even know what a nuclear weapon is. You said it's just a bomb or missile, right? What's the big deal?"

Victory gaped at her, along with Max and Daliana, but Tristan nodded in embarrassed agreement. Victory couldn't blame them for their ignorance. Not all of them had been around for centuries, as she and Daliana had, or studied military history, like Max and Lorus.

"You know what the Wasteland is? The settlers at the edge can barely eke out a living," Daliana said. More cautious expressions of affirmation. "The center of this continent used to be lush farmland around a major river. The river's gone. And not much grows there now, and certainly not well."

"So what would this weapon do to Limani?" Tristan said. "Destroy every living thing?"

"Destroy every living thing, yes," Victory said. "And every building. And ruin this land for millennia to come."

"No one knows when, or if, the Wasteland will ever become viable again," Daliana said. "I used to treat refugees from the area. The war was brutal."

"And from what Toria told me based on her contact with her partner," Max said, "the Roman commander doesn't even know what they have."

"What?" Victory said. "You didn't mention that."

"Octavian even wanted Kane to study the thing," Max said. "Chances are he found it in a bunker somewhere, missed in the global disarmament and forgotten."

"Until now." Victory's heart chilled by yet another degree. "So not only is it a weapon of incredible destructive power no one knows how to use, it's an old and unstable weapon." From what she knew and could read of them, her fellow councilmembers had shifted from uncertainty to fear. Good for them to be worried, but she wasn't about to start a panic. Continuing into the silence, Victory said, "You all know this information can't leave this room."

"We have a duty to our people to keep them aware of the danger they're in," Tristan said.

"And cause a full-scale riot?" Max said.

Now Bethany spoke up. Victory had wondered when the woman would put her thoughts on the situation forward. This should be good. "You're already hiding the fact that the leader of our government has been murdered. It's a tragedy, yes, but doesn't need to be hidden. No one has bothered to confirm the rumors that the

Roman military is at our borders. Half of my friends think it's troop exercises and aren't concerned in the slightest. How far is the military willing to go to 'protect' our people? If we fail, they'll be even more defenseless without preparation."

"And if we tell them, there'll be panic in the streets," Lena said. "Yes, a much better idea."

"We don't have time to police the city and deal with the Romans," Max said. "And we need to face reality here. The head of the government is dead. We don't have time to hold elections right now, not even internal ones. We obviously don't know who to trust among the human councilmembers, or else they'd be here with us." He paused, looking around the room to meet each person eye to eye. "So we've come up with a temporary solution."

That was Victory's cue. "Martial law," she said. "Or close enough. We are now in charge. The human councilmembers are temporarily stripped of their power unless we know we can trust them." That still didn't solve the problem of a leak in this council, but that would be dealt with soon enough. "This means we can deal with the Romans on our own terms, without having to balance Humanist politics."

"So, the military's in control of the city?" Bethany said. "That makes Max in charge?"

"No," Max said. "Not just me. All the members of the council in this room are. It's just convenient that the two most experienced military personnel in this city happen to be included."

"What about all of the weres we've recruited to fight the Romans?" Tristan said. "I know at least a few won't be happy they've been drafted."

"They'll get battlefield commissions for order's sake," Max said. "But it is a voluntary action, like volunteering was in the first place."

"I know we're all scared," Victory said. She didn't hesitate to include herself in that statement. "But we have to remain calm. We'll deal with this. This idea makes it easier for all involved to deal with both the Romans and Humanists successfully."

"And how does this deal with the Humanists?" Lena said.

Victory could always count on the teacher in her longtime friend to make sure people followed through. "Probably the one thing you guys might have a real problem with." Even she had a problem with it, angry with the prejudiced idiots as she was. "We declare the Humanist movement illegal." She awaited the outcry.

It didn't come. "Now that's the first really good idea you've had," Bethany said.

She waited for dissent. This couldn't be that easy. But nods met her from around the crowded room.

"I bet if we really dug into the city's constitution," Lena said. "We'd find something saying that. And if not, it's long past time it was added. The world has changed since Limani was established."

"And while it's a shame we should have to enforce the ideals the city was founded under," Tristan said. "We wouldn't be the first to do it."

"All in favor of the proposals?" Max said. He raised his hand first.

Victory followed suit, Lena and Bethany close behind. She wasn't about to remind Bethany that she didn't have voting power, since she appreciated the support. Soon every hand in the room was in the air.

"That settles that," Tristan said. "Okay, Victory and Max are now our fearless leaders. What do we do now?"

"Wait, what?" Max shook his head.

"No, he's right," Victory said. "I saw this coming. Martial law still means the military is in control, no matter how we pretty it up for our circumstances. Despite my age, Guild law still says you outrank me. And since Limani is now at war, the entire local Guild has now become the city's military force. So what are your orders, General?"

Victory paced her kitchen while Toria worked through a full breakfast of oatmeal, toast, juice, and coffee. Her daughter would need her strength for the upcoming day, and Victory had readied one with all the care of a mother sending her lone offspring into battle.

"Mama, now you're starting to make me nervous."

Victory forced herself to sit at the kitchen table. "Is that gladius going to work out for you okay?"

After swallowing, Toria said, "It'll have to do, since nothing else was light enough. Hopefully I won't even have to use it."

"Hopefully," Victory said. "I love you, sweetheart, and I have every confidence in your abilities, but I am very, very glad Max placed you in the reserve guard."

"I'm glad you have confidence," Toria said. "I feel pretty close to worthless. Can't even do the job I'm trained to do."

"Not without reliable magic and not without Kane to back you up." Victory hooked her ankles around her chair legs rather than stand to pace again. "And certainly not carrying a blade you're not entirely comfortable with."

Toria pursed her lips. "Thanks for the reminder."

Victory would give anything in the world to trade places with her daughter. But Max planned this sortie for late morning, to get a feel for the ground unhindered by darkness. Not all of the regular mercenary force had the heightened senses.

"I'd better go see whether Syri is ready for me upstairs." Toria placed her empty dishes in the sink and snagged an apple before heading out of the room. Victory hoped she intended to pawn it off on Syri. The elven girl needed her strength to heal.

The doorbell rang. Max was early. Toria pounded back downstairs to let him in, directing him toward the kitchen. That was Victory's cue to ready another mug of coffee, and Max entered the kitchen right as she spooned in his second lump of sugar.

"You have made my morning," he said, accepting the mug and settling into Toria's vacant seat. "We have good troops, but organizing them to include the werecreatures has been like herding cats. Sometimes literally."

"Did you get any sleep last night?" The circles under his eyes did not bode well.

"I caught a nap in my office a little before dawn," he said. "I'll be fine." Victory's silence spoke volumes, because after taking a sip of coffee, Max said, "Toria will be fine, too."

"I wish I could be with you all today," Victory said, laying her head down on the table. Helplessness was not a feeling she was used to. She'd spent far too long being the master of her own destiny, fighting either alongside Asaron or with her sword as her single ally. She'd never felt that political life made her weak, but it was still tough to bow to Max's wishes rather than demand that he push the plan back to sundown.

"Trust me, I wish you could, too."

Max's frankness reassured her far more than any platitudes he might have offered. "Thanks, hon."

"I'm serious. I've got plenty of seasoned warriors, but a lot of journeymen are being given battlefield promotions like Toria. Add in all the weres and the elves who aren't used to military discipline, and I'm almost desperate to have you helping me run interference."

"Next time?"

"Hell, yes." Max reached across the table to grab her hand, and Victory raised her head to meet his eyes. "This is a preliminary run. Gather info, figure out what we're really up against. Damn straight the next fight is going to be at night, with you in the thick of it."

"Damn straight," Victory echoed. "Finish your coffee and grab a snack from the fridge. I'll go make sure the girls are ready." She stood and crossed to the other side of the table, where she pressed a chaste kiss against Max's cheek. He would keep Toria safe.

Of course, she rather hoped Toria would do the same for him. If anything happened to Max, and with Asaron still languishing in captivity, that would leave her in charge.

Toria waved out the back window of Max's borrowed van, knowing her mother would be watching from her bedroom window, hidden in the shadows of the heavy drapes. When they turned a corner in the long driveway, she pulled her arm inside the window and settled back in her seat.

She put on a tough front for everyone around her, including her mother, but she would have given her right arm for Victory to be beside her, also geared up for battle.

Max drove into town, back toward the Hall—the staging point for the mission slated to begin at noon. It was ten in the morning, and already Toria wanted the day to be over.

Syri laid her head on Toria's shoulder. That morning, she had once again delved into Toria's mind and activated all of the battle defenses Toria had stored away. Today Syri would play Kane's part, wielding magic to protect them while Toria relied on her borrowed sword.

When Max first proposed the plan, Toria had felt it a betrayal of Kane. But this liaison was temporary, and soon she would have her real partner back.

"I have a rather silly question," Syri said, keeping her voice low.

Matching her whisper, Toria said, "Yeah?"

"Have you ever killed anyone before?"

An easy answer, but Toria hesitated, then she nodded once. That had been a long time ago, by human standards. Three years would be a blink to Syri. "It was self-defense." She looked out the window at the passing trees. "A vampire after Mama for killing her sire decades ago."

"The werepanther crisis," Syri said. "I wasn't in the city, but I heard about it. The ringleader—same vampire?"

"Same vampire," Toria said.

"I've never killed anyone." Syri replaced her head, and Toria pressed her cheek to elven-soft hair.

"Hopefully neither of you will today," Max said. He sought Toria's eyes in the rearview mirror. "You're in charge of all the promoted journeymen, Toria. I expect you to keep them out of trouble."

"Don't worry," Syri said. "We're good at staying out of trouble."

"Or at least getting ourselves out of it," Toria said, joining Syri's battle-strung giggles.

Hours later, Toria wasn't laughing. She crept through the underbrush, gladius in hand and Syri close by. Three other former journeymen walked strung out behind her, also silent in the dim afternoon forest.

She paused before they entered a small clearing, keeping to the shadows of the trees. The others halted in their tracks and stayed low behind her. While she didn't know many of them beyond sight, name, and perhaps a training session or two, she knew that Max had given her the best. "Anything?"

A dark green hood concealed Syri's blonde hair, but a few wisps escaped when she shook her head. "Nope. I think we outran them. And there's no sign through here. I think we can risk it."

With battlefield gestures drilled into her that she never thought she'd have to use with anyone but Kane, Toria motioned for the others to follow her forward. Syri took point, rifle clutched in her hands. They stuck to the tree line, skirting the clearing.

The explosions still rang in Toria's ears. She had been positioned with Syri and the others by the caravan of long-distance vehicles that ferried the mercenary force out to the major river crossing. Max nixed the bridge as too frontal of an attack, so they'd returned to the spot of the kidnapping.

Despite the fact that she itched to join the main body, Toria remained with her own small troop. All seven of them could drive, and they held the responsibility of keeping the precious vehicles safe, whether it meant picking up the mercenaries on a retreat or hightailing it out of there themselves at the first sign of the Romans and heading for the backup rendezvous.

"Remind me again what plan C was?" Syri's low voice carried back to Toria's ears.

"You mean yell 'oh shit!' and run like hell?" Toria suppressed a manic giggle. She'd been in worse situations than this, she was sure of it.

What the hell was Max thinking, putting her in charge?

After the main body had departed, Toria called for the perimeter scouts to come in. She and Syri had walked out to meet them before the first three could reach the vehicles.

The loss of the majority of the Guild's long-distance vehicles was devastating enough, but there were worse things to lose. Poor Freya had been the sole casualty of the sabotage. The nurse was the Guild's backup medic—she'd requested the rearguard since her three-month-old son remained at home with her husband. The van housing the mobile medical unit exploded first, followed in a violent chain by the other vehicles. The other three scouts were fine. The blast threw their replacements to the ground, singeing them a bit—Freya never stood a chance.

And now there were five.

Syri drew to a halt when they reached the other side of the clearing, and Toria gathered everyone around her. "Okay, back through the woods. We'll head to the secondary meeting point and wait for the others there."

"No way," Ari said. "The Romans bypassed the force already. They're probably on their way to Limani right now. We have to get back and warn the city. Do what we can there."

None of Toria's scouts had seen any sign of the Romans before the explosions. Their position had been secure. Max made sure of that before he led the others out.

"Think, girl," Syri said. "The trucks didn't explode because they were shot at."

Taba, the wereleopard, picked up on Syri's train of thought. "We were set up?"

Toria nodded once. "They must have been rigged to blow before we even left Limani. Humanist work, probably."

Except for Syri, they all gaped at her. "That's impossible," Ari said.

"You have no idea what they've been up to the past few days," Syri said.

To Toria's chagrin, every single one of them focused on her rather than their surroundings. This needed to be finished, fast.

"Care to enlighten us?" Ari said.

"We don't have time for this," Toria said. "The river docks are closer than the city. We'll borrow wheels there and head to the meeting point, secure the location for when the others get back."

"We should call back while we're there and request another medic from the hospital." Ah, another voice of reason in the group. But introductions that morning had been swift, and Toria couldn't remember the lanky guy's name. Renan? He was a new city resident, but Max had vouched for him.

"Good idea," she said. "You're in charge of that."

A low mutter from the other side of the group caught Toria's ear over the forest sounds around them. "What was that?"

Ari stepped away from Taba, lifting her chin in defiance. "I said, maybe he should be in charge of everything."

Toria's skin chilled under her thick leather armor in the stifling summer humidity. "What the hell is that supposed to mean?" They did not have time for this. She took a quick swig from her canteen.

"C'mon, we all know you're only running this show because you're the Guildmaster's favorite."

She'd always suspected that Max preferred Kane, but Ari's insinuation still made her bristle. "Maybe Max thought I was the best person for the job."

"You don't even have the respect to call him Master Asher like the rest of us," Ari said.

Syri cut off Toria's retort. "Enough," she said. "Time to move out, not stand around and bicker like schoolchildren. Did you all even have any idea that three Roman scouts are heading in this direction?"

To their credit, they all snapped into defensive positions. "Where?" Toria said.

"Oh, we're still fine," Syri said. "They're within elven hearing range, not human. But we need to straighten up and move. Now."

While not as harrowing, the jog to the docks was no less stressful than the rest of the trip so far. Toria felt Ari's eyes boring into the back of her head, but she didn't have the energy or inclination to break her momentum in order to tell the girl off.

At least the breeze caused by their passing cooled her down a little bit. She hesitated to drain the water in her canteen, unsure whether they would make it to the river before the scouts Syri overheard came upon them.

There was a subtle alteration in the humidity around her, and Toria knew they were nearing the river. Soon the docks would be in sight, and they would have a short time to breathe before she had to beg Master Rhaavi for a truck and the use of the radio.

"Heads up!"

Taba's voice alerted Toria to their immediate danger just before she felt a breeze pass her cheek, followed by the thunk of an arrow piercing a tree to her left. She dove to the ground, rolling to her side and drawing her pistol. After all of her charges hit the ground or scattered behind trees, Toria sighted through the foliage.

Before she could call out a request to Syri, her vision layered with magesight. Bless the girl for having experience with combat, however limited, and anticipating her needs. Still no replacement for Kane, but she would do in a pinch.

Crouched in the brush next to her, Taba pulled his sweatshirt off and tossed it aside, then unlaced and pulled off his boots. "Cover me," he said, the words muddling when his teeth lengthened and the bones in his face shifted. In a handful of heartbeats, a spotted leopard kicked out of a pair of jeans and ghosted out into the foliage.

Toria watched his golden shape—in both color and magical aura—slip through the underbrush. The forest, already a myriad of summer-bright greens and browns, overlaid with shadows of color that made reality appear drab by comparison. She dismissed the familiar magical shine of nature, instead concentrating on seeking out any sense of wrongness.

There. A few hundred yards away, protected by trees and thick brush. They were still now, having lost their easy targets. Three simple human auras, shades of putrid orange radiating even more fear and apprehension than her own small crew. One also contained tinges of blue, a valiant attempt at mental shielding by a weak telepath.

She had them in her sights. Any other day, she'd pull power from Kane, call down a bolt of power, and blast them into a crater.

Not an option this afternoon. She doubted that "Lightning Bolt" was one of the charms Syri had dug out of her brain to set in her own mind.

None of the other journeymen were mages of any sort, and she already knew Syri's magical abilities ran more to the mental than the combative. Time to handle this the old-fashioned way. Taba's silent figure crept around the Roman scouts, and Toria knew he would circle around behind them.

"Can they see us?" Ari's soft voice came from behind a nearby tree.

"I've got their position. Three hundred yards east, right between that pair of large oak trees," Toria said. "And you're right—they know we're here, but nothing more. Ari and Renan, circle around to the right and left, stay low. I'll go straight. Taba's blocking their retreat. Syri, stay here and keep a lookout for any surprises."

"Capture or incapacitate?" Ari was all business now, a fact Toria much appreciated.

"Incapacitate, however necessary," Toria said. "We don't have the time or manpower to deal with prisoners. Ready check?" A chorus of low affirmatives met her question. "All out. Now."

Shifting her weight and rolling onto her knees, Toria drew the gladius at her side and rose to a crouch. Renan and Ari disappeared in her peripheral vision, and she led the stealthy charge.

Field-promoted they might all be, but Toria should never have doubted any of her command's abilities. Max had overseen their training, after all.

The orange auras flared neon at Renan's wordless battle cry. Toria surged forward with the others when the three Romans scattered from their positions, blades drawn and arrow knocked. A feline scream echoed through the trees.

Renan tackled one to the ground, where they sprawled for a second before grappling each other for the Roman's gun. The rearmost scout was jerked back into the trees, bow bashed from his hands, and Toria thought she saw a glimpse of golden fur and snarling teeth. Then she had no attention to spare for the fight, clashing swords with the leading attacker.

She deflected his gladius aside with a screech of metal, knocking into his chest with her shoulder before rebounding away. Ari stood ready to cross blades with him while Toria collected herself and prepared to attack once more. Wishing for the wicked point of her rapier, Toria thrust her sword toward the scout while his attention was on the other woman.

But Octavian wouldn't send green troops out. With a dodge bordering on elven or vampiric grace, the scout extracted himself from between them. The tip of Toria's sword left a light scratch on his chest plate, nowhere near the shoulder joint she had targeted.

A gunshot rang out, and Ari screamed. Another crack, and the scout in front of her, preparing for a charge, dropped to the ground with half of his face splattered away in a mass of blood and shattered bone.

The day-to-day Toria would feel horror, revulsion, fear. But that Toria was gone, replaced by one in full battle mode. In stark contrast to her younger self, who'd impaled a vampire and dropped into immediate panic and shock, now she whirled around in search of the next danger.

Ari's scream. The other girl had collapsed to the ground a few feet away, blood gushing from her stomach. Renan's initial target lay sprawled on the ground, unmoving, and now he helped Toria confront the remaining Roman scout.

When Toria spun on him, he dropped the gladius in his hand and drew a small knife from behind his back. Renan was closest, and he dove forward. But the Roman raised his arm in one smooth motion and the knife embedded itself in Renan's chest.

Renan's momentum kept him falling forward, and he crashed to the ground.

Before Toria could react, another gunshot rang out and a matching bloom of red appeared at the scout's throat. He collapsed to the ground, twitching.

With her magesight still active, Toria stared at Renan's and Ari's dark bodies. This was…not how the skirmish was supposed to go. Taba trotted out of the underbrush, his muzzle dripping with blood. He sniffed each body, then padded over to lean against Toria's side. His shoulders came above her waist, and she buried her fingers in the fur behind his ears.

Syri emerged from the trees, slinging the rifle back across her shoulders. She knelt next to Ari to check the woman's wounds. Toria approached Renan's body and rolled him onto his back. At such close range, the Roman's knife had buried to the hilt in his chest, right where his heart was. Despite the futility of the motion, Toria felt for a pulse in Renan's neck. Nothing. Perhaps that was a blessing. Dirt and dead leaves coated his face.

The reality and terror of this situation would come crashing down on her the second she stopped to reflect. But right now, Toria was in control.

"How's Ari?" She rose to her feet and turned to Syri, who'd placed her hands on Ari's chest.

The elven woman shook her head. "Too much blood loss, too quickly." Her voice quiet, Syri pulled her hands away and rose to shaky feet with Toria's help. "I'm sorry," she said without preamble.

"Not your fault," Toria said. "There was nothing we could do."

"No, it's still my fault," Syri said, an ashen tint to her skin. "Renan blocked my shot. I couldn't get the Roman until he was down."

Toria wrapped an arm around the girl's waist and gave her a squeeze. "You did what you could. We all did."

Taba licked at Syri's fingers.

"What do we do with them?" Syri said, tilting her head toward the scattered bodies.

"Right now, nothing," Toria said, much as it tore at her stomach to say it. "We still have to meet up with the others. We remember this spot and come back for them later. Taba, I'm assuming you're stuck in that form for a bit?" The wereleopard nodded his head once, so Toria went to collect his clothing and shove them in her pack.

The birds were coming back on rustling wings, but she didn't know who else might have been attracted by the gunshots. "Okay, guys," she said. "Let's go."

Now they were three.

Victory stood above Fabbri while the woman blinked her eyes awake in Daliana's dim sitting room. "Good," she said. "You're up. Finally." Whatever Syri used to knock the woman out had been powerful. Daliana feared messing around with the spell to encourage Fabbri's return to consciousness. So they'd been forced to wait.

Not an easy task while her daughter was possibly in mortal danger. Victory sprawled back onto the armchair. Another elf had smuggled Victory here earlier, smothered in the back of the town-car with blankets and magic.

Fabbri pushed herself to a sitting position and stared around the room in incomprehension. "Where the hell am I?" Then, the reality of her current situation and pajama-clad form sank in. "You kidnapped me!"

"Yes, that seems to be going around," Victory said.

Daliana entered the room bearing a tray with three mugs and a steaming pot of coffee. "Would you care for any breakfast before we get started, Emily?" she said after setting the tray on the low coffee table before the couch.

Through half-lidded eyes, Victory repressed a smile at Fabbri's fearful reaction. The woman clutched her blanket around her, staring back and forth between the two nonhuman women. "Get started with what? Torture to go along with the kidnapping? The council will hear about this."

"Oh, relax," Victory said. "There is no council. We disbanded it when we declared martial law."

"But, Sethri would never..."

Victory straightened, drawing Fabbri's strict attention. "Sethri's dead. Your people killed him."

She expected immediate cries of denial and outrage, perhaps accusations of lies. But Fabbri could not fake her look of absolute dismay. Showing more compassion than Victory was currently capable, Daliana sat next to Fabbri and placed an arm over the other woman's shoulders. In her shock, she didn't even recoil from the elven woman's touch.

"They were only supposed to follow you," Fabbri said. "And spy on you. After what happened to Mikelos and the others, I didn't want anyone else to get hurt."

"It sounds like you're no longer in control of your own group," Victory said. "You weren't around when we discussed meeting with the Romans. That means someone else on our side of the council is reporting to you. And I need to know who."

Fabbri kneaded the blanket in her hands, and Daliana covered the awkward silence by pouring coffee.

Victory could be patient. Unfortunately, Fabbri was too smart to try to meet her gaze. That would have gotten immediate results.

"Bethany?" Fabbri did not react to Victory's guess, but she continued on. "It would make sense. She's been privy to every major meeting since all this started but she's not a real councilmember." She wished Toria were standing by her side to let her know whether the woman lied or not.

"You know, I could start naming names," Victory said, "and eventually I'll figure out who."

"Why?" Fabbri said, not taking the mug Daliana offered her. "So you can torture them for information instead?" Daliana set the disregarded mug on the tray in front of Fabbri and handed Victory the third.

Victory inhaled the warm aroma in favor of snapping right back at Fabbri. She needed this. It was approaching midafternoon, a time when all good vampires should be in bed. Preferably with their daywalkers snuggled up beside them, but Mikelos was still trapped in a hospital bed. She always forgot how much she counted on his steadying presence until he wasn't there next to her.

"Look," she said. "I know you think I'm lower than scum because I'm not human. We were looking forward to having a rational conversation with you about this. But you're really not helping."

"Besides," Daliana said. "I'm definitely against torture. I'd hate to have to get all the blood out of my carpet."

Fabbri continued to stare down at her hands, still not convinced by their assurances.

"I have been starved into a blood rage so fierce that I've killed an innocent child," Victory said, avoiding Daliana's eyes by swirling the coffee around in her mug. "I've been staked outside to wait for the sun to rise. I've had the skin flayed from my back." The chill in her own voice surprised her.

"And I've had iron spikes driven into my body to watch the skin sear around them," Daliana said, her voice cool. "We have been around a very long time, Emily. Despite our earlier flippancy, we understand the gravity of this situation. But rest assured there are lines we are not willing to cross."

A thick silence filled the room before Fabbri spoke. "Where are the two who went after you guys? I don't figure you let them get away after...after what happened to Sethri." Regret seeped through her words.

"Right below us," Daliana said. "We're keeping them in my basement, but they're quite comfortable."

Still knocked out, last time Victory checked, tied up and thrown together on an old mattress. Close enough.

"Not with the police?" Fabbri said.

"Not now," Victory said. "The police force is spread rather thin at the moment, since the Mercenary Guild went to confront the Romans."

"They will stand a fair trial," Daliana said. "Just because we've placed the government on temporary hiatus doesn't mean we've exchanged justice for vengeance."

Daliana had done some fast-talking to convince Victory and Max not to throw the men through a few windshields of their own. In retrospect, Victory figured that was out of her own self-interest, considering the elven woman's town-car seemed the logical nearby target.

"So," Victory said. She drained her coffee in a final gulp. "I can go back to guessing, or you can tell me who your insider is. Or have we not reassured you enough yet?" Despite the coffee, her patience was coming to an end.

Fabbri clutched the blanket on her lap with pale hands. "The weresnake. Lorus."

Customs Master Rhaavi took one look at Toria, Syri, and Taba, each splattered in blood, before handing over the keys to a pickup truck. Syri climbed in the passenger seat, and Taba, back to human form, hopped into the bed. They careened down back roads at speeds high enough to make Taba yelp every time she went over a pothole. No time to waste. They had to make it back to Max, warn him of the infiltration of their forces, and break the bad news of the deaths.

Her first command, too. After this, she would never be responsible for anyone other than herself and Kane ever again.

Not that she'd done a stellar job of keeping Kane safe.

Despite her best efforts, they were still late to the secondary meeting site. Max hobbled up to the truck as Toria stepped out of the cab. A red-tinged bandage bound his left calf above an incongruous bare foot. "We found the wrecks," he said without preamble. "And Freya. You guys are okay?"

"No, sir," Toria said. Taba vaulted out of the truck bed behind her, and she stifled a jump when Syri slammed the passenger door. She still felt small and lost, even surrounded by the rest of the mercenary company and warmed by the summer sun. "We were ambushed on the way to the docks by three scouts. Renan and Ari were also killed."

"Damn," Max said. "They're pulling out all the stops. No prisoners?"

Toria gestured to the empty truck. "No survivors on their side. Syri's a good shot."

Max clapped the elven girl on the shoulder. "Good girl. Taba, report to Genevieve. You two, come with me."

Even with Max's injured leg, they jogged across the clearing to keep pace with him. "What happened, Max?" Toria said. "Are you okay?"

"Lucky shot grazed my leg and shredded my boot," he said. "They were ready for us." A cluster of Max's more experienced mercs crouched around a map on the ground. "Now, I need you to tell me exactly where this ambush occurred."

Toria started to triangulate between the docks and their original starting position, but Syri was faster. "There," she said, jabbing a spot on the map with her finger. We left the bodies there."

An older merc placed a small red sticker on the plastic map at the point Syri indicated. A dozen or so other red stickers littered the area of the map between them and the river.

"The main force didn't follow us back," Max said. "But you guys ran into one of the trios of the scouts slowly infiltrating our side of the border. We know one thing for sure, though."

"The bastards don't know what's coming?" one of the older mercenaries said, noting map coordinates on a pad of paper.

"Something like that," Max said. "A frontal assault isn't going to work for us. We need to resort to more interesting methods. Whether your mother likes it or not, Toria, she's about to get recalled."

Victory managed not to drop her empty mug. "What?" When Fabbri had denied Bethany, she wasn't sure who she'd been expecting. But she had to admit that Lorus sat pretty low on the list. Now she was confused. "Why the hell would he do something like that?"

"That badger-woman was supposed to be the scapegoat," Fabbri said. "And Lorus never told me his motives. But he knew I was not pleased with the state of Limani's government system. He's the one who suggested that I run for council."

Not able to restrain her combination of nervous energy and anger any longer, Victory placed her empty mug on the tray and rose to her feet. Though she didn't resort to outright pacing, Victory crossed to the mantel and drummed her fingers against the wood. "This is insane."

The doorbell rang, and after a penetrating look in Victory's direction, Daliana left the room. She imagined the other woman was checking to be sure she wouldn't do anything to Fabbri while unsupervised. But now Victory had a different target.

Fabbri had pushed herself back into a corner of the couch. Before Victory could snap that she wasn't going to eat her, Daliana appeared once more.

"Here's our chance to find out," Daliana said. "Lorus is here. But luckily for us, Max and the others are right behind him."

Victory crowded into Daliana's living room with the other councilmembers again, but this time the tension permeating the room seethed with anger rather than the earlier fear. Max's injury warranted him a seat on the couch, and she perched next to him, Toria kneeling on the carpet at her feet. After they arrived, Toria spent almost ten minutes in the bathroom. The red skin on her hands told Victory her daughter had scrubbed them raw. She would never tell her daughter, but she still smelled blood. The afternoon's events had already traumatized Toria enough.

They were all traumatized. Having accepted Daliana's offer to borrow some proper clothing, Fabbri now sat on a kitchen chair in the corner of the living room. The space around her was clear, save for the solid presence of Lorus standing at her side. He seemed to return every glare aimed in his direction at once, his green eyes slit in true reptilian fashion. He might start hissing soon.

Instead, his voice remained steady and low. "These are serious accusations you level against me."

"Talk to Fabbri," Victory said. "She made them."

"And now we're going to trust the word of someone we should convict of treason?" The sibilants in Lorus' words grew more pronounced with every word.

"I saved the note you sent me to arrange our first meeting," Fabbri said, flinching away from the speed at which Lorus whirled on her. "It was handwritten."

"So an analysis can be performed," Lena said.

"We'd have to send it up to Calverton to do it," Tristan said. "But I have a wolf who can sense where things come from. We give the note to her, and she can tell us who wrote it."

"You're talking about Patience?" Bethany said. Tristan nodded once. "Well then, Lorus, you're screwed. I've never known that woman to be wrong in over twenty-five years."

"This is outrageous." Lorus spread his arms wide. "We have Fabbri in custody. Now we need to put this problem on a back burner while we deal with the Romans!"

"That was your plan, wasn't it, Lorus?" Daliana rose from the piano bench. "Weaken the ruling body of the city, all the while feeding information to the Romans so they'd know when to strike."

"That was the impression I got," Fabbri said. "Too bad it didn't work." She drew back into silence at the looks from around the room.

"Why, Lorus?" Lena said. "Why sell out Limani?"

The weresnake retained his moody silence, and once again it was Fabbri who spoke. "He made a deal with the Romans," she said. "He was supposed to be the new governor of the city once it was under Roman control and all the nonhumans who might oppose him were taken care of." She paused. "I was supposed to be one of the lieutenant governors."

Despite her best efforts, Victory couldn't help but gain a bit of respect for the woman. She had damned herself with her confession. If Victory didn't know better, she would swear the temperature in the room dropped a few degrees.

"In all your planning," Genevieve said, "you forgot something."

Tristan spoke over the confused look Lorus gave her. "It's not really a surprise, considering snakes don't have a proper sense of smell."

"What the hell are you two talking about?" Lorus said.

"Lies," Daliana said. "You've been making them since you walked into this house. Surrounded by a werewolf and panther, both of who can smell them literally, and two elves, who can sense them magically."

From her spot on the floor next to Toria, Syri said, "And man, are you ever fucking screwed."

"Does this mean we can arrest him and get on with the more important stuff?" Toria's sleepy voice contained a steel edge that jolted the rest of the room into action.

Gripping Victory's shoulder, Max raised himself to his feet, placing all of his weight on his uninjured leg. "Lorus Erikson," he said, "you are under arrest for treason against the free city-state of Limani. And yes, Toria, now we can focus on more important things."

"Are you sure you don't want to wait until later?" Victory gave Max's bandaged leg a pointed look. "Like tomorrow? After one of the elves has a chance to fix you?"

"I can get Daliana," Syri said.

Max shook his head, but didn't remove his attention from the maps spread on the Hall's conference table. "No time," he said. "And I'm not wasting anyone's energy on my little scratch when I've got two people still in critical condition."

Victory conceded the point. Time to act, before the Romans regrouped and hit the city with their full force at first light. After this afternoon, they should still be scouring the countryside looking for the remnants of Max's initial strike. It was a race against time to see which force could recoup the quickest. Limani had the advantage of home territory and knowing when the next attack would come—because they would be the ones making it.

"That's what the hospital is for," Toria said. "That is, you know, why Saul and Mason are there. To heal people."

"Then I'm saving them for the casualties we get tonight," Max said. "Tor, hand me that notebook?"

Passing over the blue book, Toria said, "Wow, you're optimistic." Between them, Syri handed Max the pen he was searching for.

"And you should hear how cheery you are, dear," Victory said. "Fine, Max. Suffer. Now why are we here and not the rest of your officers?"

"Because I've already briefed them on tonight's main mission and they're busy coordinating with Tristan and Genevieve's forces," he said. "Not to mention waiting for Tersiguel's pack to show up. Bloody hyenas."

"Be glad they're here," Victory said. "Tersiguel doesn't work with just anyone."

"Exactly," Max said. "That is why she, Bethany, and Daliana are with you. This afternoon you're giving them a crash course on guerilla warfare tactics so they can hit the camp from behind while my group takes on the Romans from the front with the wolves and panthers."

Victory pulled one of Max's maps toward her, covering her racing thoughts by pretending to study the area she already knew like the back of her hand. "Did we ever get an official count on the Roman forces?"

"Best estimate from what we've seen so far, both this afternoon and when we met with Octavian, is approximately two thousand men," Max said. "It's likely the vast majority is human and without much combat experience. These are local recruits, not troops from the Old Continent."

"So, if I'm taking the elves and all the other weres," Victory said, "that leaves you with barely a hundred for the frontal attack. Those are twenty to one odds in their favor, Max. When was the last time you did the math?"

Max slammed a hand down on the table. "Every damn second, Victory."

The silence rang after his outburst. "Sorry," Victory said. "The plan will work. I just haven't led a force in centuries." Much as it pained her pride to admit fear in front of her daughter, Max deserved her true thoughts on the situation.

But it was Toria who reassured her. "You'll be fine, Mama. I've heard all your stories. I doubt you've lost your touch to cause mayhem."

"Thanks," Victory said. "I'll try to live up to your grandfather's exaggerations."

"Not exaggeration," Max said. "Asaron and I have spent years discussing tactics, and he's always told me to go straight to you if I want something done that might not quite fit with my other officers' sense of honor—not that you lack honor yourself."

"No, Asaron's right," Victory said. "It's hard to fight for nearly a thousand years and not come up with your own ideas on what can and can't go in warfare. My sire is even more devious than I am."

"Which brings me to the reason the girls have joined us for this little meeting," Max said. "You two are going to get us Asaron's devious mind."

Victory could sense Toria's elation soar. "And Kane!" Toria said. "I'll get Kane back at the same time."

Max nodded. "If the first part of your goal is to set a very pissed-off Asaron loose in the middle of the Roman camp, yes, the second part of your task is to get Kane."

"That I can do," Toria said.

He held up a hand, halting her enthusiasm. "But that's not the hardest part. You three are going to find that nuclear weapon. And disarm it."

Victory crouched in a hidden pocket between two trees covered in the ever-present kudzu, out of sight of the first row of Roman tents. She surveyed the woods in the direction they had come from, keeping watch for returning scouts or sentries. Daliana's shoulder pressed into her back, the elven woman studying the movement within the camp itself. The heat of the day did not break with the fall of night, and the oppressive humidity made Victory's hair curl out of its tight braid. Daliana must be roasting in her gear.

It worked in their favor, though. The army celebrated tonight, declaring themselves the victors in the first sortie against the Limani forces. The grunt troops must not know the difference between "driven off" and "retreated."

Victory wished she knew which one was true. Damn Max for not letting her in on this from the beginning.

Daliana's low whisper echoed like a shout to her strained hearing. Clamping down on an involuntary twitch of surprise, Victory listened to the report.

"Sounds like all the celebration is happening farther in," Daliana said. "These tents are just filled with sleeping bodies, judging by the heat signatures I can see through the canvas. Haven't seen any wanderers."

Matching the other woman's soft tones and blessing the fact that elven hearing equaled vampiric, Victory said, "Support staff, then. These guys have to be up early to make breakfast and probably weren't involved in the combat today." She gave the trees another pass. Moonlight filtering through branches lit the woods like a bright stage to her eyes. "The sentry we skirted is walking the same pattern over again. Haven't seen anyone else."

"Sneaking through here is probably our best bet, then," Daliana said. A hint of question tinged the end of her words, bowing to Victory's experience.

"Sounds good to me," she said. "And support staff means supplies. Lots of supplies. Look for ammunitions wagons or trucks, and we've got our first target."

Victory gripped the bark of the tree next to her, prepared to pull herself out of her stiff crouch, when a nearby explosion shattered the world. She covered her ears and suppressed a scream, turning down the sensitivity of her hearing too late to save the ringing in her head.

Fingers touched her temples out of the darkness—when had she closed her eyes?—and the pain receded to a manageable level. Echoes of leaving the Mists after a night of dancing versus remembered days of aerial bombardment in Castille. She shoved those memories aside, and thanked the heavens these Roman troops included no air force.

Daliana's face hovered inches from her own when she opened her eyes again. "Better?" Daliana said.

"Yes," she said. "You?"

"Shields are good for some things," Daliana said. "Like preserving eardrums. But we need to move."

Once more expanding her senses to the world around her, Victory took stock of the altered situation. Men boiled out of the tents, officers screamed orders, lamps on tent poles were lit to fill the forest with light. "Someone did not follow orders." Victory and Daliana's explosion was supposed to cue the rest of the teams.

"They might have needed their own distraction," Daliana said, her gentle tones more forgiving.

"And right now we need to take advantage of this one. Let's go."

No matter who screwed it up, it might be in their favor. This section was now empty. Checking over her shoulder, Victory watched the sentry they'd evaded abandon his post.

Both women rose to their feet, remaining in the black shadows of the trees until the last possible second. Now screams drifted across the Roman encampment, echoed by a few sharp reports of gunfire.

Victory drew her sword. Daliana already had her pistol in hand. Brief regret washed through Victory. The elven woman was a healer by nature if not in true power. Never a warrior. She damned the Romans for dragging her into Victory's repressed, if not forgotten, world.

They dashed into the now-deserted section of camp. Victory drew to a halt next to an officer's empty pavilion. "There," she said, pointing to two trucks with large cargo containers hitched to the back.

"They blow up our trucks, we'll take out theirs," Daliana said.

"Keep watch." Not waiting for Daliana's assent, Victory darted through the empty space. She slipped to her knees between the truck cabs, trusting the monstrosities to keep her hidden from view.

She drew a package from her small backpack. One of Max's mercenaries moonlighted as Limani's resident demolitions expert, and it amazed her how fast the man had managed to throw these nasty surprises together. That he had such materials on hand bothered her civilian side a bit, but the mercenary in her trilled with glee. He'd even included simple step-by-step and color-coded instructions.

Another explosion from a different section of camp rocked the night. "Madness and mayhem" needed to be Limani's Mercenary Guild's official slogan.

Victory squirmed her head and torso underneath the truck, peering up into the unfamiliar workings. The mechanics of modern transportation had never been one of her major interests, despite her attraction to fast, shiny cars in the days when more engines ran on gasoline rather than electricity. The instructions indicated she should shove the small block wrapped in bright red plastic anywhere it would stay, so she wedged it between the front right wheel and axle.

A thought wormed its way through her battle-focused mind. The first explosion was Toria's cue. Somewhere in the camp, Asaron was sating his hunger. And her children were searching for an ancient nuclear device.

Place the clip on one of the blue wires to the red part of the plastic casing. Attach the other end of the wire to the metal protrusion from the small cylinder of black plastic the size of two of her fingers. Press the green button on the other end of the cylinder. Sixty seconds to run a hundred yards away.

She shoved herself out from under the truck and ran.

Daliana saw her coming, and wisely chose not to wait. Not bothering to find another hiding spot, the two women dove through the rows of tents all the way back to their original shelter, pressing themselves to the ground on the opposite side of the trees.

They had thirty seconds of tense waiting. It occurred to Victory that she should remind her partner to remove any pieces of wood impaling her torso should the trees protecting them shatter. Daliana would be fine with her bulletproof vest, but Victory didn't want an inconvenient branch to incapacitate her for too long.

"Dal—"

Both women shielded their heads and faces from explosion number three. The trees didn't shatter, but a wave of heated air blew past them. Victory tensed for a wall of flame, much more fatal to her than a measly sliver of wood, but only a heap of tent canvas crashed to her left.

The silence in the aftermath of the blast was almost deafening. Then the screams of men flowed toward them.

Victory recovered first, launching herself to her feet and reaching down to grab Daliana's arm. Pulling the elven woman to her feet was like hauling a bag of air.

"Our work here is done," Victory said. "The rest of the Guild should be on their way in. Time for you to get out of here."

"Right, let's head out," Daliana said. She started forward, then paused when Victory didn't follow. "Coming?"

"Can't." She shooed Daliana away. "Go on, I've got stuff to do."

"Like what?" Frustration leaked into Daliana's usually imperturbable voice. "The plan's gone to hell. We should get out while we haven't been spotted."

Words Asaron spent years beating into her head spilled out by rote. "No plan ever survives first contact with the enemy. Yes, we're done with Max's plan. Now I've got—"

A shout halted her mid-sentence. They dove for the forest floor again, and a crossbow bolt struck the tree trunk they'd spent far too long arguing next to.

Orienting herself, Victory dropped her sword in favor of the gun strapped behind her back. That damn sentry had returned, waving his crossbow around and screaming for them not to move. She took aim, but a bloom of red appeared at the soldier's throat before she could press the trigger.

Lying next to her, Daliana had beaten her to the punch, not having to waste time drawing a new weapon. She traded a look with Victory. "You're welcome," she said. "Now get out of here before any more come. I'll make it back fine on my own. Go find Asaron."

She squeezed Daliana's shoulder, then bounded to her feet. Recovering her sword and sheathing it with a snap, Victory peered through the trees. With the soldier down, the area was again deserted.

Time to head for the screams. Asaron was sure to be there, exacting his own vengeance against his former captors.

With one last look toward Daliana, who pushed herself to her feet, Victory stalked out of the comforting darkness and into the camp. She still gripped the pistol in her hand. Every inch of her body tingled with battle-awareness and a rising bloodlust. Her eyes tinged her surroundings with crimson, and her fangs almost ached with the primal urge to sink them into a Roman neck.

Victory knew her sire well. He would go straight to the top.

She would make sure that Octavian's neck was reserved for him.

Three more explosions followed Victory's stealthy progress across the camp. A trail of bodies also traced her meandering search pattern.

She knocked out the soldiers she took by surprise with mental commands to sleep, along with the few who surrendered at the first sight of the blood-splattered ancient warrior.

But she felt no compunction against killing those who fought back. Despite her ability to survive most mortal wounds, they still hurt. The stab wound in her right thigh and the bullet that had passed through her left shoulder did nothing to improve her mood.

She balanced on one knee, hidden in the shadows between two pavilions. Across from her stood a single tent separated from the rest. A prisoner's tent.

A short distance away sat the center of the camp, filled with higher-quality tents and larger pavilions. Officers' quarters, and the command center. It was a blur of activity, with soldiers, officers, and aides running back and forth coordinating the defense against Limani's forces.

She sensed mild panic in the air. Or perhaps it was the smoke drifting through the camp. Max was giving them more of a fight than they had expected.

No sign of Asaron so far, though she had come across an officer lying dead, his throat ripped open by the jagged edges of teeth rather than a simple knife slice. However, the wolf howls and feline screams now echoing through the camp proved the werecreatures were making their own fierce appearance.

No sightings of her daughter, either. But if Kane was free, Toria was sure to be close by after days of separation from her partner. Despite the urgings of her heart to find her children and defend them, she had to trust in their proven abilities to take care of themselves.

After a quick glance around to ensure her hiding place remained undetected, she returned her attention to the center of camp. Octavian would be there, coordinating the furious activity and directing the defense. But there were too many men, and too much light, for her to take him out like she had the others.

Victory had one other option, and evidence suggested Octavian wouldn't botch her plan. She rose to her feet, squaring her shoulders and ignoring the itch of blood drying around the scrape on her cheek. With empty hands held outstretched from her sides, she walked toward the command center.

An aide spotted her first. He called a warning to a passing soldier, who drew the longbow from his back and nocked an arrow toward her.

Halting her forward progress, Victory called out, "I request a meeting with General Octavian. I invoke the rights of Roman Article Seventeen!"

The soldier never took his eyes off her, but the aide jerked in surprise at her words and whispered in his ear. After receiving a nod, the young man bolted through the tents.

This shouldn't take long. Assuming the soldier didn't have itchy fingers and shoot her by accident.

She imagined it wasn't often that enemy soldiers declared themselves members of an ancient Roman house. No wonder the kid was surprised.

Tension permeated the small tent. Toria gripped Kane's hands in her own, stroking his palm with her thumb. The fabric of his improvised bandages brushed her bare arms, pushing her anger ever closer to the surface. Had they infiltrated the Roman camp that much more quickly than it had seemed? Worry warred with her anger, but her mind retreated from the thought that perhaps now her mother was captured, too.

"Calm, love," Kane said, his gentle voice dragging her back from the land of maybes. "I can feel your nerves vibrating from here."

She rested her head on his warm shoulder. "I'm okay," she said.

In unison, Asaron and Syri said, "No, you're not." The two older creatures shared a small laugh at Toria's expense.

"Thanks for the votes of confidence," Toria said. "I've got—"

A flash of light and rolling wave of sound announced the awaited explosion. Toria blinked away the negative images left by the sudden change, bolting to her feet and hauling Kane up beside her. Screams erupted around their tent, officers shouting conflicting orders and soldiers damning the Limani mercenaries.

"Toria, a shield?" Asaron crouched by the tent entrance, peering out at the camp. He jerked his head in her direction when she did not respond right away. "Damn, I forgot."

She'd explained her situation to them when they'd settled to wait, with Syri filling in her grandfather Zerandan's thoughts on the matter. Now helplessness struck her when she couldn't fulfill Asaron's request. A short-term external shield was a combat mage's standard work, and Kane had no energy for anything unnecessary to his own immediate survival.

"I've got it." Syri placed a light hand on Asaron's back, and a shimmer covered his features, making it hard to look right at him. "Be careful."

"Stay with them," Asaron said. Syri nodded once.

Before Toria could defend her remaining capabilities, her grandfather disappeared. He stopped long enough to strip an unsuspecting soldier of his weapons, then began his strike from within the camp.

"Time to go," Syri said. "Think you can find that bomb again, Kane?"

"I've got a decent idea," he said. Kane took the knife Toria handed him and strapped it to his belt. "Toria, have you actually tried using your powers?"

Toria knew he'd been puzzling over her situation since he learned of it. Had even felt him probing at her mind, slipping past shields that could never keep him out. Since magic came to him as easily as swords did to her, maybe he would come up with a solution soon. "Yes, more than once," she said. "And ended up with a splitting headache each time. Syri's grandfather says I've been cursed, and he knew of no way to reverse it right away. We've been muddling through for now."

"Need I remind you the quick and dirty way to remove a curse?" Kane said, replacing Syri at the front of the tent and taking his own look outside.

"I'd been trying not to think about that," Toria said. War was one thing. Fighting for your life was one thing. What Kane meant belonged to another category entirely.

Hearing her own hesitancy, Kane's voice softened. "This is war, love. The mage is an enemy soldier. It wouldn't be murder."

A week ago, those words would never have come from her partner's mouth. Events had altered him as much as they'd forced their changes on her. But he spoke the truth. Coming up with no sufficient denial, Toria said, "Let's get out of here. Syri, you've got point. I'll take up the rear."

She prodded Kane out of the tent behind Syri. The elven girl paused long enough for a quick look around, then dashed across the path. Toria and Kane followed on her heels. Toria gripped her pistol but kept it pointed to the ground while she ran, eyeing their surroundings and ready for any possible trouble. The soldiers had cleared the area, racing toward the more immediate attack.

As they ducked between two empty tents to take stock of their next direction, a second explosion ripped through the air on the other side of the camp. Now the Romans' attentions would be divided.

Toria took a split second to pity Octavian. The general's carefully ordered attack plans for the morning had been destroyed, and he would be facing her mother. Then the image of his face hanging inches above hers, hands roaming her body, surfaced in her mind and all traces of sympathy disappeared. Mama would vent her fury, and the man would be lucky to bargain for his life.

"That way," Kane said, pointing toward another corner of the camp, away from the two previous explosions. "Octavian's two pet mages had a temporary building made to hold the bomb, and they're camped right outside of it."

"You can sense it?" Toria said, hoping jealousy didn't tinge her voice.

"I can sense the absence of it," he said. "Mages have it shielded so tight that they made the earth itself invisible to me."

She trusted her partner on that one. Earth sense was his elemental gift, just as she could trace weather patterns within a dozen miles. "Then come on."

The trio ducked and wove through the Roman camp in the direction Kane indicated, staying between tents and vehicles, keeping out of sight of the scurrying troops. Two more explosions shattered the night, and they passed one pocket of fighting.

"We can't, Syri." Toria grabbed her arm before the elven girl could start toward the fight.

"But they're my cousins!"

The two elves fought back to back, flying blades keeping the Roman soldiers at bay. They had managed to get themselves surrounded, probably the sole reason no one risked shooting them down.

Kane grabbed her other arm when she would have taken another step forward. "We have a job to do," he said. "The clock is ticking."

When one of the elves let out a jubilant battle cry upon taking out a soldier, Syri stopped pulling toward them. Visibly steeling herself, she said, "Right. The mission."

The battle cries followed them away from the fight, to be joined by howls from the werewolves. An unfamiliar scream halted them again, feral and haunting, followed by yet another explosion.

"Tersiguel," Toria said, "or one of her pack."

"Must be. Whoa!" Kane snatched Syri back before she could take another step. "Shield. We're there."

They took position by an empty tent, half-collapsed from its inhabitant's mad dash to join the fight, and poked their heads around the side. A wide clearing surrounded a neat wooden hut and two large pavilions. The pavilions looked nicer than most of the officers' quarters they'd passed. They'd found the mages, then. Toria scoffed at them in her head, always disgusted by the airs foreign magic users seemed to deem necessary around "normal" humans. Victory taught her better than that a long time ago.

Lanterns lit one of the tents from within, the red one with obnoxious yellow and blue trim. The light remained steady though, with no indication of who or how many people were inside.

But she couldn't sense this shield. A new bolt of frustration raged through her.

Kane jumped as if he'd been shocked, giving her a penetrating look. "Calm, love," he said.

Well, their link still worked at least. If anything, it must be more open now that Toria had no way to control any emotions leaking through to her partner. "Sorry."

She was grateful when he did not patronize her with a response. "The area in the shield is a dead zone to me," Kane said instead. "I can't tell what we're up against in there. Syri?"

"One human mage," she answered without hesitation. "Who obviously did not take nonhuman magic into account when he crafted this overpowered beast. But they think they're setting a trap. He's got two others—nonmagical—with him in the dark tent. The red one's empty."

Now they were back in Toria's domain. "Probably ready to spring once anyone comes along. And I doubt our armor is good enough to take some concentrated blasts against whatever distance weapons they've got in there, not while we're also fending off magical attacks."

While the sounds of fighting in one half of the camp continued strong, the other half began to die down. They needed to make their move, and make it soon.

Kane wasn't going to like this. "I've got an idea," Toria said. She'd buckled on the belt holding her magical aids out of habit that morning. Now it looked like they might come in handy. She dug out her quartz crystal focus and held it out to Kane.

He cradled it in the palm of his hand, raising an eyebrow at her. "Yes?"

"Can you guys tell whether that shield is self-contained?"

Both of them eyed the invisible structure with their inner sights while she waited with impatience. She would never get used to not being able to do such simple tasks herself. She needed her magic back.

"Looks like it to me," Syri said.

"So whatever goes in, stays in," Kane said. "Got it."

Perfect. Now for the next step. "Is the shack shielded separately?"

"Yep," Syri said. "Gonna share with the class?"

"I'm thinking improvised flash-bomb," Toria said. "Disrupt their defenses. I can't create electricity for you guys, but I've still got all my passive defenses. Kane, I want you to leech the energy from my shields and channel it into the crystal. Then we throw it at the tent, and—"

"Poof," Kane said. "Leaving you completely defenseless. Screw that."

"Minor detail. Makes me less of a target," she said, "if I look like a regular fighter."

"I don't like it, but we're running out of time." Kane gripped the stone in one hand and placed the fingers of his other on her cheek.

The world dropped out from beneath her feet, and Syri grabbed her arms from behind before she could stagger away from the pressure building behind her eyes. A few seconds merged with eternity, and she shut her eyes to hide from the mingled look of pain and love on Kane's face.

An internal "pop" relieved the tightness in her skull, although the world around her still felt detached. Kane removed his hand from her face. Opening her eyes once again, she met Kane's still concerned expression. The airy feeling around her body intensified, and she resisted the urge to look down and check that she still wore clothing.

That was it. No more magic. She had nothing left to convince herself that life would go back to normal. Now she was just a regular fighter. And Kane became the only warrior-mage in Limani.

A different type of pressure built behind her eyes again, but Toria forced back the threatening tears. "Did it work?"

Kane unclenched his fingers, and the crystal he held vibrated with sparkling amethyst light. "It tingles," he said. Without further ado, he drew his arm back and sent the stone hurtling toward the dark tent. It shot through the air like a miniature shooting star, hitting the top of the pavilion with a burst of sparks and crack of lightning. A second loud shock followed the first, as the electricity found the metal tent poles and sent power surging through the entire structure.

Silence followed the short fireworks show. The odor of singed fabric drifted across the clearing to meet their noses.

"Think we pulled it off?" Kane said. "The bomb saturated the tent. I can't tell anything with my magesight."

"I'll go check." Before either could stop her, Toria crept forward from their hiding spot, drawing her sword.

She met no resistance passing the area where the shield's edge should be, but that didn't mean it wasn't still there. Feeling her partners' eyes boring into her back and ready to rush to the rescue, she kept up a steady pace until she reached the pavilion entrance. There were still no sounds of movement from within, so she drew a corner of the deep blue fabric back with a finger.

The interior was surprisingly spare—a camp cot and a few chests lined the edges, not the lavish display of creature comforts she expected. But she had expected the bodies of the two soldiers sprawled unmoving in the center of the tent. Longbows lay within reach of their lifeless fingers, reaffirming the decision Toria had made not to charge right in.

Fingers snapped once, and a putrid green light illuminated the back corner. It encompassed a gaunt young man dressed only in breeches in the tent's oppressive unmoving air. He lounged on a few pillows in the corner, apparently at ease despite the dead bodies at his feet. Spiraling tattoos decorated his naked torso, one particularly intricate knot on his lower abdomen glowing with a yellow tinge.

"And she keeps coming for me," the mage said, a touch of legitimate surprise in his voice. "How charming."

Toria stepped into the tent and pointed the tip of her sword at the mage. "Who the hell are you?" She didn't have time for niceties.

"Your puppet master."

Before she could make a snarky inquiry, he snapped his fingers a second time. Toria felt every muscle in her body tense beyond her control. The hilt of her sword dug into her palm, and she worried the sudden slickness she felt was blood rather than sweat. Pain ran through every joint in her body, and her teeth ached with the pressure of her jaw clamping together.

The pain wasn't good. On the plus side, she'd found the mage who'd cursed her.

He was silent for a beat, but the strain on his face told Toria he was attempting something she wasn't going to like.

She relaxed as much as possible, but every muscle screamed with cramps. Despite her best efforts, a high-pitched whimper escaped her gritted teeth.

After a second whimper, as she desperately wished for her shields back, the pressure lessened. The mage's eyes opened, and he studied her through narrow slits.

"Someone else has been draining your power," he said. "Not quite what I'd intended."

The rest of her muscles remained rigid, but her teeth stopped grinding together. An overwhelming urge to call out to Kane for help washed over her. The mage's yellow tattoo flickered under his silver shields.

No way would she be used to lure her partner into a trap. Manipulating the mage's mental control, the words that finally slipped from her were, "Nalamas! I've got him!" Then every muscle in her body seized, and it became an effort just to breathe.

She *never* called Kane by his last name. It took her two years to learn how to pronounce it right.

Feet pounded across the clearing toward the tent, Kane's boots followed by Syri's lighter steps. Her teeth snapped shut again, and she began to curl in on herself, the weight of the pain pushing her to the ground.

The tent flap snapped open behind her, but she had no way to give them further warning. The mage lunged to his feet, a mocking smile spreading on his face.

"Right then," Kane said. He laid a gentle hand on her shoulder, but his other secretly pulled her pistol from the holster at her lower back. Relief, both physical and mental, spread through her.

The mage's grin transformed to horror, and a pistol cracked inches from Toria's head. The yellow tattoo disappeared in a spread of crimson when the bullet buried itself in his stomach and disrupted the magical energy with his own blood.

He fell back on the pillows with a howl of agony, clamping both hands over the wound. Toria stood up straight, muscles still aching but under her own control. With her shields gone, magesight flooded her field of vision as her magic poured back into her, turning the dark tent into a miasma of corrupt magical energy.

Kane, keeping her pistol squared toward the mage, stalked across the tent toward him. "I would kill you," he said, "or challenge you to a duel. But you're the one tied to the bomb." He hauled the mage to his feet by the arm as the man kept his hands pressed over his wound.

A glimmer of clean violet caught Toria's eye in the corner of the tent. She stalked over and pulled aside the cloth covering a low trunk. Lying on top of the trunk was her rapier, still neatly sheathed. The blade might be new and untouched by her magic, but the hilt of the sword contained years of her imbued magical signature.

She sheathed her replacement sword, then clutched her rapier with both hands, a single tear tracing its way down her cheek. Things had to get better from here on out. Now she was whole again.

"This is mine," she said to the mage, a snarl in her voice that vented all the stress of the past days of trauma.

Syri covered Kane while they followed Toria out of the tent and to the small wooden structure. Giddy with power flowing through her veins once again, she pointed to the padlocked door and blew it open with a focused bolt of energy. They didn't need the mage to disarm this nuclear warhead. She could take anything—

"Steady, girl." Syri's fingers intertwined with her own, reeling her back before she could become drunk on her reborn power.

They entered the shack together. Upon the bare dirt ground sat a metal cradle holding the cylindrical object she recalled from Kane's memories. He hadn't exaggerated the nauseous aura the weapon produced, waves of roiling ochre contained by a gunmetal shield the same color as the Roman mage's.

But the electronic keypad lay dead. No conveniently ticking numbers marked how much time they had left to prevent the utter devastation of her beloved home. "You wired it to yourself," Toria said, whirling on the mage who had collapsed at Kane's feet upon entering.

He nodded, once. "The power itself was easier to work with, so I bypassed the control system." He gasped out through the pain. Kane heaved an exasperated sigh and ripped another strip from his tattered shirt. He wadded the cloth and pressed it to the gunshot wound, folding the mage's hands back over it.

Toria's scientific tendencies briefly overtook her hatred of the man. "Idiot. You could have killed yourself. There's a good chance you would have died anyway when it blew if you tied it to yourself too deeply."

"I know," he said. "You think I had any choice?"

"Well, you've got a choice now," Kane said. He drew his dagger and idly flipped it from hand to hand. "Tell us which of your little tattoos is tied to the bomb, or I'll start cutting them out at random."

Before the mage could begin gibbering or Syri could protest, Toria said, "No need." His pants had ridden up when he'd hit the floor, revealing a tattoo on his right calf glimmering with the same swirling mass enveloping the bomb. She slid the pants leg up a few more inches with the tip of her sword. "That one."

The tattoo was new relative to the more faded ink work on his torso and upper arms. A delicate spiral began on his inner leg, partially hidden by a heavier star. It glowed in the same fashion as the one now hidden behind a bloody bandage.

"At least knock me out first," the mage said. It almost disappointed Toria that he didn't put up more of a fight. "And make sure I don't bleed to death after you do it."

"You're helpful all of a sudden," Syri said. "Why the fuck should we even let you live?"

"Because of all the military secrets I hold?" The mage returned her feral grin. "I doubt you three are authorized to let such a source escape your hands."

"Fine, bargain all you want," Toria said. She nodded once to Syri.

The elven girl placed a hand on the mage's head. Light flowed from her fingers into his skull, and the mage slumped to the side. If it was the same trick she'd pulled on Fabbri, he wouldn't wake up for anything. Syri gestured to his leg.

Kane's turn. Her partner was not as bloodthirsty as he'd wanted the mage to think. Kane visibly steeled himself before placing the edge of his blade to the side of the tattoo and slicing through the skin, peeling away the layer holding magic anchored with ink. Blood dripped through his fingers as he sliced.

The shield around the bomb shattered and faded while Kane cut, the ochre magic flowing through the air and reabsorbing into the mage's skin. It dispersed throughout his body, soothing a few of the lines on the mage's face.

He had tied so much of himself into the bomb that it was no wonder he'd put a link on Toria's magic. Some of her sympathy faded when she realized he would have eventually started to pull energy from her to feed the bomb's power. But she'd made a promise, and ripped some of her own shirt to have a new bandage ready once Kane finished.

"We good?" Kane waited for her signal before removing the knife. Blood covered his hands and pooled on the floor beneath the mage.

The bomb was completely inert. No magic, no electrical power, just a dull undertone of violence that should never have seen the light of day again. Toria said, "We're good." She handed the bandage to Syri, who wrapped the mage's leg with deft fingers.

"So now what do we do with him?" Kane said. All of their adrenaline had worn off, and he sounded as tired as Toria's aching body felt.

"Run like hell before any Romans get the bright idea to check on their precious toy," Toria said. She dialed down her magesight. Now her partners weren't glowing vessels of power so much as worn-out people. She couldn't wait to begin rebuilding her shields. After about a hundred years of sleep.

"There's a truck on the other side of the mages' pavilions," Syri said. "Probably dedicated just to them. I almost feel obligated to take it."

Grateful a little humor still existed in the world, Toria matched her smile. "Let's go. We'll take their toys, too." Sounds of continued fighting leaked in from outside. But their mission was complete.

Time to go home.

Article Seventeen of the Roman Constitution contained a tricky bit of language. A holdover from the old Imperialate, before Emperor Gordian IX had created the Roman Parliament in the last century. With the caste system demolished, official houses of nobility had been tainted to the point of being almost unrecognizable to anyone without dual degrees in genealogy and heraldry.

But five hundred and thirty-seven years ago, Victory married into the house of Galerius. It only lasted six months before she left Leto for his womanizing and gambling, but Octavian didn't need to know that.

The law required the Roman soldiers to escort Lady Victory Galerius into Octavian's presence for an audience. Access was all she needed.

She cooled her heels under the watchful gaze of the soldier. The explosions tapered off, but the fighting around them never ceased. She was grateful for the chance to—metaphorically—catch her breath. Though she still owned property in the Roman Empire, and Mikelos still held many financial interests from his days of musical fame, her own past as a lady of the nobility seemed a much more impressive way to demand a face-to-face meeting with the general. Calling on Article Seventeen had occurred to her as a possibility for getting within range of Octavian the day before, but she'd never solidified the plan. She could wing it. That was her specialty.

The aide came scurrying back, three more soldiers trailing behind. He gave her a low bow; the soldiers followed suit after the aide gave them nasty glares.

Looked like this might work after all. Victory gestured with her empty hand for the aide to rise.

"I apologize for the wait, my lady," he said. "General Octavian is willing to see you." He fumbled in a pocket and withdrew a small green cloth. "However, the general offers you this token in return for your firearms. You are more than welcome to retain your bladed weapons."

She wouldn't quibble over trivialities, despite the fact that Article Seventeen gave her the right to retain all weaponry. They were at war, after all. A point to Octavian for not being stupid. In silence, she dangled the pistol from her pinky for the soldier on her right to retrieve, then stood with her hands held a few inches from her sides.

Reassured that she wasn't about to replace the pistol with a knife, the aide approached with the handkerchief. He handed it to Victory with another bow. She assumed the small coat of arms belonged to Octavian. Presenting it for her keeping implied that she remained under his protection during the audience.

"Thank you," she said to the aide. "Please lead on."

The soldiers fell into an honor guard around them, escorting Victory and the aide through the camp's command center. Shouting officers who coordinated with other areas of the camp via radio fell silent when they passed, staring at the scruffy armed vampire being given the deference due any Roman lady of birth. Rumors must be spreading like wildfire already.

Spotlights lit a group of tables near the largest pavilions. General Octavian stood ready to greet her, distracted from his stance of attention just once to sign a clipboard for yet another aide. His support staff dropped what they were doing when Victory halted a few feet from Octavian. The officers saluted as one, and Octavian bowed.

He held the position for the full three seconds decreed for a high-ranking military official to give a member of the lesser nobility. He did the political dance well, even dressed in fatigues and dirt-scuffed boots.

Victory inclined her head when he rose. "Thank you for the chance to parlay," she said. "If there is any question of my use of Article Seventeen, I assure you I can be found in the history books in the seventh dynasty House Galerius, as Leto Galerius' first wife."

"Thank you," Octavian said, "but I don't think a check will be necessary."

Convenient, since such a check would be impossible in their current situation. She folded his handkerchief into a small square before tucking it away in her pocket. She withdrew a delicate white satin glove that had been wrapped around her belt. Its twin had been ruined years ago by a much younger Toria playing tea party. So it caused her no hardship to toss the glove to the dirt between them.

Octavian stared at the glove, then traded bemused looks with the officer next to him. "You can't be serious," he said to Victory.

"Deathly serious," she said, "as it were." She kept her gaze level, resisting the urge to give her own short bark of laughter. The situation had indeed shifted from the strange to the downright absurd.

"Didn't your little town outlaw dueling fifty years ago?"

"Luckily, we're three miles from the city limits," she said. "Are we going to get on with this, or do I need to insult your manhood or something equally juvenile?"

After exchanging one more nod with his fellow officer, Octavian said, "Then I see I have no choice but to accept. Dare I ask the reason for this little stunt?"

"Sure," Victory said. "If I win, I have effectively decapitated your army and left them no choice but to turn around and go home."

"And if I win, I imagine I've just killed an obnoxious vampire whose forces will fight all the harder. I'd hardly call that fair."

"Too bad you already accepted the challenge," Victory said. "Your choice of weapon, sir." She could feel the smirk emerging on her lips at the effort to retain dignity in the face of such a bizarre scenario. Asaron would be proud.

"I will confer with my officers," Octavian said, a note of stiffness appearing in his voice. He was not as amused, evidently.

"Take all the time you need." She'd surprised him. That was a good thing. Now how long she could drag this little drama out?

The minutes stretched while a huddle of men surrounded Octavian, and runners were sent back and forth with messages and directions for other areas of the command center. The rest of the war did not halt for her, after all. Victory took the time to study the officers around her, all of whom stared at her with blatant curiosity until she met their eyes. Then they were back to work, pretending they'd never paid any attention to her, nor that they'd found themselves unable to meet her direct gaze.

"I've made my decision." Octavian's announcement jerked her attention back to the man in front of her. He stood flanked by subordinates, solid resolve emanating from the entire group. "The weapon shall be pistols. My second shall be Commander Tiberius Ibrahim."

"Silver bullets, I assume?" Victory said.

"Of course." Octavian made a slight gesture with one hand, and yet another aide ducked into one of the pavilions behind them.

"Excuse me, sir," Ibrahim said. "But the lady has no second herself, leaving the requirements for a formal duel unfulfilled." His voice dripped with satisfaction as he probed for any hole in Victory's farce to exploit.

A soldier's shout of warning rang out behind Victory, and rifles all around the command center sprang to attention. These must be the elite guard, to be outfitted all with firearms. She turned on her heel, keeping her hand from her own sword lest Octavian decide she had broken their terms of truce.

A lone figure emerged from the shadows between two of the grander pavilions—a tall man, battered and blood splattered. He pushed messy red hair out of his face, leaving behind another bronze streak.

It was the loveliest sight Victory had seen in days. He'd probably been waiting to make such a dramatic entrance.

"I'll be her second," Asaron said. "I almost wish she'd chicken out so I could take you on myself." He walked across the silent clearing to take his comforting place on Victory's left. "But alas, my girl would never do such a thing. So let's get on with this."

Octavian had sent two soldiers running during Asaron's speech, but the elder vampire laughed while the men passed by. "Don't worry," he said. "The kid is long gone, too."

"I'm not even going to ask," the general said, a growl entering his voice. "Since it seems I have no control over my own camp anymore."

The aide returned from the pavilion and presented a wooden box to Octavian. The general opened it to reveal two ivory-handled pistols. With a curt nod, he directed the aide toward Victory.

The young officer approached with hesitant steps, stopping far enough away that Asaron was forced to step forward to give the pistols a proper inspection. He wiped his hands on his battered leather trousers before handling the fancy weapons. He checked the chambers, popping out the single silver-plated bullets and reloading them with deft fingers. Asaron gave a double thumbs-up to Octavian before returning to Victory's side.

While Octavian had his aides mark out the official twenty paces that would separate the duelists, Asaron said to Victory, "You sure about this, love?"

"I can take one bullet," she said. "Just...make sure that's all they get the chance for, okay?"

He captured one of her hands in his larger ones, pressing her fingers to his lips. "Mikelos will haunt me to the end of time if I let something happen to you."

"I know," Victory said.

"Are you going to kill him?"

Before she could respond, Octavian called out from across the command center. "If you're quite ready."

Asaron joined Ibrahim to the side of the marked out line, the two seconds creating an incongruous pair. Victory took her place where another soldier indicated, accepting her weapon with a simple thanks. The soldier did not return her politeness, but that was to be expected.

She hefted the pistol, preparing herself both mentally and physically. Down the line, Octavian stood with military precision, waiting for Ibrahim to call the beginning of the duel. Victory cocked the gun and leveled it at Octavian, nodding her own readiness.

"I hereby revoke my protection of the Lady Victory Galerius," Octavian said. "You may proceed, Commander."

"Yes, sir," Ibrahim said. "On my mark, sir, my lady." He raised an arm to the dark sky.

Victory drilled holes in Octavian's head with her eyes, but he avoided her direct gaze. She felt his own attention aimed at her heart.

"Mark."

She wasted no precious time before squeezing the trigger. She kept her arm steady while simultaneously shifting the rest of her body, side-stepping with a short burst of vampiric speed.

A bloom of red appeared over Octavian's stomach at the same instant a searing pain shot through Victory's right shoulder. She'd forgotten how much silver burned under her skin, unlike the simple electric tingle above.

Chaos broke out across the command center. But most importantly, the bullet missed her heart, the last spot truly vulnerable to a vampire her age. She remained on her feet.

Judging by the shock on Octavian's face as he clutched his stomach and stared at her with wide eyes, he hadn't been expecting her to still be standing.

Two of Octavian's officers ran toward her with swords drawn, past their wounded general already being tended by Ibrahim and a medic. Asaron slammed into one of them from the side, tackling him to the ground and distracting the other long enough for Victory to wrestle her sword from its sheath.

Feeling her strength flow out of her along with the blood from her shoulder, she managed to swing her sword underneath the soldier's guard and catch him between his pants and bulletproof vest. The tip of the blade pierced his skin, and she flung him aside, twisting the sword out of him with the flick of her wrist. He landed with a howl, blood pumping from his stomach.

Victory didn't give him a second look. She stalked toward Octavian, and Asaron joined her side, wiping fresh blood from his mouth.

They drew to a halt a few feet away from where Octavian had been lowered to the ground. The medic had pressed bandaging over the general's wound, frantically trying to stem the flow of blood. Victory smelled stomach fluid. Even if they managed to fix the wound, Octavian was at huge risk for infection. Ibrahim drew his sidearm and stood to face them.

"Stop!" He cocked the pistol and aimed it back and forth between the vampires, unsure of who posed the greater threat. "You got what you wanted. Now get out of here before I have both of you killed."

Victory exchanged glances with Asaron. They couldn't stop now. Not when they were so close to cutting out the heart of this fruitless invasion. Fighting had mostly ceased around the camp, leaving only the screams of wounded. Having no idea who had emerged the victor, she couldn't take any chances.

Asaron drew the knife tucked into his belt and let it fly at Ibrahim. It stuck in the commander's neck, forcing the man to drop his gun and clutch at this throat. The medic bolted to his feet and ran as Ibrahim collapsed over Octavian's legs.

In another burst of speed, Victory stood over Octavian, placing the tip of her sword against his throat. Soldiers all around the clearing aimed guns, crossbows, and longbows at her, poised to fire.

"If you kill me," Octavian said, gasping out the words around his pain, "you won't make it out of here alive."

"Good thing I'm already dead, then," Victory said. "This is what you get for taking on Limani. This is the message your men will take back to the Emperor."

"I am glad to die for my—"

Victory couldn't wait any longer, judging from the amount of her own blood soaking her leather vest. She pressed down on her sword, using her own weight to push the blade through Octavian's throat. The tip glanced off his spine, leaving a jagged, spurting gash.

A collective howl went up around the camp, and Asaron dragged Victory to the ground with him. Bullets passed over their heads before a second shout called off the soldiers' hasty actions.

"Let's get the hell out of here, shall we?" Victory said. She gritted her teeth before a gasp of pain could escape her mouth. Asaron had most of his weight on her injured shoulder, but she wasn't going to complain about him saving her skin.

They grabbed hands and rolled to their feet, balancing their weight against each other for momentum. Now she noticed Asaron also bled from multiple wounds—he hadn't reached her side unscathed. "Run!"

Drawing on reserves of strength she hadn't known still existed, the two vampires dashed from the camp. She wasn't sure who hauled who most of the way in the blind blur as men and tents gave way to trees and brush. But the next thing she knew, dark woods surrounded them. Starlight brightened a road a little farther ahead.

"Come," Asaron said. They made it the rest of the way, but Asaron collapsed onto the side of the road first. Victory sank to her knees next to him. "See?" Asaron said. "We're good."

"We're both going to bleed out before we make it home," Victory said. The wound on her shoulder screamed. The silver bullet in her body prevented any healing, and she felt herself draining away by inches. And Asaron had too many bullet holes to count, despite the amount of Roman blood he'd taken once freed from imprisonment.

"Stop. Hear that?" Asaron peered down the road, and Victory followed his gaze with eyes that felt hard to keep open.

A truck appeared, chugging along the road as if it didn't know a war was on. A truck with a Roman license plate on the front fender. Cursing this sudden bad luck, Victory pushed herself to her feet using her sword for balance. Not that she knew what she would do if the truck was full of soldiers bent on revenge.

The vehicle slowed, finally halting right next to where Victory stood. She raised her sword with hands that couldn't quite tell whether they still had fingers attached to them.

The passenger-side window rolled down, and a head popped out. "Hey, Mama!" Toria said. "You and Grandpa need a ride home?"

EPILOGUE

Mikelos slipped his hand into Victory's underneath the council table. While strange to have him by her side in this setting, it also felt reassuring after the whirlwind events of the past few days. But he helped to fill the room, disturbingly empty without Lorus and Fabbri, both in police custody. And Sethri, ready to be buried the next evening.

A speakerphone sat in the middle of the conference table. From it emanated the strong voice of the young Roman emperor, dimmed only by the distance of an ocean. The council had nominated Victory to be acting head, due to both her political experience and knowledge of how to deal with temperamental nobility from her days as a professional bodyguard.

"So now that you've ruined my plans to expand my territory on the New Continent," Emperor Benedictus said, "and alerted the entire British Empire to be on guard against future attacks, how do you propose to amend this problem?"

"Need I remind you, sir," Victory said, "that your use of a nuclear device breaks international treaties, never mind your attempts at expansion. So I don't believe Limani owes you any sort of apology."

The rest of the council gaped at her, though Mikelos sat back in his chair. He'd done his share of standing toe-to-toe with nobility.

"Well, the British ambassador here in Roma has been clamoring for apologies since the news broke yesterday of the attack on Limani," Benedictus said. "And we've not even done anything directly to the British."

And here the emperor began to show his true youth, at least in the political arena. The old emperor might have trained his nephew up a bit more before passing away and feeding him to the wolves.

"If you'll take a piece of advice from an old mercenary who has dealt with the British," Victory said, "they don't really need an excuse to clamor for anything."

"I'd hate to ask your opinion of the Empire, then." A short chuckle emerged from the speaker.

He was lightening up. She could work with this. "While honorable to a fault, I feel your typical Roman citizen believes Might makes Right."

From her other side, Max stifled a laugh. One of the human members of the council, on the other hand, looked ready to pass out from embarrassment.

"I thank you for that, my lady," Benedictus said. "Your honesty is a refreshing change from my ministers here in Roma. I don't suppose I could tempt you with the honor of a state visit? I realize I have much to learn yet about ruling."

"It is quite tempting," Victory said. "But right now, my place is here in Limani. However, I believe I could offer you a piece of advice?"

"Be my guest," Benedictus said.

"Don't apologize to the British," she said. "They will be sated by a formal apology to Limani. Which can be made at a conclave between all three countries designed to revisit the old treaties. Since I'm the only person in any of our three governments still alive who was part of the original treaty discussions, I feel obligated to admit it is time for some changes to be made. Territorial negotiations can certainly be made part of the new meeting."

Silence from the speaker. The emperor probably hit the mute button for a short discussion with his own advisors, surrounding him as the rest of Limani's council surrounded her. Everyone in the room on her end of the line tensed, waiting for a response.

"My lady Victory? Are you still there?"

"Yes, sir," Victory said. "I'm not pressuring you to make a decision now, of course. Just offering my opinion on the situation."

"And a good opinion it was," Benedictus said. "Let me first announce here the need for a conclave between the Roman Empire, the British Empire, the official city-state of Limani, and any other countries wishing to attend, in order to discuss global matters in this new era."

"Thank you," Victory said. "Limani will be glad to attend."

Toria sat with Kane and Syri in the back of the baking trial room, ready to sneak out at the first opportunity. They'd come to support her mother, one of the prime witnesses in Lorus' trial for treason against Limani.

It had been an arduous trial, stretching through the long days of summer. Treason was serious business in Limani, and this was the first trial for such in over seventy-five years. Lorus never claimed innocence, but evidence of his guilt had been carefully drawn over the space of the last two months.

Now the room was packed to the brim, while television cameras shared the scene throughout the rest of Limani.

"How are you feeling, Syri?" Kane narrowed his eyes at the elven girl. "Too much yet?" A woman in the row ahead of them turned her head to glare at his interruption of the proceedings.

Syri had been stuck in the hospital for two weeks after the final battle, due to aggravating internal injuries from her original attack. Even now she wasn't quite a hundred percent. But what most amused Toria was Kane's attentiveness to the girl, who'd been inseparable from them since her release from the hospital. She was even coming to Europa with them in the fall, to attend the conclave called by the Roman Emperor.

"I'm fine," Syri said, waving Kane back. "Shush."

The central tribunal officer stood from the long table at the far front. Every little movement in the room ceased and silence descended over the crowd. He cleared his throat, and Toria felt everyone draw closer.

"In the trial of the city-state of Limani versus Lorus Erikson," he said, "Lorus has been proven guilty of state treason and has been sentenced to death by hanging. No appeals will be granted due to the defendant's previous documented confession."

He banged his gavel, and the room exploded. Toria lost sight of her mother in the front row when people around them bounded to their feet. Cheers, jeers, and even various expressions of dismay surrounded them.

"Let's get out of here," Syri said. "It's done."

"Finally," Toria said.

Fabbri clasped Victory's hand as they stood at the edge of the pier. She would board a Roman cargo ship bound for the British colonies as soon as the deliveries to Limani finished unloading. "Thank you for everything," she said. "I'm sorry things turned out the way they did."

"I am, too," Victory said. "Such is life."

Fabbri picked up one of the packs at her feet. "So it is. Though to be fair, banishment is preferable to death."

"So it is," Victory said.

Two dock workers approached, ready to bring Fabbri's belongings on board the transport. "Guess this is it," Fabbri said. "Take care of the city, Victory. And good luck in Roma."

"I will," she said. "Good luck yourself." Victory moved away while Fabbri helped the men gather the rest of her bags. The encounter had been awkward, but she'd been the one to volunteer to see the woman out of Limani territory, now that Lorus' trial was over. Missing the man's execution at noon hadn't pained her in the slightest.

She returned one last wave as Fabbri boarded the ship, then turned back toward the customs house where Mikelos waited in the air conditioning. She sank into the chair next to him in the empty waiting room and let her head fall to the side to rest on his shoulder.

"She off?" Mikelos said. He looked up at her from his pages of musical notation.

"She's gone," she said. "The world can go back to normal now. At least until the fall."

"You excited to go back to Europa?" Mikelos patted her knee before rising to his feet. "Visit the old stomping grounds?"

"I'm more excited for next week's emergency elections, when I no longer have to act as interim council head." Victory followed Mikelos out of the waiting room and out to the town-car. The horn from the cargo ship sounded, and they paused to watch it back away from the pier. "But yes. The trip will be good. The world needs it."

The surreal situation did not hit Toria until mid-song on the Twilight Mists dance floor. She froze, staring at the other dancers and people lounging on couches or chatting at high-top tables. "What are we even doing here?"

Kane and Syri had been dancing rather inappropriately together next to her, but she assumed that had to do with the fact that Duncan, Kane's ill-fated date from earlier in the summer, was staring at them from the bar. They broke away from each other.

"It's Thursday night," Kane said. "Thursday night is half-price drinks and industrial music. I'm here for the drinks and the boys. You're here for the music and the drinks and the boys. Syri's here because she's been attached to us all summer. And possibly for the boys."

"You're the only man for me, darling," Syri said.

Kane laughed. "Still not interested. What's wrong, Tor?"

"This!" Toria waved her arms around. "These people! They're acting like nothing happened this summer."

Kane took her hands in his. "Come on, hon, it's not that bad." He must have seen the stress in her eyes, because he said, "Should we call Daliana for dinner tomorrow?"

Toria had occasionally seen Daliana in her official capacity since high school, and both she and Kane had visited her multiple times over the summer. The elven psychiatrist had been booked solid for weeks as the residents of the city absorbed the recent events, but she was willing to see them at her house over meals rather than during office hours.

"This isn't some flare-up of my nonexistent posttraumatic stress disorder." Toria shook her head. "This is dehydration. Let's get beer."

Once the three were ensconced on their own couch, beer acquired, Toria continued. "This isn't over. This won't be over until the conclave in Europa. Which we can't attend. Despite the fact that we are the reason there is still a Limani to attend the conclave."

"Is that what this is about?" Syri said. "Not being able to go next month?"

"Fall classes start in two weeks." Kane reached across Toria to clink bottles with Syri before taking a swig of his beer. "I'm not taking a semester off and messing up our graduation date. Sorry, love."

"I could go," Syri said. "I graduated college last century."

"No, you're not going anywhere without us," Kane said. "Not until we figure out just how much of your magic is entwined with ours after being in Toria's head. Zerandan's orders. And Victory's."

A knot began to loosen inside Toria, and a bit of tension drained out of her tightly wound soul. "So life can go on as normal, and we can go back to being treated like children."

"So life can go on as normal," Kane said, "and we can dance. After we finish our beer."

Toria draped her arms over the top of the couch to either side of her, drawing Kane and Syri closer. "We really are stuck with you now, aren't we?"

"You complaining?" Syri said.

Toria laughed. "Not complaining at all."

Photo by Brian Roache

ABOUT THE AUTHOR

By day, J. L. Gribble is a professional medical editor. By night, she does freelance fiction editing in all genres, along with reading, playing video games, and occasionally even writing.

Previously, Gribble studied English at St. Mary's College of Maryland. She received her Master's degree in Writing Popular Fiction from Seton Hill University in Greensburg, Pennsylvania, and Steel Victory was her thesis novel for the program. This is her debut novel.

She lives in Ellicott City, Maryland, with her husband and three vocal Siamese cats. Find her online (www.jlgribble.com), on Facebook (www.facebook.com/jlgribblewriter), and on Twitter and Instagram (@hannaedits). She is currently working on more tales set in the world of Limani.

CPSIA information can be obtained at www.ICGtesting.com
Printed in the USA
BVOW08s1759130715

408387BV00003B/84/P